There wa ***in***
Patrick's e

For a split second, while he was standing in the library, Catherine had thought she'd seen something more. A flash of interest, a hint of sympathy. But that was impossible. Patrick Shaw hated her and her family.

She studied him, the way he held the cat so gently and glared at her so fiercely.

He had the perfect body for a horseman. Long, powerful legs. Muscled back. The question came unbidden: What would it be like to have a man like Patrick?

"If you receive a ransom note, will you let me know?"

Catherine caught the worry in his voice and, for the first time, she considered that he might actually be innocent.

CAROLINE BURNES

Caroline Burnes has published thirty-five Harlequin Intrigue novels, many of them featuring horses, cowboys, or the black cat detective, Familiar. From the age of four, Caroline wanted to be a cowgirl and write mystery books. Though she is far from a cowgirl, she lives on a farm in south Alabama with six horses, six cats and six dogs. One of the cats, E. A. Poe, is a prototype for Familiar. Although she spent most of her riding career jumping, she recently took up team penning, a sport that demonstrates that cows are far smarter than humans.

CAROLINE
BURNES

THRICE FAMILIAR

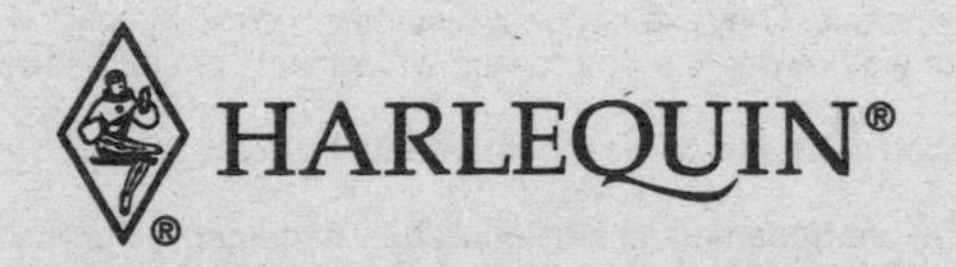

TORONTO • NEW YORK • LONDON
AMSTERDAM • PARIS • SYDNEY • HAMBURG
STOCKHOLM • ATHENS • TOKYO • MILAN • MADRID
PRAGUE • WARSAW • BUDAPEST • AUCKLAND

This book is dedicated to Susan Tanner, fellow writer, rider and traveler; Carolyn Nyman, cat lover, friend and teacher; Gloria Howard, who made the dream of horses possible; and Corrine Morgan, friend, gardener and chef extraordinaire.

ISBN 0-373-80953-0

THRICE FAMILIAR

This edition published by arrangement with Harlequin Books S.A.

www.eHarlequin.com

Printed in U.S.A.

CAST OF CHARACTERS

Catherine Nelson—Her lifelong dream turned into a nightmare, and now her life—and love—are at stake.

Patrick Shaw—He was out for revenge—with a vengeance.

Familiar—The feline detective would need to do some fancy pussyfooting this time to protect his human friends...and his own sleek black hide.

Limerick—The future of Beltene Farm.

Kent Ridgeway—A gambler who's used to winning; how far will he go to take this prize?

Allan Emory—He may already be guilty of kidnapping. Is he desperate enough to kill?

Colin Shaw—The black sheep of the Shaw family.

Eamon McShane—Is he protecting his family—or setting Patrick up for a fall?

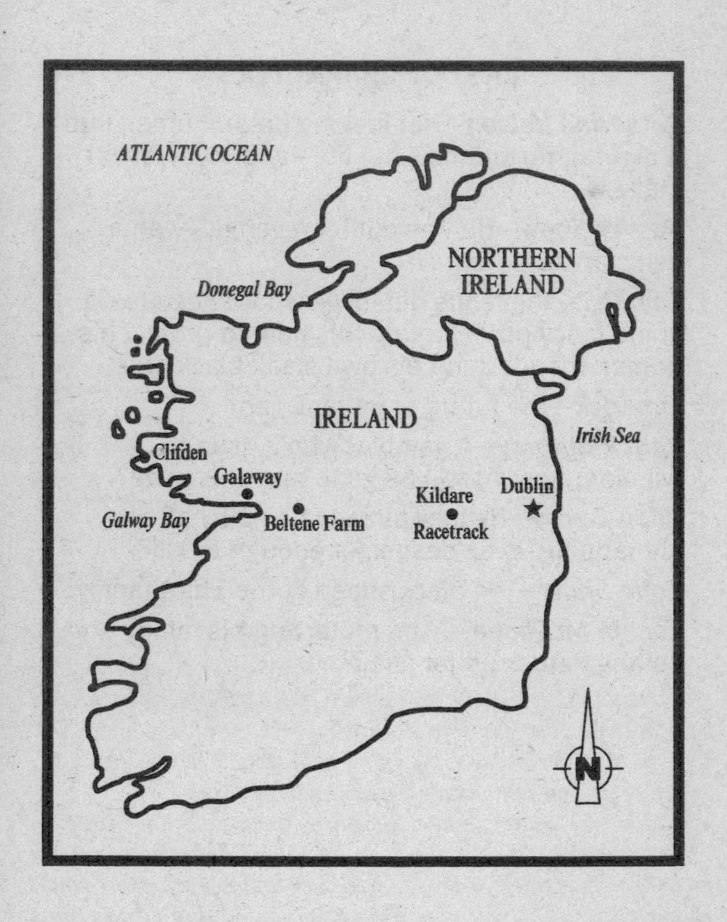
ATLANTIC OCEAN
NORTHERN
IRELAND
Donegal Bay
IRELAND
Irish Sea
Clifden
Galaway
Dublin
Kildare
Racetrack
Galway Bay
Beltene Farm
N

Chapter One

I cannot believe that my life has come to this. Abandoned by my own Eleanor in the squalor of—dare I utter the word—a barn. Not your small, pleasant red variety of barn. This is an enormous rambling structure with forty stalls and a dozen workers moving about at all times.

And I'm supposed to live here. Outdoors. Eating out of a bowl that hasn't been washed in days. Drinking rainwater, if I'm lucky enough to find some.

How is it possible that I've been subjected to such a demeaning situation?

Barn cat. Think of the image this conjures up. Lean, scruffy cats always alert for the tell-tail movement of a rodent. Oh, that's not a pun, that's a gag. A real gag! They're probably going to expect me to catch rats. And eat them.

It doesn't matter that I've been smuggled into Ireland. There's not enough bracing air in all of Europe to rid my nostrils of the smell of hay and leather and horses. How could Eleanor do this to me? Dr. Doolittle, well, I don't expect any more of him. He's only a man. But Eleanor, she should know better than this.

I have a multitude of complaints about the travel arrangements, too. First of all, I resent being sedated. Second, the cage is too cramped, with poor ventilation. Third, I could have stayed in Washington and minded my own affairs with perfect safety. Ever since the bombing I've been on the lookout for my old nemesis, Arnold Evans. I know he's out and about and still trying to get even with Eleanor and Peter. Believe me, I won't make the mistake of forgetting about him or that bomb blast that nearly killed Eleanor. I won't forget or forgive. The trouble is, Eleanor won't either. She won't give Arnold another chance to hurt me or Peter. That's why I find myself in this degrading situation.

The dame packed me in this case and imported me into Ireland in an effort to keep me safe. In the whole country of Ireland, though, it seems she could have found me better accommodations than in the loft of a horse barn on the west coast of the Emerald Isle. She says it's just a temporary upset of our summer plans. The meeting on human rights scheduled in the peaceful coastal town of Galway has turned into an effort to stop a possible bombing in Northern Ireland. She's in Dublin with a hot ticket for Belfast and danger. That amnesty group she and the good doctor are working with is doing everything they can to prevent another tragedy.

And I'm left here, in a cage, in a barn, in the country, on an island, with no prayer of getting out for a little exercise and a snoop around for some vittles. I'm missing Wheel of Fortune *on television and the new Nine Lives' flavor that was due out this month.*

And my protector, if you can call the man such, is a solitary soul with an attitude. The dame can certainly pick the hard cases. Patrick Shaw. He lives up here in the barn above his beloved horses. I've been watching him and the only time he seems alive is when he's working with one of those large, temperamental equines. When he touches them, there's some kind of instant communication. Especially that big gray devil, Limerick. Too bad he hasn't developed the same bond with his human counterparts. He's a little brusque, if you ask me. I keep trying to see why Eleanor thinks he's such a wonderful man. Or at least wonderful enough to be trusted with me for two whole weeks while she's away. I just don't see it, but then again, I'm partial to tall, slinky legs, sexy eyes and the female gender. Patrick definitely doesn't qualify there. He's lean and about as soft and cuddly as a field of rocks.

He's not even a cat person. Maybe if I could whinny I could attract his attention. I want out of this cage. I'm acclimated. If he's so concerned that I won't know where I am why doesn't he put me up on one of those horses and give me a ride around the grounds? Anything to get out. I'll try the whinny.

STARTLED BY THE strange noise coming from the cat, Patrick hurried to the cage. He wasn't overly fond of felines, but he'd given Eleanor and Peter his word that he'd care for the black cat they seemed to regard with such affection. And he honored his word. Always. But especially to the couple who'd helped so many of his friends. Eleanor and Peter Curry had done a lot of work to bring peace to Ireland. For Patrick, that peace was a personal and a political concern.

As he unlatched the cage and lifted the big black cat into his arms, he sighed. In the past year he'd lost his dreams of freedom and peace. The farm that had been in his family for generations now belonged to someone else. Instead of boss, he was a hireling, a "manager." Horses that he had bred no longer belonged to him, and the only reason he remained in County Galway was the big gray stallion that had once been his future. His invitation to stay was based on the magic he worked in getting a horse to run from the heart. If it wasn't for his record as a trainer, he would have been asked to leave as soon as the ink had dried on the deed.

"Can I trust you on your own?" he whispered in the cat's ear. His brogue was as soft as his touch. He held Familiar with one hand and stroked him with the other. There was nothing that could be done to save his horse farm, but maybe Eleanor and Peter could help his country. Two weeks' care of the cat was little enough to ask in return.

"Eleanor says you're a smart lad. She said you'll learn the barn and stay out of trouble. Now don't disappoint her. She's too fine a lady to be troubled by a prowling cat. And I've got the devil's own spawn due here in five minutes to torment me to death.'' He put Familiar on the ground and walked away.

Tail twitching, the black cat hurried after the man as he disappeared down the center of the barn.

''Miss Nelson will be here any minute,'' Patrick said as he walked to a cluster of grooms. ''Check the tack room once again. If there's a speck of grain on the feed room floor, I'll have someone's head, and that's a promise. Be sure Limerick's blanket is spotless, and that his halter has been oiled.''

''That's a fair amount of work for one woman who'll walk in, twitch her nose, give a few orders and leave.'' The man who spoke had a thicker accent, gray hair and an abundance of wrinkles. He walked with a slight limp, evidence of a bad encounter with a horse. ''She's a banker, not a horsewoman. What does she know?''

''I don't like it any better than you do, Mick,'' Patrick said, not bothering to hide his displeasure. ''But if it pleases Catherine Nelson to have spotless blankets and oiled halters, then we shall have them for her.''

''Aye, what would please her would be...''

General laughter erupted among the grooms at Mick's bawdy remark. For the first time that day Patrick's mouth played with the idea of a smile. At last the smile won out and his blue eyes danced. ''That'll be enough of that. I don't believe Miss Nelson is known for her sense of humor or her fondness for the opposite sex.''

''And what exactly is Miss Nelson known for?'' The soft female voice carried a load of sarcasm.

Patrick and the grooms stopped laughing. They turned to confront the woman who stood at the open door of the barn in immaculate riding boots, tan breeches and a black hunt jacket. Tall and slender, her shadow stopped right at the toe of Patrick's boot.

He took in the shape of her leg, lean and booted, the curve of her hips and waist. Beneath the expensive material of her jacket he could see her breasts rising and falling softly, dangerously. She was mad and struggling to control it. She had more than a bit of spirit, and that was something he enjoyed in his horses and his women. "She's known for giving ridiculous orders and having a bad temper," Patrick said evenly, knowing that he was deliberately baiting her. The men around him stood very still.

"Just as my barn manager is known for his arrogance and rudeness." She lifted an eyebrow. "Instead of hating us, Mr. Shaw, you should be glad that my father bought your family's business. It would have been auctioned off piece by piece and horse by horse. At least this way the farm was maintained and you have a job. Which won't last long with that attitude no matter what kind of a magician you are with the horses." She walked outside, gave a signal to someone, and turned back to Patrick. "Bring Limerick out of his stall. And do be sure his blanket is clean and his halter is well oiled." Without a backward glance, she walked into the sunshine.

"That's a cold one," Mick said softly. "Many a man would shrivel before that Medusa."

"A smart man would run," agreed Jack, a young groom. He looked at Patrick, but the taller man was staring at the empty door through which Catherine Nelson had disappeared. The look on Patrick's face was anything but that of a man who intended to yield the battlefield. "Don't even be thinking you can best her, Patrick," Jack whispered. "She's a devil and she owns you lock, stock and barrel."

"Get on with your chores," Patrick said. His blue eyes were hard even though his voice was soft. "I'll bring Limerick out myself."

"She's here because you haven't worked him in a week," Mick said. "I told you she'd be on your back. They mean to race that horse next week no matter what condition his knee is in. It doesn't matter to them if they cripple him or not. Why should it matter when they can just buy another toy to race?"

"That's enough!" Patrick's words were harsh. "Get to

work or you'll find yourself begging along the roadsides. It's only by Miss Nelson's generosity that any of us have jobs. And that's something she never intends to let us forget."

As Patrick strode down the barn, Mick shook his head. He spotted the black cat sitting by the wall. "Ah, the American cat. It's best for you if you take yourself off from here. If Miss Nelson sees you she might take it into her mind that you aren't part of the Nelson plan. Then you'll be in a pickle and Patrick right alongside you."

Familiar arched his back and rubbed against Mick's leg.

"So, you aren't intimidated by the likes of Catherine Nelson, are you?" He scratched the cat's ears. "Neither is Patrick. And that doesn't bode well for his future."

Mumbling to himself, Mick went to make sure the foals had been brought into the barn for their evening feeding. His mumbling ceased as he stepped into the sunshine. It was hard to be in a bad mood when the sun was shining and the grass was as green as a new bud.

Inside the barn Familiar sought deep shadows.

AH, THINGS ARE picking up. Instead of a bucolic holiday in the country, I get the feeling that Eleanor and Peter aren't the only ones dealing with an explosive situation. Catherine Nelson. What a babe. She carries herself like royalty, and she's got the face and figure to support the title. If she ever let that red hair loose from that braid, I'll bet it would go all the way to the top of those long, long legs. Really a classy piece of work in those boots and breeches. Maybe an ice queen, though. She's cold. But I suspect that Patrick runs just as hot. It's a tit for tat situation here. Now I'd better scoot to see how Limerick will fare in this contest of wills. I'm laying my bets on Patrick.

THE BIG GRAY stallion nosed his velvety muzzle into the halter that Patrick held. With a quick movement, Patrick latched the hook and stepped back to allow Limerick to enter the barn aisle. The stallion's stall was in a separate portion of the barn, removed from the mares and geldings. Patrick used the cross ties to secure him in the center of the aisle and quickly readjusted his green blanket before Catherine Nelson could arrive. He heard her before he saw her.

"He's the best prospect I've seen in years. That's one reason we've kept him over here in Galway. We didn't want to attract any attention. When we take him to Kildare County on Saturday we want to take them by storm."

Patrick's fingers clenched the cross tie as he watched Catherine walk into the barn with a tall, well-muscled man also dressed in riding clothes. His boots were polished to a high gloss, his tweed jacket immaculate. Just as always.

"Patrick, this is Kent Ridgeway. Kent, this is our trainer, Patrick Shaw."

The two men eyed each other, neither extending a hand nor making any gesture of common courtesy. Patrick knew Kent Ridgeway. They'd competed against each other for years, though they'd never met face-to-face.

"For God's sake, Kent," Catherine said with exasperation. "You two act like dogs ready to be thrown into the pit together. Surely you know Patrick's work. His horses have won everything in the country. As I understand it, Patrick's bloodlines have consistently put yours in second place."

"They're your horses now," Kent said easily. His gaze strayed over to the gray who had begun to paw the ground. "Yes, I'm familiar with the Shaw name in horse breeding. It was exceptional at one time. Tell me, Patrick, was it bad management, fondness for the bottle, or gambling that lost Beltene Farm for you?"

Patrick gently pulled in his breath. "I'm not certain that it's any of your business why I chose to sell my farm, Ridgeway."

"Kent!" There was genuine disapproval in Catherine's voice. "Patrick's right. That is none of your concern. If you're going to act like a boor I'll get someone to drive you back into town."

"Sorry, Catherine." Kent smiled at her. "I didn't realize how personal the question would sound. Forgive me, Patrick. I wasn't thinking." He smiled at Patrick, his blue eyes hard.

"Enough foolishness. Let's get the blanket off this big fellow and give Kent a chance to look him over." Catherine stepped forward and took the green blanket off the stallion before Patrick could protest. "Would you saddle him up and call Timmy to ride him?" Catherine was busy running her hands over the horse's legs. She missed the expression that blazed on Patrick's face.

"Did you not get the message I sent about Limerick's right knee?" Patrick asked softly.

"Indeed I did." Catherine's slender fingers pressed about the knee in question. "There's no soreness or swelling. He seems fit to me. Saddle him up."

"He's not sore because we've been resting the knee and giving him hydrotherapy along with hot rubs." Patrick's hands itched to pull her out from under the horse and shake her. Limerick's injury occurred because of one of Catherine's ridiculous orders—to keep him stalled. The horse was so anxious to get out of his stall that when he got a chance he had tried to leap over the door and had banged his knee.

"You're not resting his knee, Patrick. You're mollycoddling this animal." She finally looked up. If the thunder on Patrick's face intimidated her, she failed to show it.

"He needs another two days of walking and trotting. If you put him on the track pounding around now, you'll undo every bit of good I've done him. Then he won't be able to race Saturday or for the next three weeks!"

"It seems your employer gave you a direct order." Kent stepped forward. He put his hand on Catherine's arm. "I suggest you obey it."

"I suggest—" Patrick lowered his voice and smiled "—that you go straight to hell."

"Enough!" Catherine stepped between the two men. "I can see that this is more about male ego than about horses." She stormed toward the main section of the barn. ''I'll take care of it myself.''

''You're treading on thin ice, Shaw.'' Kent walked up to the horse and put a hand on Limerick's shoulder. The stallion shifted away from him and stamped the ground nervously.

''I'll take my chances.'' Patrick eased up to the horse, speaking softly to him. Limerick shook his head up and down.

''Catherine keeps you on because she feels sorry for you. She doesn't want it on her conscience that she sent another Irishman on the dole.'' Kent smiled. ''She has a big heart for a Brit, doesn't she?''

''Why are you so concerned about who Miss Nelson hires or doesn't hire?'' Patrick's fists were clenched white at his sides. Every few seconds the right one twitched, as if it had a mind of its own.

''Let's just say I have an interest.''

Patrick started. ''You don't mean to say that she's so stupid she's involved with the likes of you? She couldn't be that much of an idiot, not even if she poured half her brains out her ear and scrambled the rest.''

Kent smiled. ''You don't think much of me, and the feeling is mutual. If you ever had anything worth having here, you've ruined it. If you don't run a racehorse it isn't much good.''

''That shows what you know about horses. I...'' Patrick stopped. Catherine was walking rapidly toward them, a reluctant Timmy following behind with his racing saddle over his arm.

''Saddle up Limerick and let's get out to the track,'' Catherine said to the jockey. ''I didn't come here to watch men argue, strutting their testosterone levels and acting like fools.''

Timmy cast a silent appeal toward Patrick.

''Hold, Timmy,'' Patrick said softly. ''You'll be putting the saddle away now. Limerick isn't going anywhere.''

Timmy turned on his heel and started back down the barn.

''Timmy Sweeney, you'd better think who signs your paycheck before you take another step.''

Catherine's clear voice stopped the jockey in midstride. He turned back to look at Patrick.

"I won't put Timmy's job on the line," Patrick said. He unclipped Limerick's halter. "But I don't believe Timmy can saddle him if he's moving around." With that, he started out of the barn with Limerick following obediently.

"Wait just a minute!" Kent moved to catch Limerick's halter.

The stallion's head whipped around and his bared teeth caught Kent's jacket. With a jerk, the horse pulled half the sleeve away.

Patrick kept walking.

"Damn you, Patrick Shaw. This isn't the end of this. You can't behave as if that horse is still your property."

Patrick never turned around. "Go back to Dublin, Miss Nelson. I've heard you're quite good over fences on the hunt when you're not toting up your father's money at the bank. Go back to what you know and leave the training of these horses to someone who knows what he's doing. Limerick will race. And when he does, he'll win. But he won't race until he's ready."

Catherine watched helplessly as the tall trainer left the barnyard and walked down the tree-shaded lane. The gray was following him like a puppy.

She turned her attention to the man who stood rubbing his arm.

"Are you hurt?"

"No," Kent said. "He's one arrogant bastard, Catherine. I hope you don't intend to keep him around here much longer."

Catherine noticed Timmy still standing near a wall, his saddle over his arm. "That's all for today. Thank you." As furious as she was with Patrick, she didn't want to discuss his future in front of other members of the staff. If she decided to fire him, he'd be the first to know, not the last. And at the moment, she felt like booting him off Beltene Farm—except that he was the best man with a horse she'd ever seen, even if he did pamper the animals too much.

"Let's go to the house," she said, allowing Kent to take her elbow. "I'll get some ice for your arm."

"No wonder these people think they still run things. You're going to have to do something about that man. I didn't drive all the way from London to be told by the hired help that I couldn't watch a horse work."

"He's raised that stallion since it was a foal. It must be difficult." Catherine cast one last look over her shoulder. Limerick was still following Patrick around like a giant puppy.

"Difficult!" Kent was outraged. "You're not feeling sorry for that man, are you?"

"Not exactly sorry. It's just that he seems to have a special bond with Limerick. Kent, you should see him ride." She sighed. "Those horses come alive for him. They want to please him. I've never seen anything like it. And Limerick is the best he's produced."

"The horse is ill-mannered and dangerous. It bit my sleeve. If a horse in my stables had behaved in such a fashion, I'd discipline it. Shaw simply allows these animals to do whatever they wish. They run if they want to, they bite if they decide to do that." He raised his hands in the air. "What's next?"

"A glass of champagne and some cheese." Catherine put her hand through his arm. "Let's not let this ruin our day. Limerick will run Saturday. That's a promise. Patrick Shaw may think he's won the war but he's only fought the first battle. If that horse is sound, he'll run. And he'll win."

A SLIVER OF MOON hung just above the horizon, giving barely enough light to help guide the horse trailer that moved toward Beltene Farm. There were no lights on the trailer, and no one from the barn came out to greet the lone driver. The man got out of the Land Rover and went into the barn. Only a few moments later he returned, leading a large horse wrapped in a green blanket. The horse walked willingly into the trailer.

From the barn loft a small black figure watched. The cat's

tail twitched several times, but he was as silent as horse and man.

Less than five minutes after he'd arrived, the man was driving away. He drove the road blind, without any assistance from headlights, until he was nearing the main intersection. There was no traffic, and he pulled the trailer onto the road and picked up speed.

Familiar heard the sound of footsteps below him on the barn floor.

"That should fix the high-and-mighty Catherine Nelson."

The voice that spoke was filled with enough anger to make even the brogue sound harsh and ugly.

"It could very well fix us all," a second man replied.

"You're always looking over your shoulder to pay a price, Mick," the younger man said.

"That's because I'm old enough to know that there's always a price to pay." Mick's voice was sad. "It's a bad situation when we come to this. A bad situation."

"They had no right to come in here and buy up everything we've worked for. They make us out to be nothing more than servants. This is less than what they deserve."

"Not by their standards. And not by the law."

"The law, is it? Is that what you're going to start living by now?"

Mick sighed. "What we've done is stolen a horse. That's the cold and simple cut of it. If we're caught, we'll pay the price."

"When should we tell Patrick that the horse is gone?"

Mick snorted. "We'll tell him nothing. Let him find out on his own."

"But we should tell him," the younger man insisted.

"You'll keep your mouth shut and that's the final say. Do you want to start the hue and cry this minute, when the van is hardly gone around the bend?"

"You've no stomach for this." The younger man turned back into the barn. "I'll get my jacket and we'll be gone."

Mick stood for a minute staring into the empty night. The wind had picked up and it was cold, even for late summer. He stuffed his bare hands into the pockets of his jacket and hunched his shoulders. "It's a bad night's work, and only the young are foolish enough to think no one will pay." He spoke to the night and then turned back into the barn.

Chapter Two

Patrick stood beside the cold fireplace remembering the room from when he was a boy of twelve. He'd stood waiting in just the same spot to confess to the sin of breaking the O'Keefe's front window with a ball. Twenty years had passed since he'd been inside the house. Twenty years and a lot of hardship.

When John Nelson, Catherine's father, had bought Beltene Farm for her, he'd also purchased the adjoining property. He'd left the stables as a working farm, but he'd renovated the O'Keefe house to serve as his weekend estate in the country—and Catherine's headquarters. What had once been the library in the old O'Keefe house was now the office of Catherine Nelson.

Patrick walked to the window as he waited. The stables weren't visible from the house. The road separated the two properties, but that wasn't nearly enough distance as far as he was concerned. It was bad enough selling the stables, but now that Catherine had expressed her intentions of moving from Dublin to the farm to take a serious interest in the horse business, Patrick knew that she would be too close in every respect. Too close and too pushy. The fact that she was beautiful didn't help matters, either. He found himself reacting with two diverse and contradictory impulses. It was a condition he'd been warned about often enough, by his mother, his friends and his church.

The door opened, and the redhead walked into the room. Light from the windows struck her face, and Patrick almost didn't believe that the woman who stood before him was the same one who'd been in the barn. Hair down well below her shoulders, Catherine wore a short skirt and sweater. Gold earrings dangled from her ears and patterned hose called attention to her long legs. She looked young and adventurous, not the cold and bossy woman he tried to remember. Her first words brought back the chill.

"I hope you've come to apologize for your behavior yesterday." Catherine walked past him to the desk, where she took a seat and motioned him into a chair. She sat because she did not want Patrick to see that she was uncomfortable. He seemed to fill the room, just as he did the barn. The men at the bank where she'd worked were different. They took up their space and no one else's. Patrick took it all, with a casual grace that was unnerving. She had to make him understand that she was in charge of Beltene. If she failed to show her strength now, he would never respect her as his employer. "The way you behaved was rude and—"

Patrick stood. "I did not come to apologize. I came to tell you that Limerick is gone." He'd meant to deliver the news with a bit more finesse, but he had to remember that Catherine Nelson's ignorance and power could ruin the animals he'd devoted his life to. He could not afford to be tender or kind.

"Gone where?" Catherine's furrowed brow was indication that she hadn't yet grasped the situation.

"Just gone." Patrick steeled his voice and his emotions. "I was hoping you'd tell me where he is."

She tilted forward in her chair, bracing her arms against the desk. "Are you telling me that my father's most valuable racehorse is gone? His stall is empty and there's no sign of him?"

"Yes, ma'am." Patrick took a perverse pleasure in his servile response.

Catherine slowly stood up. "Limerick has been stolen?"

"I did not say that. I said he was gone. If you didn't take him, though, then apparently he has been stolen."

"As simple as that, someone walked into my barn and walked out with a horse?"

"It does seem hard to believe."

She leveled a steady gaze at him—a gaze that had made executives in the bank step back. "You're taking this awfully calmly, Mr. Shaw. Aren't you concerned about the horse?"

"As you pointed out yesterday, Limerick is no longer mine to care about." Patrick stared at the floor as he spoke, giving nothing away by expression or voice. "I did want you to know as soon as I was told...so there would be no confusion or accusations."

Catherine found it difficult to absorb the news. Beltene was a big place, with stable hands constantly about. "No one heard or saw a thing?" Her voice registered disbelief.

"That's exactly the way it happened." Patrick watched the beginning of the quiver at the left corner of her mouth. He wasn't certain if she was going to cry, curse, or come out swinging. He dismissed the idea of tears. Catherine Nelson wasn't soft enough to cry. "According to your instructions, I'd spent a great deal of time working with Limerick's loading and unloading. He was awfully well trained about getting into the horse van. He liked to travel."

Catherine ignored the last barb. Her brow furrowed deeper with concentration. "Sit down, Mr. Shaw. We've got to figure out who has Limerick and how to get him back. If it's someone in the barn, acting alone or under your instructions, have them return the horse and all will be forgiven. I'm going to give you that one chance because I believe you could have been motivated by your concern for the animal." She looked at him, her gaze unwavering. "I may not care for you personally, but I don't believe you're a common thief."

Reluctant admiration made Patrick concede to her command. He eased his lanky frame into the chair. Instead of going to pieces as he'd anticipated, Catherine had done the exact opposite. She didn't know beans about horses, but she wasn't a total idiot, either. "There's no need for a general amnesty. There's no one at the barn guilty of any crime."

"Then let's get to some facts. When did you discover he was gone?" She took out a pen and paper and began to make notes.

"Just before I walked over here. I mixed his feed and took it to his stall. That's when I noticed it was empty." He watched the way her pen looped over the page. Elegant handwriting.

She looked at her watch. It was still early morning. Just after seven o'clock. "Maybe one of the grooms has taken him for a workout?"

"No one touches Limerick but me." He spoke coldly to crush the hope in her eyes.

"How convenient." The softness was gone. "I want a list of all the grooms who stayed at the barn last night. I want the entire staff assembled in the barn in fifteen minutes. I'll be over there, as soon as I call the police."

Patrick had been ready to rise from his chair when her final words stopped him. "Do you think it's such a good idea to bring the authorities into it?"

"Of course. A valuable animal has been stolen." Catherine felt her exasperation rising. Patrick was looking at her as if she were completely daft. "Why wouldn't I call the police?"

Patrick's jaw twitched once. "Remember when Speedo was stolen?"

Catherine nodded. Who could forget that horrible case? The horse had been held for ransom and then killed. The very idea made her stomach knot.

"It was said the men who stole the horse wouldn't have killed him if the authorities hadn't been called in. Once they were cornered, they reacted badly. It might be better, for Limerick, if we…if you waited to see if there is some kind of demand made."

Catherine put her pen down. "Should I be expecting a ransom demand?" She held her breath.

"I suggest you wait for a call, or at least until the post arrives, before you rush around making any outlandish accusations or riling the staff." Patrick saw the look in her eyes. "All of the grooms have been with me or my father for at least five years. Some over twenty. You can't accuse a man of being a thief and then expect him to forget it the next day."

"I don't believe I asked you for a lecture on the collective ego of *my* staff." Catherine stood. "Don't touch anything near Limerick's stall. I'm sure my father will insist that I hire a detective, and the insurance company will also want to send someone to look into this." She brushed her hair back and set her earrings into motion. The gold glittered in her hair.

Patrick stood, hands clasped in front of him as he watched Catherine begin searching the directory for the appropriate telephone numbers. She looked up. "Is there anything else?"

"I just thought it was worth a mention that you've never once inquired about the horse's health. If he's been taken for ransom, he might be well cared for. If he's been taken because someone knows his potential, he might be dead. But then, he's just another investment to people like you."

"No one would kill such a magnificent animal." Catherine's face blanched. "That's a terrible thing to even bring up. Limerick is extremely valuable. He has the potential to sweep the English and French tracks. No one in their right mind would steal him just to hurt him."

"I wish that were true."

Catherine snapped the pencil in her hand. "You're merely trying to scare me, aren't you? You take pleasure in making me think of the worst things possible."

Patrick could not stop the rush of pity he felt for her at last. Her face was white, startling against the red of her hair. "They can't run him. He's too distinctive in his coloring and his conformation. They can't register the foals if they breed him—

unless they falsify his records." He stopped. He'd made his point.

Catherine's green eyes glazed with worry. "We have to get him back. Before he's injured."

For a split second Patrick thought Catherine might cry. The woman was hard as volcanic rock baked in the hot sun for ten thousand years. Tears were biologically impossible for her. Yet they glittered dangerously at her lower lids, threatening to slip down her face.

"I'm sure Limerick will be okay." Patrick was surprised at the tenderness in his own voice. Where had that come from?

"And how are you sure?" Catherine rounded on him with words as sharp as a slap. "Unless you know who has him."

"You're a hard woman to give a bit of comfort." Patrick moved toward the door. He was as mad at himself as at her high-handed tone. "I'll have *your* staff assembled, Miss Nelson. I hope you have sense enough to take their offers of help, if they dare to give any." He walked out of the room and shut the door behind him with a solid slam. She was the most infuriating woman he'd ever met.

When he got to the barn he called up the workers. There were fifteen in all, with one missing. "Where's Mick?" he asked.

"One of the foals stepped on his bad foot this morning. He took himself home for a hot soak," Jack said. He gave Patrick a knowing look. The grooms, trainers and stable hands looked speculatively at Patrick. They all knew that Limerick was gone. They all believed he'd taken the animal.

"Don't touch anything near Limerick's stall. Miss Nelson is calling the police. There will be an investigation, so I suggest you all try to remember where and with whom you spent the night last night."

"And what about yourself?" a trainer asked, grinning. "I hope you have an alibi, Patrick. You'll be the first they suspect. You went up against her royal highness and you'll pay the price."

"They can suspect me all they want. I don't give a damn for their suspicions. When they can prove something on me, then I'll have a worry."

Patrick shifted his attention to the barn door. Catherine had slipped up on him once, but it wouldn't happen again. He was watching for her. She arrived promptly, already changed into riding breeches and a sweater, her long hair pulled into a severe chignon. Patrick expected Catherine to be on time. What he didn't expect was Kent Ridgeway to still be with her. The British trainer had undoubtedly spent the night at the country house.

That idea made Patrick's temper flare. Ridgeway was a successful trainer, but then no one kept statistics on how many of his horses broke down after a short racing season. No one but him and a few other trainers who abhorred Ridgeway's practices. Ridgeway's horses ran and they won. And then they suffered the consequences of his win-at-any-cost program. With leg injuries and temperaments spoiled by mistreatment, many had to be destroyed. Yet Ridgeway was an honored guest of Catherine Nelson. The fact rankled.

"Miss Nelson, I would appreciate it if we could keep this meeting among the staff." Patrick shot a pointed glance at Ridgeway. "A stranger will only make a bad situation worse."

"Mr. Ridgeway has an interest in this matter." Catherine's tone was glacial. Her fury at Patrick's suggestion was plain for all to see.

"It isn't a good method of doing business," Patrick insisted. "An outsider will only heighten what's sure to be an emotional meeting. We're all very concerned about Limerick."

"Mr. Ridgeway may not be an outsider for long."

Even expecting the worst of Catherine, Patrick was stunned. He looked away from her, dropping his gaze so that she could not see the emotions in his eyes. His vision chanced upon the black cat sitting sphinxlike down the barn. The strangest feeling that Familiar was drinking in the entire scene gave him the distance from his anger that he needed. He struggled for composure and finally won.

"Is Mr. Ridgeway coming to work here at Beltene?" Casual interest was all he dared express.

"That's really not your concern, but the answer is no. I'm considering sending some of the two-year-olds down to his training facility. He can condition them faster than we're doing here. They'll also be convenient when the English racing season opens. I want Beltene to hit the next racing season with a horse in every major event. But none of this is relevant now. We're here to discuss Limerick."

"Not relevant!" Patrick shouted. He couldn't help himself. He'd rather see them sold for plow horses than crippled by Ridgeway. "You'd give that man my horses to break down. I—"

"They are no longer your horses." Catherine's calm voice cut through his outrage. It stopped Patrick in midsentence.

"A fact I won't forget again." Patrick matched her, glare for icy glare. He could only be thankful his father was not alive to witness this moment. Thomas Shaw would surely be turning over in his grave at such a tragedy. And there wasn't a damn thing Patrick could do. If Catherine decided to put Ridgeway in charge of every horse on Beltene, Patrick could not stop it.

"If Mr. Shaw will allow us, we'll get on with this. As you all know by now, the most valuable horse at Beltene has been...taken."

Mumblings swept among the men. Several looked at Patrick, some with glee and others with worry.

"I want the grooms on duty last night to come with me. Everyone else will remain here. Use the time to try and remember anything that might be of help in locating Limerick. If he's still alive—" Catherine's voice trembled slightly "—we want him back." She turned abruptly and walked toward the barn office where Patrick kept the records on each horse. Ridgeway followed.

Five men in the group shifted uneasily and started forward. "I knew there was going to be hell to pay for this," one of them said. He swung his gaze around the cluster. "If one of you has taken that horse, I hope you bring him back before we all lose our jobs. I've got a family. My children need shoes and books. In case you haven't noticed, jobs are scarce."

"Keep your mouth shut and stand together," Jack warned him. He led the others to the office door where Catherine waited.

"Sean is upset." Timmy came up to Patrick. "He's afraid we'll all be fired."

"Sean stays upset. If the sun shines, he wants rain. If rain is soaking the earth, he wants dry weather."

"Will we all be fired?" Timmy touched Patrick's arm. "I can still get on at one of the stables in Kildare. If I'm accused of horse theft, no one will ever hire me again."

Patrick stared at Timmy. "You're the best jockey I have. It would hurt me to see you go, but I can't make predictions on the future. The mind of Catherine Nelson is a dark and twisted thing. You'll have to make your own decisions about what to do."

"Did you take Limerick?" Timmy rubbed his forehead with his fist. "If you did, bring him back. I know you're worried about his knee, but is one horse worth all of the men who work here?"

"I don't attempt to give you advice, Timmy. I'd appreciate the same consideration." Patrick's look left no room for further conversation.

I'D SWEAR that it was Patrick I saw leading that horse out of here last night. But it was dark, and I didn't get a clear look. The million dollar question is, who else would that horse follow around like a big dog? It's a puzzle, that's for sure.

With two resolved mysteries under my belt, I've given myself the official title of T.O. That's Trained Observer, to the uninformed. T.O.s notice the fine detail, the telling nuance. For example, everyone was so busy watching the Ice Queen and the Lone Ranger at each other's throats, no one paid any attention to that British fellow. Except me. He's about the same size as Patrick. He's a horse trainer. He was looking at the Ice Queen as if he intended to melt her bones. Hmm. Is that the reason I sense the old chap despises Patrick? Could be a simple case of jealousy. Or it could be more.

Looks like my confinement in the country is going to be more interesting than I thought.

Catherine deserves some serious contemplation, too. Now that's an easy task. For all of that frost she generates, there's something in her eyes that tells me she's not as cold as she likes to portray. Cat's eyes. I'll bet, given the right set of circumstances, that one could make the fur fly. I've always heard that no water boils so fast as that from a freezing spring.

Well, okay, maybe I did make that up, but it sounds right. Especially where Miss Catherine is concerned. If only Eleanor were here. I can see that things are going to come to a head very quickly. And it is my moral obligation to look out for Patrick, even though he isn't the best host I've ever visited. He just needs a bit of refining, I suppose. As interesting as all of this may be, it doesn't help resolve who took that big gray horse.

Speculation never made a solid case, so the T.O. must begin to gather evidence. Lucky no one around here seems to take any notice of me. Anonymity is great, except I'm ready for breakfast. I refuse to eat that horrible crispy stuff he put out for me. I can't believe my Eleanor wasn't stricter with him about my dietary needs. At any rate, the main house is across the road. I wonder if I trotted over and chatted up the cook if I might get a few luscious tidbits. I can smell the ocean from here so I know there's bound to be some tasty seafood in that kitchen. Patrick spent twenty minutes last night mixing up oats and corn and barley for that horse. And he pours a bowl of dry food for me. That man has a lot to learn about cats. Cats and women. And I do believe that Catherine and I might just be the team to clue him in.

After I solve the mystery of Limerick.

And that's after breakfast.

Oh, saunter, saunter. I haven't had to warm up a cook in quite some time. It'll be good practice for me. The kitchen is always the place to pick up the local gossip. Right at this minute I'm curious to find out how Kent Ridgeway fits into the scheme of things.

"WHERE DID THAT CAT come from?" Catherine's voice stopped Familiar and every stable hand within hearing.

"Patrick's keeping him for a friend." Timmy spoke up.

"Has it had all of its vaccinations?" Catherine took a step backward as the black cat turned to look at her. She could swear his green eyes went from curious to furious. One minute he'd been simply looking at her, and the minute she'd said "vaccination," he glared. His green eyes were slits of displeasure.

"I'm sure this cat is fine. He's from America. His owners are here on business and they were called away suddenly. Patrick's only keeping him a few days." Timmy was almost pleading.

"America?" The cat seemed intent on her, as if he'd excluded everyone and everything else from his attention. "He is a handsome animal." The barn lights were reflected in his sleek black coat. When no one answered her question, she snapped, "Tell Patrick to take him 'round to the clinic and be sure he's had all his shots."

"He's a special case," Timmy supplied. "A rare exception he is, to get into Ireland like he did."

"I still want to make certain that he's vaccinated. For his sake as well as—"

"Yours? Afraid he might bite you?" Patrick's voice held a clear challenge. He'd quietly followed Catherine. "I think if they let Ridgeway into Ireland they should certainly let a well-behaved cat.''

''I spoke with the men who were on duty,'' Catherine said, ignoring his remark. ''They deny hearing anything. They were all industriously working in some other area of the barn. Sean pointed out, in fact, that since you're living over the area where Limerick's stall is, that you'd be the logical one to hear any disturbance.''

''That is logical.'' Patrick bent over and scooped Familiar into his arms. ''I heard nothing.''

''So you've said.'' Catherine forgot about the cat and approached the trainer. There was a dangerous glint in Patrick's eyes. For a split second, while he was standing in the library, she thought she'd seen something more. A flash of interest, a hint of sympathy. But that was impossible. Patrick Shaw hated her and her family. He hated everything she stood for as a successful member of one of the British families that had decided to make Ireland their home.

Intruder. Interloper. Outsider. Those were some of the prettier names she'd heard behind her back. Some of the others were far worse. True, she'd never heard Patrick utter any of those phrases. He didn't have to open his mouth. She read contempt in every line of his body whenever she asked him the simplest question or offered the tiniest suggestion. Were he not the best trainer in the British Isles, she'd find it more than a simple matter to dismiss him. That and the fact that she felt some degree of sympathy for what had happened to him through his family's decisions.

Beltene, named for beltane, the pagan spring holiday on the first day of May, had been in his family for five generations. They'd created a name and a breeding line that was limited but legendary. But they'd lost it. No one had taken it from them. Poor management and bad decisions had put them in the red. Her father had paid a fair and reasonable price for it. More than he would have had to if the banks had had their way. Instead of being grateful that his family heritage had been left intact, he resented her father—and even more so, her.

"Have you notified the police?"

Patrick's question went right by her. She was studying him, the way he held the cat so gently and glared at her so fiercely. Something in his eyes accelerated her pulse.

"Have you notified the police?" Patrick repeated. Not only was the woman insufferable, she apparently went into dazes. She was staring at him and the cat as if she'd never seen either man or feline.

"I'm sorry." She blinked her eyes. "No. I decided to wait for the post, as you suggested."

Patrick let his back relax slightly. "If you receive anything, will you let me know?"

Catherine caught the worry in his voice. For the first time she considered that he might actually be innocent. "Yes, I will."

"Thank you." Patrick walked past her without another word.

Catherine was left standing alone in the aisle, watching his lean hips. He had the perfect body for a horseman. Long, powerful legs. Muscled back. What would it be like to have a man like Patrick Shaw, to lay in his arms and welcome his kisses? The question came unbidden, and she felt again the acceleration of her pulse.

It was an idle and stupid thought. A dangerous thought. Patrick Shaw was a handsome man. She'd noticed that long ago. He was also a man of great dignity. It crossed her mind that he wasn't the kind of man who would steal so much as a biscuit, much less a racehorse. But she had to remember that he was a man capable of making a terrible enemy. If that's the route he chose.

Catherine entered the small office that Patrick used and found Kent sitting at the desk, files on each employee open before him and his hand just replacing the telephone receiver.

"I've put through a call to Dublin. Sam Prescott is one of

the chief investigators there. He's a personal friend of mine. I'm sure he'll take a special interest in this case.'' He stood and walked over to her. He casually touched her hair. ''I'm sorry, Catherine. We'll get the horse back. I promise.''

Catherine tried to check her irritation, but she failed. ''You shouldn't make promises you can't keep. Unless you know where the horse is, how can you promise to keep him safe? Besides, I'll call the Galway police department after lunch. There's no cause to involve Dublin in this.''

''Limerick is insured for half a million pounds, Catherine. Your trainer, Mr. Shaw, has relatives who've been involved in some of the troubles in Northern Ireland.'' Kent went back to the desk and pulled out the appropriate paper. ''I thought I'd simply expedite matters.''

''Between you and Patrick you'd think I didn't have a brain in my head.'' Catherine took the paper from his hand. ''I can read, Kent. I know about Patrick's brother. I can weigh information. And I will.''

Kent leaned back in the chair. ''You are rather touchy about this. I can see Shaw challenges your authority at every turn. I'm sorry, darling, I didn't mean to do the same thing. I only wanted to help.''

''Oh, blast it all to hell!'' Catherine dropped the piece of paper on the desk. ''I'm sorry, too. I just can't believe that Limerick is gone. Disappeared. Without a trace and without a single person even hearing him go.''

''Catherine,'' Kent's tone was amused, ''surely you don't believe that Shaw and his helpers are innocent? You're not that naive. My advice to you is to dismiss every single one of them. That will break their little conspiracy of silence. Someone had to see that horse go. If you want Limerick back, alive, you're going to have to be as ruthless as they are.''

Chapter Three

Catherine's hand shook as she held the single page of cheap white paper. Letters, cut from newspapers and magazines, sloped left to right in a schoolchild's imitation of a sentence. As childish as the letter looked, its intent was deadly.

"Keep your mouth shut or horse dies. Will be in touch." That was it. Two very simple sentences that made the marrow of her bones harden with fear.

Kent's footsteps echoed on the wooden floor outside her office and she hurriedly tucked the letter into the top drawer of her desk. She was just in time as the door opened.

"Did the post arrive?" he asked.

"Yes." Catherine swallowed. Some impulse told her to keep the letter to herself. Kent was only trying to be helpful, but he pushed her too fast. She needed time to think, to weigh the advantages and disadvantages of every action. If the person holding Limerick wanted ransom, she was willing to pay. Realistically, though, there was only so far she could go. That was as far as her own personal savings stretched. Her father would never, ever agree to pay a ransom. Many people viewed him as a hard man. He'd become a successful banker because he never let his emotions rule the bottom line, and his motto was Never Yield To An Unreasonable Demand. No matter how much he valued a horse, he would never pay a ransom demand. For herself, Catherine wanted the stallion home, safe and sound. She'd pay whatever it took, if she had enough money.

"Well, was there anything in it?" Kent waved his hand in front of her eyes. "Was there a note in the mail?"

"Kent, what are we going to do about the race Saturday? We need to scratch Limerick, but we don't want to draw any attention to the fact that he's missing." She couldn't bear to lie outright to Kent. He'd agreed to stay at Beltene for another few days, just to help her out. With fifty horses in his own stables, he had more than enough on his plate. Yet he'd put aside his own responsibilities and obligations for her. She owed him honesty at least.

"We'll make sure he's scratched. There will be talk, of course, but we'll try to minimize it." Kent began to pace the office. "We'll say he has a stone bruise on his hoof. People already think you're slightly mad to allow that fool Shaw to run your horses up and down the rocks here. They'll believe he struck a stone."

"Patrick feels that the roadwork conditions a horse and at the same time allows them to settle and relax. He says that track work alone doesn't fully develop—"

"I'm well aware of Shaw's radical approach. But tell me, who produces the winners. Wicklow or Beltene?"

"That's hardly fair, Kent. Beltene never had the funds to send horses all over the world like you have. The Shaws have produced some fine animals. Leprechaun's Charm, for one. Pot o' Gold for another."

"Irish national winners. With silly names, I might add."

"They could have gone further. Patrick's father didn't believe the rest of the world mattered. The Irish Sweepstakes was his goal, and he took it with both horses."

"And squandered it on a radical son."

"That's past history. I'm worried now about Saturday."

"I'll take care of pulling Limerick from the race." He went to her and smoothed the frown from her forehead. "Just leave it to me, Cat."

He leaned down to kiss her as she looked down at the files open on the desk. His lips brushed her hair. "Thank you for all of your help, Kent. We have to keep this very quiet. If we don't box the people who have him into a corner, maybe they'll keep him safe."

"I think we should call Inspector Prescott. This biding our time is a stupid waste. It only gives the thieves more of a head start."

"No. I'm going to give them twenty-four hours to make their demands known." Catherine's mind was in full throttle. "Then we'll call the Irish army, the National Guard and every other agency available."

"What makes you think twenty-four hours will make a difference?"

"Intuition." She smiled at him, her most charming smile. "Woman's intuition. And that's something no man can argue against, so you might as well not try."

"Ah, that's not fair play." He reached out and caught her hand, drawing her to him until she was only inches away. "I'll take care of canceling Limerick from the race for you. But I'm not going to tolerate this intuition business for long."

Catherine extracted her hand. "Tolerate? That's a rather presumptive word, isn't it?"

Kent smiled. "You know I have more than a passing interest in you. I don't think it's presumptuous of me to want to take care of you."

"It's presumptuous that you think I need taking care of," Catherine pointed out, but there was no bark in her tone. "I am quite capable of looking out for myself."

"I hope so, Cat. You don't know what you're dealing with when you go up against the likes of Shaw. At any rate, I hate to go, but I have to get back to England. I'll stop by Kildare on my way to Dublin."

Catherine felt her body relax. She'd met Kent at the racetrack, a handsome man who was popular with all of her friends who owned horses. They'd been thrown together socially, and before she knew what was happening, she was seeing him on a regular basis. His passion for racing almost matched her own, and it was a tremendous relief to find a man who could share her interest. But it was clear that he had more designs on her than just as a companion at the track. The trouble was, she didn't feel the same. While Kent was an entertaining companion, he didn't stir the feelings in her that Patrick Shaw did. And that was even more troubling.

Kent fit so smoothly into the contours of her life, and Patrick was like an abrasive edge. He rubbed and jarred and challenged her entire world. He was not an easy man, but the excitement he generated was undeniable. And forbidden. His anger toward her ran too deep.

"When will you return to Beltene?" she asked softly, forcing her concentration back to Kent.

"As soon as possible. I'll call you from Wicklow," he said. "If you get a ransom note, are you going to pay it?"

"It depends." She'd gnawed at that question all morning long. "I resent the idea of ransom, but I'd pay what I could to get him back."

"Limerick is a valuable animal."

"More valuable to me than anyone."

"Except maybe Shaw." Kent tapped the files on the desk. "I know you don't like to think your help could do something like this. But as I told you, it would serve several purposes for Shaw. First, revenge. I don't have to point out how sweet that would taste to him. Second, he'd have the money to leave here and start over. Shaw isn't the kind of man who takes easily to working for others, especially a woman."

"I think you might be wrong about Patrick." She stepped to the office window and looked out on the lush green pastures. "He might relish revenge and money for a fresh start, but he doesn't strike me as a thief." She turned back to face him.

"Doesn't strike you, eh?" Kent raised his eyebrows. "Is that more woman's intuition?"

"Don't be snide." Catherine had to laugh at the expression

on his face. Sometimes he could be so unrelentingly proper. "My woman's intuition tells me that there's a hint of jealousy in your behavior."

"I care about you, Catherine. A lot. You know I want to marry you. I'd have to kill that bastard if he did anything to hurt you."

"Kent!" Catherine was shocked at the vehemence in his voice. "I hardly think it will come to that. I don't believe Patrick is involved in this." She held up her hand so that he would let her finish. "But I promise you I will be extremely guarded. If there is the slightest indication that he's involved, I won't hesitate to turn him over to the authorities. A man who would steal a horse deserves a term in prison. Any man."

PATRICK WAS IN the east pasture checking on a mare and foal when he saw Ridgeway's car pull out of the estate grounds and take the main road toward Dublin. He was glad to see him go. When he'd owned Beltene, the likes of Ridgeway had never been allowed to set foot on the property. A man like Ridgeway wouldn't have been hired as a cool-down boy or a tack cleaner. But the Nelsons were a different matter. They had plenty of money and no sense.

He spied the foal he wanted to check. One of the grooms had said the bay filly was limping. They'd tried to catch her, but she'd run away. Afraid of causing more injury, they'd stopped and gone to get Patrick.

"Easy, girl." Patrick spoke low and continuously as he approached the mare. "That's a fine filly you've got there, Penny. She's exceptional. But her foot is sore and I'd like to take a look at it."

The mare rolled her eyes, showing whites. She was wary of him, but she didn't bolt and run. The filly nervously nuzzled at her side. Whenever she stepped down on her right front leg she gave to the pressure. Patrick felt a surge of worry.

"Come along, sweetie. Let's have a look at that leg. Whatever is wrong, we've got to get it tended to." His voice continued, soft and reassuring, as he eased closer to the mare and foal. When he could reach out and touch Penny's neck, he stroked her softly. His hand worked its way down her shoulder and onto the filly. Both animals quivered as if they wanted to turn and flee for all they were worth, but they stood. After a second of Patrick's hand on her, the filly calmed. Her delicate nostrils flared as she extended her nose and sniffed his hand. Very carefully, her lips touched his thumb. Limping painfully, she walked toward him.

Patrick picked up the filly's sore leg. She trembled again, pulling back slightly to signal her fear. He scratched beneath her belly, just behind her front legs, and she relaxed again.

His fingers probed the hoof, searching for bruises or anything that might have lodged in the tender frog of the foot. When he found nothing, he let his fingers slide along her leg. The tendon was puffy and warm to his touch. When he exerted the smallest amount of pressure, the filly pulled back.

"Easy, girl, easy." He released her foot and stroked her neck, scratching where the tufts of mane were just beginning to lose the wispy look of a foal. "It's to the barn for you. You're not going to like the idea of a bit of water on that leg, but I think some cold hydromassage and then a splash of liniment should fix you up. It seems you've romped yourself into a pulled tendon."

From a small beech beside the stone wall of the pasture, Catherine watched the scene between man and filly play out. She'd clearly read the filly's fear and her desire to flee when Patrick began to approach. She'd also seen the way his touch had calmed her, drawn her to him.

She leaned closer into the tree when Patrick looked her way. It wasn't that she was spying, it was just that he always made her feel like such an intruder. She'd heard of people who had "the touch." Heard and never believed. Now she'd seen it with her own two eyes. Patrick Shaw had a way with horses. Probably with all animals. What would his touch do to a woman?

Even as the thought passed into her mind, she felt heat flush through her. He didn't even have to touch her—just the thought made her giddy. She was acting like a complete fool.

The stone fence was solid but low. She hopped over it with little effort and walked toward Patrick.

"Can I give you a hand?" she asked.

Patrick didn't look surprised at her appearance. "I left a halter by the gate. Would you get it for me? I need to take this little one in."

"Sure." Catherine walked over and picked up the large red halter. She knew, then, he intended to lead the mare and let the baby follow. Once in a stall they could better manage the foal.

Catherine slipped the halter over Penny's head and handed the lead rope to Patrick. "Is she seriously hurt?"

"Just a bit of a sore tendon. It doesn't seem bad. She's a fine filly, too. Out of Charm and the mare we call Penny." Patrick smiled. "I'm afraid we don't often stick to the registered names. Too much for an average mouth."

"I know the mare," Catherine said, falling into step beside him. She looked over and saw that his eyes were more intensely blue than the sky. The wind rumpled his dark hair. Black Irish, a long-ago mixture of Moorish invaders and Viking conquerors.

"Have you noticed that none of the farmers around these parts allow their horses to graze by the sea at night?"

The question seemed completely out of left field. "No."

"It's because of the enchanted sea horses."

"Sea horses." Catherine cut a look at him. "You're playing me for a fool."

"Not on my life. They're as old as Ireland and they come out of the sea, and some lakes and rivers. They'll frolic in the pastures and when they go back to the waves and the foam, they lure the farm horses to follow. Once a horse enters the sea, he's never found again. And that's why no one dares to leave their horses grazing by the sea."

It was an interesting bit of folklore, and beautifully told. Patrick's voice warmed her as thoroughly as the sun. She found herself caught in his bit of fancy.

"I'll remember that," she answered, surprised to find she was short of breath.

"One day, perhaps, you'll be lucky enough to see a sea horse."

"I'd settle for getting Limerick back."

They were halfway across the pasture when Catherine spoke again. "Since you're not going to ask me what was in the mail, I'll tell you. There was a note. Two sentences cut out of newspaper letters. It said, 'Keep your mouth shut or horse dies. Will be in touch.'"

Patrick never slowed his stride. "And what have you decided to do?" He wondered suddenly if Ridgeway had been sent to personally talk with the law.

"I decided to wait twenty-four hours."

"What does your father say?" Patrick shot one quick glance at her. Her face was troubled, and he knew instantly that she'd consulted no one about her decision. She'd taken the matter into her own hands, and she'd taken his advice. A gust of wind fanned her hair, pulling some of it loose from the twist at the nape of her neck. The bright curls caught the sun as they tangled in her eyelashes. Patrick raised his hand to brush her hair back, then stopped. What on God's green earth was he doing?

"I haven't told anyone about the note." She brushed the stray hair from her eyes.

"Except me," he said. A half smile touched his face. "I'd reassure you if I could without incurring your wrath." The humor left his voice. "It's going to be a long twenty-four hours."

"Yes, it is." She stepped in front of him and opened the gate. Patrick led the mare through with the filly at her side.

"Patrick, if they demand money, will you take it to them?" She hadn't intended on asking that question, but watching him in the pasture she'd made a decision. If anyone should go and retrieve Limerick, it should be Patrick. He'd know instantly if the horse had been hurt, and he'd know what to do.

"We'll take that fence when we come to it," Patrick said. "May I ask you a question?"

"Turnabout is fair play."

"Why did you suddenly decide I didn't take Limerick?"

"Because you're the perfect suspect. It would be insane for you to steal him, because everyone suspects you. That makes me believe you wouldn't take him."

"I see." The tension had returned to his voice. "It's good to know how your mind works." He clucked to the mare and led her into the barn.

Catherine stood in the sunshine listening to the sounds in the barn and in the pastures behind her. All of her life she'd wanted nothing more than to work with horses. She'd dreamed horses, read about horses, drawn horses and ridden since she could walk. If she'd had her way, she'd have gone to school to study animal husbandry and agriculture and training. But her father had insisted on a business degree. He'd wanted her in the bank at Dublin. And she'd done that, for him. Even though she felt as if she'd lost nine years of her life. Four years of schooling and five long years of figures and loan applications and business deals. But as a reward, her father had purchased Beltene, and he'd finally given his approval for her to quit the bank and manage the horse farm. She had her dream at last.

And it was turning into a nightmare.

Limerick was the stallion on which she'd pinned her hopes. His potential was so clear to her. He had the ability, the natural talent, to take every race on the continent. Maybe even America. And then return as a stud. Twenty-four hours ago, it had all been possible. With the Saturday race, he would have been on his way. And now?

She couldn't sit and wait for something to happen. She made sure the gate was closed and followed Patrick's path to the barn. There had to be something else she could do.

Talk among the grooms and jockeys stopped when she walked down the barn aisle to where Patrick was soothing the little bay filly before he started treatment on her leg. There was an immediate tension among the men, as if they all expected she'd come to fire them. Or worse.

Only Patrick ignored her. His full attention was focused on the filly. For the first time in years Catherine found herself wishing that she had developed some rapport with her employees. It had never really mattered to her at the bank that she was "the boss's daughter." It mattered greatly now. She was not a part of the barn team. The harsh truth was that she might never be. The men looked to Patrick, not her.

"I was wondering if any of you had come up with ideas about who might have taken Limerick." She looked around the group. She recognized Timmy, the jockey, and Jack, one of the grooms. The others she didn't know. "If he's returned unharmed, I promise there won't be any charges filed."

No one answered her. No one looked at Patrick. They looked down at the ground or off to the side.

"I want to get Limerick back." She felt as stiff and awkward as a teenager, and she hated it. "The horse is of tremendous f-financial importance to the stables. I'm s-sure you know that." Damn! She was stammering all over the place and sounding as if it was only the money she cared about. "But that isn't my only concern."

She caught Patrick's eye. He was looking at her with interest, as if he really wanted to hear what she was saying. The usual resentment he displayed was not apparent.

"What I mean to say is that I don't want anything to happen to that horse. And not just for financial reasons. He's a special animal. Anyone with eyes can see it. I want him back here safe and sound." She took a breath. "Can you think of anything that might help? Maybe there was someone about asking questions. Have you spoken with anyone about Limerick? I'm not accusing anyone. He's a magnificent horse and it would be natural to brag about him. But if we could begin to put together a list of people who'd shown an interest in him, maybe the same name will pop up more than once. I feel that he's been taken by someone who intends to ask for a ransom."

"That's what I've been thinking," Timmy said. He cleared his throat and spoke a little louder. "The truth is, I've talked about him to several other jockeys. Just to say that he was something special and that Beltene would have a surprise for everyone once we brought him out."

"I can't believe it was a local who took him," Jack said. "At least, not anyone we know. They wouldn't do such a thing to Patrick. Everyone around here knows how long and hard he worked to get Limerick ready to race. Patrick's put the last three years of his life into that horse." He glanced at the trainer and then quickly away.

The fact that the stallion no longer belonged to Patrick hung in the air, unspoken.

"The locals wouldn't do it," Patrick said, breaking the tense silence. "Not for themselves, at least. They could never keep a horse like that secret. The gossip in this county spreads faster than lightning bolts thrown to earth."

"Maybe we should think of who Limerick would willingly leave with." She felt more comfortable. The men were at least talking with her, giving her a chance. And it was due to the example that Patrick set.

"Patrick had him well trained," Timmy said. "He'd go in the starting gate and the trailer without even blinking. He was solid there, so it wasn't a challenge to load him up."

"Is there anyone he disliked?" Catherine was desperately searching for a pattern. "Or would he follow anyone?"

"He hated that man who came out to appraise the farm." Patrick spoke again.

"That's right!" Timmy smiled at Catherine. "The gentleman got too close to the stall and Limerick reached over and picked him up by the shoulder pad in his jacket. I thought the poor man would have a heart attack. Patrick has taught Limerick too many tricks."

Catherine smiled, a genuine eye-crinkler. "So he did show discriminating taste. I didn't like that man, either. What was his name?"

"Frederick Tipton." Timmy had a note of excitement in his voice. "He was asking a lot of questions about Limerick, too. He was acting like it was insurance business, but I wondered why he was asking us instead of you, Miss Nelson."

"I'd say the man acted suspicious. Achingly suspicious," Jack added.

"Excellent." Catherine beamed. "That's it. We can all think about this and try to find likely suspects."

"And then?" Patrick asked. He kept his hand on the filly as he turned the water on. At the first pulse on her leg, she jerked, but he circled her with his arms and held her until she ceased struggling. Very gently, he loosened his grip.

"Why, then we'll begin to check these people out."

"Are you thinking of hiring a detective?" Patrick asked.

"That would be the best way. That way we could keep it secret. I mean, the authorities wouldn't have to be involved."

"I don't know, Miss Nelson. You should notify the insurance agency." Timmy's face was worried. "I don't know if the insurance company has to pay out if you don't tell them right off. I mean, you want Limerick back, but what if he's...dead?"

"And what if he is safely tucked away somewhere?" The man who spoke was tall, a fair-haired man with a thick brogue and self-composure. "I'd swear the horse is not far from here." He looked at the men around him. "I'd be willing to bet that someone in this group knows exactly where he is." His gaze shifted to Patrick and held.

"Do you have evidence of what you say, or have you been out in the bogs talking with the fairies?" Patrick's question was gentle, but his undertone was cold anger.

"I happened to follow the hoofprints to the point where I believe the stallion was loaded. The tire treads turned right onto the main road."

"Judging from the performance of the last horse you trained, maybe you'd make a better investigator than trainer," Patrick said. "It seems you're suited to the snoop."

"Let the man talk." Catherine signaled him to step forward. "What's your name?"

"Eamon McShane, assistant trainer."

"Not fit to groom." Patrick threw in. "He was due to be fired when you bought Beltene. My advice is to fire him to-day."

"For God's sake, let the man speak his piece," Catherine said, her voice sharp.

"Shaw doesn't want me to say any more because he knows that what I have to say points the finger of guilt at him."

"If you're to be pointing any fingers, you'd better have what it takes to back it up." Patrick shrugged off the hand that Timmy laid on his arm.

"Or what, Shaw?"

"Or I'll make you curse the day you were born."

"You see?" Eamon turned to Catherine. "An innocent man has no fear of the facts. Maybe I can save a call to the coppers and the insurance gents. Why don't you ask Patrick Shaw to bring his Rover and trailer up here? I marked out the tracks. It would be interesting to see if they match up. I'm willing to bet my job that it's a perfect match."

Chapter Four

Catherine stood at the front of the barn beside Eamon McShane. Patrick had not hesitated at getting his vehicle and driving it over. He hadn't hesitated, but he'd displayed a cold aloofness that spoke of possible guilt. Just at a time when she'd begun to put a little trust in the man, she found reason to suspect him. Kent's words came back to her. Who had a better reason? Who had more access?

The white Rover pulled into the yard only feet away from the tire track that Eamon McShane protected. Patrick let the Rover stop, then backed up to leave a clear track.

"It's a match," McShane proclaimed even before he'd really examined it.

Catherine bent down, hoping against hope that there would be a visible difference. Something even her untrained eye could discern. The tread marks looked identical.

"Perhaps I'd better contact the authorities," she said. Patrick got out of the Rover and walked over. She found she didn't want to meet his gaze, but she did. "It's appears to be a match," she said.

"Which proves what?" Patrick's blue eyes bored into her, daring her to accuse him aloud.

"I don't know what it proves, but it does give me pause." She knew some of the stable hands were watching from just inside the barn door. She'd been on the verge of making some connection with them. Now, once again, she was the enemy.

"Did it ever occur to you that someone else might have driven my vehicle? Or that maybe I'd driven up here two days ago to load a horse, as it happened?" Patrick threw a glance at McShane. "Or perhaps you might ask Eamon McShane if I wasn't on the verge of firing him for gross incompetence. Leaving horses without water. If he didn't have three small children and a wife with child again, he would have been gone whether you bought Beltene or not."

Catherine found herself caught between the two men in what was obviously a personal battle.

"Shaw has that horse. You can bet your life on it," McShane countered. "He'd rather see him grazing in a cropper's field than running for the Nelson family."

"That's enough." Catherine stepped between the two men before the accusations erupted into physical violence.

"What are you going to do?" McShane asked.

Catherine looked at Patrick. Once their eyes connected, she couldn't look away. He was mad, yes, but what else did she see in those blue depths. Frustration? Sadness? She couldn't be certain.

"There's only one thing I can say for sure," she said, feeling her way as she went. "If Patrick has the horse, then I have no concerns for his safety. I appreciate your help, Eamon. Keep your eyes open and feel free to speak with me at any time. Now I think it would be best if everyone returned to his duties. I know I have business at the house."

Before any more questions could be raised, she walked away. Her head was pounding with the many possibilities of destruction. She wanted to trust Patrick. Needed to trust someone. But as soon as she thought that, she realized it would not help. She had to figure this one out on her own. Advice was well and good, but the ultimate decision rested with her.

As she crossed the road she saw the big black cat standing outside the kitchen door. Before her very eyes she saw Mauve, the cook, open the door and put a china bowl on the stoop. She'd never heard Mauve say a kind word about any animal, especially a cat. She loathed the creatures. More in amazement than anything else, Catherine shifted her route so that she went to the back door.

"My God," she whispered. The bowl was part of the best china in the house, and it was full of plump buttered prawns. The cat looked up with a single meow as he polished one off.

"You are quite the little beggar," she said softly. "If you've charmed Mauve, then you deserve whatever she gives you. But beware, don't try that on me. You've still got to get those vaccinations."

Familiar licked his lips and walked directly toward Catherine. He executed a perfect figure eight around her legs and then rolled over on his back for a stomach rub. When she didn't oblige, he raised up on his hind legs and reached for her hand with his front paws. Catching her fingers lightly with his claws, he fell onto his back, pulling her hand with him. Catherine was forced to stoop.

"Hey!" She tried to withdraw her hand but found that although he wasn't clawing her, he held her firm.

"You're a determined little rogue, aren't you?" She stroked his soft fur and was immediately rewarded by release and a purr.

"So this is how American cats behave. Pushy and charming."

"Miss Nelson!" Mauve the cook was standing in the door. "I couldn't help but feed the little creature. He was so pitiful and hungry. He cried and cried."

Catherine continued to stroke Familiar's stomach until he flipped over and gave her his back. "I can see you had to feed him the prawns on our best china, too."

"Mercy me." Mauve put her hand to her cheek. "I just did it without thinking. It seemed to be what he wanted."

"I didn't think you liked cats, Mauve?"

The cook looked at the cat and then at Catherine. "I don't.

But that's no ordinary cat. I'd say he's magical. That's it exactly. The little devil bewitched me. He forced me to use the fine china and give him the prawns."

Catherine couldn't help herself. She laughed out loud at the cook's outrageous excuses. "I doubt he's a witch's ally, but Patrick said his name is Familiar, so I'd watch him in the future."

"In that case he can have anything he wants. I'll not go against the likes of him." Mauve was chuckling at her own foolishness.

"I told Patrick to see to his shots, but until he gets to the clinic what harm can he do? He seems friendly enough."

"Maybe he'll catch that big rat that's been living in the woodshed."

Catherine laughed again. "I doubt he'll eat rodent that he has to catch if you're serving him seafood at the back door."

Mauve reached down and picked up the now empty dish. "Well, he's a handsome cat. I hear he's from America. Some friends of Patrick's moved to Galway and then had to go to Belfast. He's only here for a few weeks."

"I used to have a cat when I was a little girl." Catherine remained kneeling and stroking Familiar's back. "He was accidentally run over, and it nearly killed me. I haven't wanted another one since."

"Beth's cat has a new litter if you take it into your head to have one."

"I might at that." Catherine stood. The interlude with the cat had been a welcome respite from the troubles that settled on her shoulders like a ton of rocks. "I'll give it some thought." She started into the kitchen, unaware that Familiar was right at her side. Mauve saw the black cat maneuver his way into the house, but she said nothing. Miss Catherine had let the rascal in. He was her problem.

THE COOK WAS a piece of cake. A little purr, a bit of pitiful caterwauling, and she was ready to give me whatever I wanted. A real soft touch, even though she initially threatened me with a broom. Interesting point of observation. In the brief time I've been in Ireland, I haven't seen any stray animals. Cats and even those slobbering, fawning, disgusting dogs aren't thrown out and abandoned like they are in the good old U.S. of A. What's going on over here? Maybe a better question would be, how can we get it to happen in America? Ah, well, a bit of something to discuss with Eleanor and Peter when they get back.

Now that I'm in the house, I hope Catherine doesn't turn temperamental and toss me out. One night in the loft of the barn was plenty for this furry feline. Catherine looks like the silk sheets type to me. Probably a nice green. Something to bring out those amazing eyes. I can imagine that red hair on a pillow. What a picture! And I'm just the cat to cuddle on the foot of her bed. These Irish nights get a little nippy, let me tell you.

But there is an ulterior motive. I want to take a look at some of the goings on up here at the big house. Something isn't right with Patrick. It's really gnawing at me. I can't believe that one of Eleanor's friends would do something like steal a valuable horse. But just about the time I'm ready to say he's innocent, some new evidence turns up. My eyes and ears are open. The next step rests with the thieves.

THE WALK to Mick's cottage wound through fields neatly divided by stone walls. Mares and foals grazed in three pastures, and Patrick let his practiced eye roam over them. All seemed at peace as he stepped over a wall and took a shortcut through the fields. He had no time to linger and enjoy the horses on this day, but he couldn't stop his thoughts from drifting to the past.

As a young boy he'd been obsessed, sneaking out of his father's house in the middle of the night to ride bareback around the property on horses that had been declared off limits to him.

For a moment Patrick allowed himself the luxury of falling into a past far more pleasant than his present. There had been a young stallion named Flint, a steel gray animal with a dead-calm attitude—until the rider was in the saddle. The horse had the speed of fifteen fire-singed demons and the attitude of Satan himself.

After eleven jockeys had given him up as unridable, Thomas Shaw finally made an attempt. It was a brief episode. Patrick's father was laid up in bed for a week with four cracked ribs.

But Patrick had been sneaking out of the house in the middle of the night to ride the stallion. He'd used the only bit he could reach—a rubber training bit—and no saddle. And he and Flint had flown down the road, taking any fences that happened to get in the way of their wild ride.

Patrick had been too afraid to tell anyone that he could ride Flint. He was only seven and he'd been forbidden to go near the stallion, or any of the more temperamental horses.

When Patrick's secret was discovered, as he found all such secrets ultimately were, his father wasted no time in finding a set of silks for young Patrick and putting him up on the big gray in a race. Flint won handily and Patrick's career, brief but sweet, as a winning jockey was launched. Too young to ride at regulation tracks, and too big to ride by the time he was old enough, his only days as a jockey were in grammar school.

Putting aside the past, Patrick watched the smoke rising from the peat fire in Mick's chimney. It would be good to warm his hands, and possibly his belly. Mick kept a bottle of good Irish whiskey, and at the moment, Patrick could use a drink. Unconsciously he wiped the back of his hand across his eyes as if to erase the mental image of Catherine Nelson from his mind. When he dropped his hand, she was still there, a red-haired tigress of a woman, giving orders and leveling accusations. Complicating his life at a time when he could ill afford another snarl.

Patrick groaned softly. The green-eyed Catherine was not

likely to disappear. Tapping lightly at the door, he entered before he heard Mick's welcome.

"I came to make sure you were resting that foot," Patrick said, stepping into the kitchen and moving on into the sitting room. Mick was before the fire, a glass at his hand with an inch of amber liquid. "I was thinking about that hellion Flint."

"Ah, Flint. I think about him a lot," Mick said. "I'm getting to be an old man, dwelling in the past. But you could sit that devil like you were hooked to his spine."

Patrick smiled and took a seat in another cane-bottom chair in front of the fire. "He was a fine animal." He sighed. "Limerick reminds me a great deal of Flint. There's the same heart there, the same willingness to give everything if he's only asked properly. We have to get him back here...whether we want to or not."

"It broke your father's heart to sell Flint to the Kimballs."

"It broke mine, as well," Patrick said. He didn't like to think of what had happened to Flint. An overeager owner and a bad trainer had conspired to push him too hard and too fast.

"If your da' had had the funds to campaign him..."

"If we'd had a bit more money it would be a different story to tell now." Patrick's voice was laced with bitterness. "If Colin had only decided to get himself killed in a simple fashion instead of making a martyr of himself, then the family wouldn't have come to such a pass."

Mick picked up a bottle from beside his chair. There was a clean glass beside his own and he poured a measure of whiskey into it and handed it to Patrick.

"I see you were expecting a guest," Patrick said, forcing himself to beat back the anger and frustration that came whenever he thought of his older brother.

"I knew you'd be along. There's too much to discuss." They sipped the liquor in companionable silence for a moment.

"How's the foot?" Patrick asked.

"No better or no worse. I didn't want to be around the barn today. I have no use for Catherine Nelson, none in the least, but I find it hard to watch her twist in the wind. Did she call the police?''

''No.''

The two men shared a look as the fire danced in front of them.

''Why not? The horse is the best asset she has.''

Patrick sighed, staring into the flames as if they would burn the truth out of him. ''She's afraid to put pressure on the people who took him. I recalled the story of Speedo to her. She wants Limerick back, alive. She's willing to pay as much as she can without having to go to her father.''

''She said so?'' Mick sat forward.

''In so many words.''

''If she was so damn fond of the horse why wouldn't she give him time to heal his knee? Why pay money for something that you ruin because you don't have another few days?''

''You'll have to take that question to someone who has two coins to rub together. Since I can't afford to buy anything, I can't speak to the matter of ruining it.'' Patrick got up and paced before the fire. ''I don't think she knows any better. She's got that fool Ridgeway chattering in her ear, telling her how I mollycoddle the horses, and she's too ignorant to understand how delicate a horse can be.''

Mick nodded. ''She's green. And a bit spoiled. That's a dangerous combination. How much ransom do you think she'll pay?'' Mick looked at the fire as he asked the question.

Patrick paced faster. ''I believe she'd give her last penny.'' Patrick turned to face the older man. ''Damn her! She thinks she can buy his safety. Money isn't the answer to everything, except if you don't have any.''

''It's a quandary, Patrick, my lad. But if she's willing to pay a ransom, then she'll be busy putting it together. That would give the kidnappers a chance to find a really secure hiding place for the horse. How long, do you think, before she takes it to the police?''

Patrick stopped pacing. He returned to his seat, rubbing the bridge of his nose. A fierce headache was forming between his eyes. "That depends on how much influence that ass Ridgeway has on her. If she believes Limerick's safe, then I believe she'll want time to raise the ransom. I can promise you one thing, Mick, when she gets ready to go after the culprits, she's going to hit with everything she has. I get the feeling she's not the kind of woman who stops in midstream."

"Aye, she's not a quitter, no matter what else you can say about her." Mick gave Patrick an appraising look. "It's a pity for a woman with her face to have such a temperament. She reminds me of that chestnut filly your father bought at auction."

"Crimson Flyer." Patrick remembered the horse well. He smiled. "She was a challenge, but when she was finally broken, she was a pleasure to ride."

"Perhaps Miss Nelson will prove to be a pleasure, but I pity the man who's sent up to break her to the saddle."

Patrick couldn't help but laugh. That was one thing about Mick—he was bawdy enough to chase away the blues, at least for a limited time.

"What are you going to do about Limerick?" Mick asked.

"What can I do?" Patrick answered. "It's a waiting game."

"And the grooms? How are they taking it?"

"They all think I took him, and a few are spoiling to see me take the blame."

"Don't worry about Jack. It's a shame he caught me, but he didn't know for certain it was you, and he won't rat on an old man like me. McShane is another matter. You should have fired him when you had the chance. He's a worthless layabout."

"You're right on that count, but there's no undoing the past."

Mick looked out the window. "It's time to feed the foals." He pulled his feet under him and prepared to rise.

Patrick stood and put a hand on the older man's shoulder. "Take a rest, Mick. I'll feed the little ones for you. I can tell it's going to be a long, long night and I'd just as soon have plenty to do. You'll see to it that Limerick is fed? I can't leave the grounds. I'm sure they'll have me followed."

"I'll see to Limerick. In a week we can sneak him back to the stables just as easily as we took him. His leg will be healed and he'll be fit to run for the Queen's jewels if that's what Catherine Nelson wants."

"I couldn't stand by and see him ruined. Like Flint. I just couldn't." Patrick's hands were clenched at his side. "Even if I hang for horse theft, I couldn't allow that to happen."

"It'll take her at least a week to raise the ransom. We'll send another note and keep her stirred to the point of boiling. When Limerick is back safely, she'll forget soon enough about who took him."

Patrick arched an eyebrow. "I hope you're right about that, old friend, but I'm not so certain. Especially not if she suspects that I had anything to do with it."

CATHERINE PUSHED the books away from her and flopped back in her chair. Her shoulders were knotted and throbbing from tension. She'd been able to pull together twenty thousand pounds, without her father noticing the drain on her personal and the farm accounts. That was it, though, and she knew it wouldn't be enough to ransom a horse as valuable as Limerick.

The first time she'd seen the horse, she'd recognized his potential. Not because of his conformation or bloodlines. She'd seen it in his eyes, in the way he carried himself. She'd known he was a winner, even if she didn't know all the ways she'd known. Now he was gone.

She got up and wandered to the window. She couldn't see the barn, but she could see the pastures where two young colts were rearing and charging each other in a game of tag. This was everything she'd ever wanted, but it wasn't happening the way she'd dreamed.

The day was ending, and she had no idea where Limerick might be, or what was happening to him. She tried to keep her mind away from gruesome thoughts, but she couldn't help herself. As she watched the colts frolic, her eyes sought Patrick. Even when she realized that she was consciously thinking about the head trainer, she didn't stop herself. It did no good. It was better to admit that the man was constantly in her thoughts. It occurred to her that it was the very fact that he had no use for her that made her want to prove herself to him. She wasn't a born-to-the-saddle horseman, like he was. But she loved the animals and the sport. Why couldn't he give her a chance to show that she was a capable businesswoman and farm manager?

As she watched the light begin to fade from the sky, she felt a pang of regret. She had come to Beltene with the attitude that she was going to show everyone who worked there who was boss. That was how things were done in the business world. When a company was bought out or merged, there was the total assertion of power by the winning side. The vanquished had to understand the power of the conquerors. It was a system as long and brutal as the history of humanity. And the Irish knew it well.

At that thought she felt a flush of color rush up her neck and into her face. She'd made a mistake. She should have come in with kid gloves instead of brass knuckles. Now she had to figure out a way to rectify it. As she'd sat in her office trying to find ransom money for Limerick, it had occurred to her that the only people who really cared if Limerick was returned safely or not were the men who worked for her. To them, Limerick was more than an investment. He was a horse, a living creature valued above all others. A vision of the future.

He was also Patrick's horse.

As if she'd called him up, Patrick came across the field into her line of vision. She couldn't see him clearly, but she knew his walk, the way he carried himself, and she felt a simple surge of pleasure at the thought of him.

"Enchanted sea horses, indeed," she said aloud, remembering the legend Patrick had told her. "It would seem that

Limerick has been spirited away by the fairies. Or that's what some people would have me believe."

The tire treads troubled her enormously. They seemed incontrovertible proof that Patrick was involved in Limerick's disappearance. Would he be so stupid as to use his own vehicle to steal a horse? Patrick was not a stupid man.

But he was a daring man. It was possible that he'd enjoy the idea of flaunting his theft in her face. He knew better than anyone else how much Beltene depended on Limerick. He was the heart of the farm, the future of it. Without him, Beltene would fade into oblivion.

She pushed aside the draperies to get a better view out the window. Patrick had stopped beside one of the two colts that had been playing earlier. He seemed frozen, but Catherine knew there was some communication going on between man and horse. In a few seconds, the colt walked up to him and nuzzled his chest.

The man had a way with horses. And he also had a very unsettling effect on her.

Chapter Five

The large manila envelope was padded, the address typewritten on a plain postal label with local postage from Galway. Thinking of fingerprints, Catherine held it gingerly as she slit it open with a letter opener. It was no surprise to see the videotape. She'd been expecting it all along. She was torn with relief and fury. Relief that Limerick was still alive; fury that someone had taken him and reduced her to a position where she was totally powerless to protect the stallion.

She could hear Mauve rumbling about the dining room, checking dishes and setting the table for lunch. The rest of the house staff were busy upstairs. The den was free and Catherine took the tape and went there to plug it into the VCR. Until she'd determined a course of action, she wanted to keep the tape a secret.

In the sixty-second shot of Limerick, she saw three things. The horse was still in Ireland, and somewhere along the western coast. The slope of the land, the stones and fences, the vegetation—it all smacked of the Connemara region. Of course, she wasn't an expert. She noted the old wooden structure in the background. Was Limerick safe? Were there things he could injure himself on? In the video he pranced and shook his head, and there was the brief glimpse of a man's hand reaching out toward him—and the horse extending his nose toward the hand. Then it ended.

Catherine rewound the tape and played it through three times more before she froze the video on different frames. The camera angle didn't allow for her to see much of the background. The camcorder had been held from high up and aimed toward the horse and ground, as if the cameraman deliberately wanted to limit the horizon view. It would also indicate that the cameraman was standing on top of a vehicle or a rock or steps of some kind to get such a high angle.

When she got to the shot of the hand, she stopped. It was a large hand, a man's hand. That was no surprise. The tip of a sleeve was evident—nondescript jacket, no jewelry. It was a left hand, and the man did not wear a watch. That was something to think about.

The hand also looked rough, callused, an outdoor hand. But the nails were clean. She rewound the tape again and clicked off the VCR. So Limerick was alive and in good health. That was the message the horsenappers wanted to send to her. That meant she had more time to put money together in preparation for their demands. Strangely enough, there was no demand attached to the tape.

At that thought she felt a stab of apprehension. How much would they demand? The letter, the video, that was all preparation. A few days of torment and worry, then the ransom note when she was at the peak of her anxiety. These were very sophisticated horsenappers. They'd studied their subject and knew well how to manipulate her.

With the tape in hand she returned to her office. She locked the video in her desk drawer and got out the figures she'd compiled. It was slow work, but she'd managed to eke out twenty-three thousand pounds for ransom. It had taken all of her personal savings and the retirement she'd earned. Everything she could cash in or convert had been included. Would it be enough? It all depended on who had Limerick.

The dark-haired Irish trainer materialized in her mind. If Patrick had the horse... At the thought, she got up and went to the window. In the last day she'd gotten into the bad habit of walking to the window and looking out, hoping to see him in the fields or riding along the road. He used to work Limerick up and down the roadways, over fences and around the county. It was a practice that appalled most racing trainers. But the Shaws had used alternative training to great effect. In fact, Limerick had even been put to the plow, pulling large stones out of the pastures. He'd developed a broad and strong chest because of it, too. As had Patrick.

Once again Catherine found her mind drifting to the absurd. Patrick Shaw was not a figure to dwell on.

Her thoughts were interrupted by the phone, and she picked it up to hear Kent's voice.

"Have you determined to take this matter to the police?" he asked.

There was a tightness in his voice that immediately made Catherine balk. She was tired of people, particularly men, trying to push her around.

"I'm still considering my options." Her voice was equally tense.

"You're being pigheaded, and I can't understand why." Kent backed off. There was a degree of amusement in his tone. "Is it Shaw? Are you feeling sorry for the chap, what with the fact you've bought his farm, cleared his debts, left him with a line of credit and given him a cushy job? Is that why you're sympathizing with him?"

"Your sarcasm goes unappreciated." She didn't want to get into a row with him. Not now. Not when she was feeling so uncertain about her decisions.

"If you don't report the theft, the insurance isn't valid. I checked it out. You have a reasonable time frame, but you're tampering with a total loss if you don't take the proper steps."

"Thank you, Kent. I appreciate your efforts." She forced her voice to sound sincere. He had only her best interest at heart. The least she could do was show a little graciousness.

"I thought I'd drop back on Sunday with the van and pick up those two-year-olds. There were six, correct?"

Catherine hesitated. Patrick's rage at the thought of Ridgeway touching those horses came back to her. It wasn't necessarily ego with him. He was concerned about the horses.

"Catherine?"

"Kent, I'm not certain I can afford your services. If Limerick is gone, that well may be the end of my racing career." She wasn't exaggerating her plight. She'd gambled on Limerick.

"I'll give you a line of credit, darling." Kent chuckled. "And there are other methods of payment."

"Kent!"

"Just teasing. Listen, I know your father's good for the bill. Harold Nelson may not like the decisions you've made, but he won't let his name be ruined for a bad debt."

Catherine sighed. "You're right about that. Of course I'd never hear the end of it."

"What about it? Shall I bring the van?"

"No." Catherine didn't know why she was refusing such a generous offer. Nine months ago, when she was still negotiating for Beltene, she'd determined to send the six animals to Wicklow for training. Now it didn't seem like a good idea.

"Is something wrong?"

"Of course not. It's just that I won't be put in a position where I can't pay my bills. It won't hurt to wait a week. By then I should have Limerick back."

"Catherine—" Kent broke off. "Well, shall I come up Sunday?"

"That would be delightful." Catherine tried to sound enthusiastic. "It would be good to have you to discuss things with."

"My advice is don't pay any ransom. Your father would agree with me, but I know you well enough to know you'll pay whatever you have. You haven't come to realize what it's like not to have money, how desperate these people may be. Even if they get the money, they might not let Limerick go."

"I intend to pay the ransom, if I'm given the chance, and I

can only pray that I'm given the chance.'' Catherine shivered. She only wanted to get Limerick back safely.

''I'll ring off now and see you Sunday. I know you don't want to fire Shaw, but I think you should. If you'd like, I can tell him for you.''

''Thank you, Kent, but I can manage my employees myself. If and when I decide to fire anyone, I can do it in person.''

''It was just an offer. You hide it well, but I know how tenderhearted you can really be. That's one of the things that attracted me to you.''

''Tenderhearted but not stupid,'' Catherine said, injecting a note of humor into her voice. ''But thanks for your offer. You're a good friend.''

''One day I hope you'll view me as more than a friend.''

A light tap at her office door was a signal Catherine was delighted to hear. ''There's someone at the door, Kent. We'll talk Sunday.''

''Yes, we need to talk. Sunday.''

Catherine replaced the receiver. Of all things she didn't need now it was Kent pressuring her to feel something. It was just too much.

''Come in,'' she said, eager to see anyone at all. But the sight of Eamon McShane, blood crusted in the corner of his mouth and his right eye blackened, wasn't what she'd bargained for.

''That bastard Patrick Shaw beat me up and threatened me.'' He stepped into the room. ''Left me in a ditch, bleedin', and I'd be there today if my wife hadn't come out lookin' for me.''

Catherine stood slowly, assessing the damage to the man. He was bruised and battered, but he was walking properly, without any difficulty. ''Have you seen a doctor?''

''No need. What I want is action against Shaw. He can't go around bullying and beating up on people. He doesn't own Beltene anymore and he can't act like he's the king of Ireland.'' McShane's swollen face was red with anger. ''I wanted you to see what he's done.''

"Take a seat," Catherine said, pointing to the chair. "I'll call Mauve. She'll know what's best for your cuts and bruises."

Excusing herself, she went to the kitchen and got the cook, hurriedly explaining that someone had been injured. For the next fifteen minutes, Mauve clucked and washed, her strong fingers probing bruises and finally exploring McShane's teeth.

"No serious damage," she assessed. "You'll hurt like hell for the next few days, but you'll live."

The furrow between Catherine's brow eased slightly. She thanked Mauve and let the cook return to her duties. When she was alone with the groom, she crossed her arms. "Why did Shaw attack you?" she asked.

"I was out looking for that horse. See, I figure he's around here close by. The more I thought about it, the more it seemed to me that Patrick would put him where he could keep an eye on him every day. He and Mick are in it up to their ears, I tell you. They don't care that you could fire the lot of us. They've never cared about anyone or anything except their own selves."

McShane's hatred of Patrick was as easy to see as his bruises. It piqued Catherine's curiosity, especially knowing what she did about Patrick. "Were you aware that one of the conditions Mr. Shaw insisted upon before he sold Beltene was that I keep on every single one of his employees, at least for a year?"

McShane wasn't impressed. "He always liked to play the important man."

"He made sure that your job was guaranteed. It doesn't sound as if he were totally self-involved."

McShane's laugh was short and bitter. "It's irony to watch you defending the man who stole your horse." He got up. "It's none of my affair. I can take care of getting even with Shaw in my own good time. I don't need you or anyone. Patrick Shaw will get his, I'll see to that."

"Did you see the man who attacked you?" Catherine kept

a firm grip on her temper. "If you can positively identify Shaw, then I'll take up the matter with him. I can't have my employees bludgeoning each other."

"I didn't get a clear view. The cretin came up on me from behind or he wouldn't have done me so much damage."

"If you didn't see him, how did you know it was Patrick?"

"He grabbed me around the throat from behind. He has a crooked finger on his left hand. I saw it."

Catherine had never noticed the finger. What she did notice was that McShane was eager enough to pin the beating on Patrick to lie about it. "I'll speak with him about it," she said.

McShane snorted rudely. "Thanks very much. Scold him properly for fighting while you're at it."

"That will be all, McShane." Catherine walked to the door and opened it.

"You can talk to him all you want, but be alerted that I intend to pay him back in his own coin. You tell him for me to watch his back. I'll slip up on him and work him over just like I got. Tell him. At least I'm man enough to give warning." McShane walked through the door and never looked back.

Catherine listened to his footsteps traveling the length of the hallway to the front door. When she was certain he was out of her house, she closed the door to her office and turned back to her desk. Sitting in the window beside her chair was the black cat. Catherine hadn't noticed him before, but he was perched on the windowsill. He was a wily rascal with a knack for finding any open door or window. She'd awakened with him asleep on her green silk comforter, curled against her side. No one could say how he'd gotten into the house.

"You'd better go back to the barn," she said, reaching through the window to stroke his silky fur. "Patrick will be looking for you."

HE CAN LOOK till his eyes roll out of his head for all I care. I'm not spending another night in that drafty old barn when I can warm my spine against those lovely legs.

But that's a thought for later. I'm more interested in what's going on with Eamon McShane.

Patrick left the barn last night just after two. Since I've discovered the open bathroom window on the first floor, I can come and go as I please. That's the first rule of the Trained Observer—find a route of unobserved entrance and egress. That's how it happened that I was sitting on the stone wall when Patrick strolled out the back door of the barn and cut across the fields. He went to Mick's. And after that? I can only guess because they got in Mick's rattletrap of a truck and drove away. It had something to do with a large gray mammal who is reputed to be worth millions of dollars. Or pounds, as they call it here.

I must be getting cranky in my old age, because this pound business is making me testy. Pounds have to do with butter and cheese. With fish and steak, ground round and shrimp. Money shouldn't be measured in pounds. It's almost a sacrilege. The pound is a vital measurement, not a mere monetary unit. Ah, well, what do people who live on an island know? They don't know what a mile is, either. I'm trying to eavesdrop and find out where they're going and Mick says it's only twenty kilometers. I mean, can I walk it or will it wear my paws down to the nub? If I were running things, the entire world would have miles and dollars and cats on the thrones of power. See, monarchy is one thing we should have in America. A royal family with a royal cat. That's the ticket.

Enough of this tirade. I've got a little snooping to do around the barn. I was watching the video through the den window. Limerick is fine, which is no surprise to me. I think, though, that I'd better pay him a little visit. And then I want to check out Patrick's digs for a brown jacket that looks as if it's had a hard life.

CATHERINE WATCHED as Familiar jumped off the window ledge and walked toward the barn. He was an arrogant creature, but extremely affectionate. Why was it that she had the feeling that he knew more than he let on? There was something about those golden eyes, an intelligence that was a bit unsettling.

For the second time that afternoon, a light tap on the door alerted her that someone was waiting to see her.

"Come in," she called as she walked back to her desk.

"There's a gentleman to see you." Mauve stepped into the room and softly closed the door. "He said he was an old friend, but I didn't know. He's in the parlor."

"Thanks, Mauve. I've never known Beltene to have so many visitors. Maybe I should think about getting a butler."

"Now, that would add a bit of polish to the house," Mauve agreed. "Just find a good-looking man who's single and it would suit my fancy."

Catherine chuckled. If the men at the barn sometimes made her feel like an outsider, Mauve had done her best to make her welcome. The cook was humorous and always ready to talk about men, or the lack of them, in her life.

"Did the man give his name?" Catherine asked.

"He said he wanted to surprise you."

Catherine made a face. "I see." She started toward the door. "I usually love surprises."

When she walked to the parlor, with Mauve at her heels, she saw only the man's boot. An expensive English riding boot. The rest of his body and face were hidden by the wing of the chair.

At the sound of her step, the man stood, turning to face the door.

"Allan." She was completely flabbergasted. Allan Emory had been the man of her dreams—until a year ago when he "let her down gently" to marry a duchess. The wedding had never materialized. She'd hoped never to see him again.

"Catherine." He stepped toward her and lightly kissed her

cheek. "You look marvelous, especially under the circumstances. How are you holding up?"

"What are you talking about?" The question contained some heat. What was Allan doing on her doorstep with this false air of solicitude?

"I've heard. It's terrible." Allan picked up her hand and kissed it. "I'm here to do anything I can to help."

Catherine jerked her hand away, then looked at Mauve. "Could you bring us some tea? Or maybe some brandy. I think I need something stronger." She had no idea what Allan was talking about, but she wanted whatever it was kept within the confines of the parlor.

"How thoughtless of me," Allan said, dropping his voice. "You haven't told anyone yet, have you?"

She heard Mauve shut the door. "Told them what, Allan?"

"I know Limerick has been stolen." Allan grabbed both of her hands. "I've come to help."

She withdrew her hands from his. "And how do you intend to do that?"

"Moral support. Whatever. If you think he's in the area, maybe we can mount a search. Farm to farm. If the locals have him, we can intimidate them into giving him up."

"Oh, really?" Catherine felt the bite of her temper. "What shall we do? Torch their farms? Perhaps take their children?"

Allan caught her tone and shrugged. "I'm only trying to help."

"How did you find out about Limerick?"

He walked away from her to the fireplace. A crystal decanter contained an arrangement of roses. Leaning into the flowers, he took in their perfume. The afternoon sun slanted into the room and caught his blond hair, the tan skin. "These are delightful. Do they come from Beltene gardens?"

"Who told you about Limerick?" Catherine stared at the handsome man she'd once fancied herself in love with. It seemed like a million years ago. "The only people who know about the horse are my staff. I went to great pains to make certain no one else knew. How on earth did you find out?''

''When I saw that Limerick was scratched from the Kildare track, I asked a few questions. I found it interesting that Wicklow's owner had scratched your horse. Very interesting.'' He walked away from the roses and gave her a look.

''So Kent told you?'' Catherine found that even more unlikely. Allan was often at the track, as a bettor. But he had nothing to do with the training of horses. He had nothing in common with Kent Ridgeway. Except her. And the knowledge that Limerick had been stolen.

''Kent didn't actually tell me. I put two and two together, based as much on what he didn't say as what he did. He was too evasive. Almost as if he didn't want me to speak with you. He's acting as if he had some personal interest here.''

Catherine ignored the implied question. ''I asked Kent to scratch the horse.''

''Because he's missing?''

''He's fine. I just—''

There was a light tap at the door as Mauve entered with the brandy. ''Connie found a letter on the drive. The postman must have dropped it on his way out. It's on the tray.'' She put her burden on a table and left the room, carefully closing the door.

Picking up the envelope, Catherine noticed several things. The handwriting was neat, as if the writer made sure to make each letter uniform. It was printed, not written. The envelope was addressed to Miss Catherine Nelson, Beltene Farm. There was no postage at all.

Allan's gaze bored into her, so Catherine flipped the letter over. The flap had been sealed with old-fashioned wax and the crest of a horse head. Sliding her nail under the flap, she opened the letter and read it silently.

''The horse is in perfect health. Whatever you do, don't panic.'' She looked up to find Allan staring at her intently.

''What is it, a ransom note?''

She tucked the single page back inside the flap. "An invitation."

"To what?" Allan demanded. "How can you think about social engagements when the future of Beltene is missing?"

"Allan, what are you doing in Connemara?" Catherine turned the question back on him. She had to think of some way to keep Allan's mouth shut about Limerick. The note indicated the horse was okay. If she could only keep everything calm, she might get him back.

"I came to help you find your horse."

"Thanks, but no thanks. This is something I'm handling myself." Catherine saw that he wasn't paying any attention to her. "I don't want your help, Allan. I fully expect to get Limerick back."

"I've booked a room in Galway. I'm staying here until Limerick is found, dead or alive. I came to offer you some money for his ransom, if you need it."

Allan's generosity made Catherine really look at him. "Why?" she asked. With Allan, she'd learned, there was always a why.

He smiled slowly. "I want a piece of him. If you need the ransom money, then I'll give it to you for fifty percent of the horse."

Catherine felt the blood rush to her heart and then to her brain. She'd never experienced such a blinding fury. "You'll loan me the money for fifty percent of the horse?"

"Calm down, Catherine. Not loan. Give. If it comes down to a ransom, I'll pay half for half the horse. That's a fair business deal."

"I'd rather die than be a business partner with you." Catherine hurled the words at him. Her fingers clenched around her brandy glass. The smash of the crystal against his face would be extremely gratifying.

"I realized you'd put up some resistance to the idea. That's why I brought cash." He motioned to a suitcase on the floor on the opposite side of his chair. "That's fifty thousand pounds, cash. If you can come up with your fifty, that should be able to ransom Limerick.''

''And what makes you think they're going to demand a ransom?'' Catherine's voice was shaking.

''That's what they always do, isn't it? A few silly little notes, maybe a video, and then they come across with their demands. You meet them and, if we're lucky, we get the horse back alive.''

''If we're lucky...'' She didn't like the sound of those words.

''It's a gamble, love. You know how much I love a good risk.'' He went to her and removed the brandy glass from her lifeless fingers. ''You, on the other hand, never learned to enjoy risk. But I've been giving it a lot of thought. Perhaps I can teach you.''

Chapter Six

Patrick ran his fingers down Limerick's front leg. The tendon was clean and straight, the flesh firm and not sensitive. He moved up to the knee, probing gently, exerting more and more pressure. Limerick lowered his head and nuzzled Patrick's hair.

"He's sound," Mick declared.

"Another two days. I'll start conditioning him tonight." Patrick had to make sure. Once Limerick was returned to Beltene, the stallion would be off to the track. By means of the desperate horsenapping he'd succeeded in pulling the big gray from the Kildare opening race, but there would be another match, and another. Catherine Nelson had her reputation riding on Limerick, and he would run—and win—for her. As soon as he was totally sound.

Mick shifted from side to side, favoring his bad foot. "It'd be best if we took him on back, Patrick. It's been four days. Miss Catherine is tired of waiting for a ransom note, and she's tired of waking up each day with her most prized possession gone. She'll be taking it to the coppers if we aren't careful."

Patrick, too, was amazed that Catherine had not gone to the authorities. In fact, her entire demeanor was a puzzle. The first two days of Limerick's disappearance, she'd been frantic with anxiety. Then for the past two days, she'd acted as if she had some secret connection to the horse's safety.

"Hey." He pushed at the horse's muzzle. Limerick was breathing in his ear, nibbling at the edge of it.

"Do you think we should send another video?" Mick asked. "It would make her feel that he's still safe."

Patrick shook his head. "I don't think it's necessary, and each time we do anything, it increases our risk." He rubbed his hand over his unshaven face. It was barely daybreak, and the long days and nights were beginning to tell on him.

The location that he and Mick had chosen to hide Limerick was extremely secluded. It was a long and bumpy drive over fifteen kilometers of rut and bog. Then it was a six kilometer walk. Feed had to be carried on his back, and water brought up from a spring. None of that mattered in the long run, because Limerick was completely safe and he was getting the rest he needed.

"You should leave the horse to me," Mick said softly. He was concerned for his friend. As much as the long hours and hard work were telling on Patrick Shaw, it was also his conscience. Patrick wasn't the kind of man who took another's property. Only his grave concern for the horse would ever have provoked him to steal Limerick. His concern *and* his love for the animal.

"I heard that McShane told Miss Nelson that you'd beaten him." Mick leaned on the fence. It had taken the gossip three days to get from the house staff to the barn staff, but it had finally arrived, as did all of the gossip.

"He can say anything he pleases. I didn't touch him and he knows that."

"What's his gripe with you?"

"Personal." Patrick's lips clamped shut, a sign he would talk no more on that particular subject.

"I heard his wife had a fancy for you, would that be it?"

"Peg McShane is a decent woman." Patrick's lips grew harder.

Mick nodded to himself. He'd ferreted out the secret, sure enough. "She's a decent woman who's been indecently treated. It's no sin to want a man to treat you with a bit of kindness. Even the animals expect as much."

"Peg was just wishin' and talkin'." Patrick's brogue intensified for a moment. "I talked with her because she reminded me of Lucy."

"Aye, she does, now that you say it." Mick recalled Patrick's sister. She'd died as a teenager. She'd been in the wrong place at the wrong time—looking for her older brother Colin in Belfast.

"Eamon must have thought there was more to it than a friendly conversation."

"The man is daft. He isn't capable of thinking."

"And you kept him on because of Peg."

"And the children."

"She'd be better off if a horse kicked that one in the head."

Patrick's lips curved up in a smile. He pulled a bottle of liniment from his pocket and splashed some into his hand. With firm and gentle strokes he began to work on Limerick's leg and knee. "Now that's a picture, Peg with three little ones and a husband with a hoofprint on his forehead."

"It would look well in a wooden box carried by six pallbearers."

Patrick chuckled. "I wonder who did smack his ears for him. Not as if he didn't have it coming from a number of sources. Timmy said he isn't doing his work and some of the other men are tired of picking up the slack for him."

"He knows, because of you, he has a year to lay about if he chooses."

"A man can change." Patrick stood up.

"If he has a mind to, or if God smites him hard enough." Mick grinned. "I suspect it was Jack that got him, but maybe you should give him a beating. He'd know well enough who had hold of him then."

"You're a violent man, Mick," Patrick said, shaking his head in mock concern.

"I don't like that bastard. He's been following us around,

peeking 'round corners and spying up lanes. He's trouble, mark my words."

"Trouble for Peg and the children. Let's head back. It's a long haul and I want to be there for first feeding."

"You're going to have to sleep sometime, Patrick."

"I will, when Limerick's safely home and all accounted for."

Patrick ran his hand down the gray stallion's neck. In return, Limerick lowered his head and pushed it gently into Patrick's chest. "See you later," Patrick whispered in the horse's ear.

Limerick followed them to the fence and stopped. "Well, would you look at that," Mick said. A large black cat was sitting on the stone fence. "Is that your American cat?"

Patrick walked over to the cat and stroked his fur. "It is, indeed. He must have been asleep in the Rover."

"And he followed us all the way up here?" Mick looked around. There was nothing to see but the rolling pasture, a few sparse briars growing along the stone wall.

"He'll have to follow us home," Patrick said.

"Meow," Familiar agreed, jumping to the ground and starting down the path.

Limerick gave a soft whinny, and the cat turned back to watch as Patrick gave the stallion a last pat.

"Limerick could be gone from here any minute he chose," Mick noted as he stepped over the low stone wall.

"He knows to stay. He knows what I want him to do."

"I don't doubt that for an instant. From the day he was born, he looked to you." Mick's voice faded into the still night. The stars were thick with a half-moon dangling in a cloudless sky. Simultaneously, the two men turned up their collars against the cold, crisp air and began the long walk back to the vehicle. Familiar led the way as if he'd traveled it all of his life.

CATHERINE STOPPED SHORT of the barn door. Patrick and Mick were coming across the pasture, both walking as if they'd not slept in days. The large black cat was in front of them. She'd noticed his absence in her bed during the night and wondered what adventure he'd gotten involved in that would keep him out in the cold. Now she knew. He'd been with Patrick and Mick, wherever they'd been.

Unable to sleep, she'd gotten up early and gone to the barn to ride. In the four days that Limerick had been gone, she'd been so busy hanging on to her own emotional roller coaster that she hadn't given much thought to what she might do on horseback. But yesterday she'd gotten the second handwritten note, sealed with a blob of wax and the same horse head impression. It had said that Limerick would be returned safely. Since there had been no ransom note, Catherine had begun to allow herself to be lulled by the reassurances of the anonymous writer, a writer she'd assumed was Patrick Shaw.

When she thought of other possibilities, she felt as if she might begin to shake so hard she'd never stop. She'd committed herself to an action—or lack thereof—in failing to report the stallion's theft. Now she could only wait, hoping that the writer of the note knew what he was talking about. The wolves, in the shape of Allan Emory, were circling her door, and she'd put her faith in the fact that one of her own employees had her horse. She looked sharply at Patrick as he entered the barn.

A dark shade of stubble marked his strong-jawed face. His dark hair, usually neatly combed, was curled softly. It was out of character for him to appear in the barn unkempt. Mick was dragging, too, and even the cat acted tired. The suspicion that had been growing blossomed into certainty. Patrick had her horse. She knew it—had known it. So why wasn't she more upset? She should haul him before the authorities and have him jailed. She could do it, or at least, her father could. It might not be legal or fair, but the Nelson name carried a tremendous amount of weight. It would be simple enough to do, so why hadn't she?

It was a question with too many answers, all not completely rational.

"Good morning." She stepped in front of the men as they approached the barn door. The startled looks on both their faces was her reward. "Sick horse?" She directed the question to Patrick. "You look like you haven't slept in days. And you're late."

"I didn't realize you were clocking me in and out." Patrick couldn't help the fact that he bristled. Since he was ten years old, no one had forced him to account for his time or activities. He'd done a man's work, without shirking, and he had no intention of letting a woman dictate his movements.

"How about a ride?" Catherine asked.

"Help yourself. The riding horses are on the left front. Pick whichever you want."

"You don't understand. I'd like for you to ride with me."

Patrick had been avoiding her gaze, but he looked up. Something in the green of her eyes made him pause with the sarcastic remark unsaid. There was a sudden, unexpected surge of pleasure in the idea of a ride with Catherine Nelson.

"Excuse me," Mick said. He gave Patrick a warning glance before he entered the barn. "I'll talk with you later, Patrick."

"Make sure Lily's eating," Patrick called after him. He turned to fully face Catherine. "So it's a ride you're after."

The innuendo in his words made Catherine's pulse jump. "Just a ride. I thought it would be nice. Educational. Maybe we could ride in that direction." She pointed in the direction from which he and Mick had come.

"Aye, that's a lovely ride, over by Mick's cottage. He's having some bad nights, you see. The pain in his leg keeps him awake."

"Oh." Catherine felt a pang of contrition. Had Patrick really been sitting up with a sick friend? Her gaze slid over to him and she saw the crust of oats on the front of his brown jacket. Exactly the kind of mark a horse would leave if he nuzzled someone with affection after eating.

"Would you like a few minutes to shower?" she asked innocently. She took a half step toward him and reached out to brush the oats from his chest.

Patrick froze. Without a doubt, Catherine knew that he had the horse. So why hadn't she done something? Their eyes met and held, green against blue.

A gentle wind sifted through the barn and ruffled the strands of hair that had worked loose from her long braid. The tendrils tickled her cheeks and she brushed them away with a quick, casual gesture.

"I'll meet you in ten minutes," Patrick said, breaking the spell that had bound them. "I need to change into some riding clothes."

"What horse would you like? I'll have him saddled while you change."

"Get Tam for me. I think you'd enjoy Mayo's Motion. She's a bit spirited—" his eyes challenged her "—but I feel certain you can handle her."

"In ten minutes." Catherine turned away, walking toward the front section of the barn where several grooms were busy brushing horses and checking hooves. Her heart pounded with each step she took, and a strange rushing of blood affected her hearing.

Patrick Shaw had Limerick. He'd deliberately taken him, forcing her to pull him from at least two races. He'd jeopardized her strategy for making Beltene a success. He'd thwarted her authority as owner. He'd done everything he could to make her life unbearable. So why was she getting ready to ride with the man?

"Please saddle Mayo's Motion and Tam," she said to the first groom she saw. It took her a second to recognize Eamon McShane where he stood against a barn support. When he stepped into the light, she could see that the purple around his eye was fading to green. "I hope you're feeling better, Mr. McShane," she said.

"Well enough." He turned away. "I'll get your horses. Who'll be riding with you so I can get a saddle?"

"Patrick on Tam." A sudden thought occurred to her. "Saddle them and I'll be back in ten minutes," she said, hurrying in the direction she'd seen Mick take.

I HOPE THERE'S *long-distance phone lines to wherever Eleanor and Dr. Doolittle have gone, because their good buddy Patrick is getting ready to take a fall. He's taken that short step off a steep cliff and if any little thing goes wrong, he's going to hit bottom hard.*

Even an obtuse humanoid ought to be able to see that Patrick's intentions are completely honorable, but the grim fact is that he's stolen a horse. I believe he did it for all the right reasons. I believe he had no other choice. But if anything happens to Limerick, no one else will believe in him. They'll think he was bitter over the sale of Beltene and decided to strike back any way he could.

Oh, Eleanor, there might be trouble in Belfast, but there's more brewing here than Irish tea. Ice Queen is beginning to thaw a bit, but the Lone Ranger is making it terribly difficult. I think I'm going to have to intervene in this situation.

If I can sneak around and follow Patrick to Limerick's hidey-hole, then someone else can, too. That's what really unsettles me. He's put a two-million-dollar horse running around in a half-fenced pasture with barely enough stable to keep the wind off him.

Oh, well, I always think better on a full stomach, and last night was quite a workout. I wonder if Mauve might have some fresh sea trout, or perhaps another bite of buttered prawns. Those were exceptional, I must say. I've never had better, not even on Pennsylvania Avenue, when I was carousing that neighborhood in my renegade days. And the cream here! To die for. My coat is already taking on a sheen that wouldn't be possible in the States. Not even the injury from the bomb blast last year is giving me any trouble.

Life is sweet, for those who know how to live it well. Yes, humans have a long way to go on the evolutionary chart. Work, ride, use those biped muscles to labor and sweat, while I, superior in my knowledge as well as my manipulative abilities, stroll to the kitchen for some food and a few kind words from the obliging Mauve.

"MICK!" Catherine caught sight of the older man as he limped toward the west pasture. He was making very good time for someone who suffered a foot injury and looked as though he hadn't slept.

"Yes, ma'am." He turned slowly to face her, as if he'd thought about ignoring her call.

"I'm worried about Patrick. Is there anything troubling him?"

Mick furrowed his brow in mock concentration. "Not that I know of, Miss Catherine. He seems happy to me. He's a bit concerned over Limerick, but he believes the horse is safe. Unless you've heard otherwise?" Mick gave her a cagey look.

"I've heard nothing." Catherine decided to give as little information as possible. She'd been dying to talk with Patrick about the handwritten notes, but something held her back. The notes had to have come from him. Why would he endanger himself to that extent? It didn't make sense.

"It's a strange case." Mick shook his head sadly. "No ransom note, eh? Maybe the thieves will tire of dealing with that spoiled horse and bring him back."

"I haven't heard a word from the thieves since that first note. If they don't want ransom, what could they want?" She had to work hard not to smile. Mick was far too easy to manipulate.

"Must be the thieves had some other reason."

"Must be. Can you guess what?" She looked down at the lush winter grass, toeing her boot into it. "I wouldn't be nearly so worried if I was certain he was okay. It's just that I have no idea what the thieves are up to. Ransom? Breeding? Have they taken him simply to hurt me?" She gave him an innocent look.

"I wouldn't think a man would risk spending the best part of his life in prison just to get at someone else. No, I'd say revenge wasn't the motive." Mick rubbed his stubbly face with his hand. "More likely, maybe it was someone trying to provide a bit of help."

"Help?" Catherine felt her pulse increase. She was on to something. She could tell by Mick's awkward demeanor and his earnestness. He wanted to tell her, to explain. But he could only go so far, and she knew why. He was as guilty in taking the horse as Patrick.

"Help to be sure that he was...protected." Mick stumbled through the sentence. "I have to go and check on Lily. She's a beauty and I don't want Patrick yelling at me that she didn't get her morning ration."

"But what kind of man would steal a horse to make sure the horse was protected?"

Mick didn't hesitate. "The kind of man who works for a woman too stubborn to listen to him." He clamped his mouth shut when he finished.

"I see." Catherine felt her spine tighten.

"No, I don't think you do." Mick pushed the brim of the flat green hat back a bit where he could stare at her with piercing blue eyes. "There are men who do what they think is right, no matter what the consequences. Not for themselves, but for those they love. You should never push a man like that to the extreme. When you do, the fault of whatever happens is yours." He pulled the cap back down. "Now if you'll excuse me, I'm off to do my chores. You pay an honest wage, Miss Nelson, and I intend to give an honest day's work."

"Thank you, Mick," she said, watching the old man walk away. His limp was more pronounced, as if he'd used up a measure of strength to talk to her.

She walked back to the barn to find Patrick holding the two horses. He'd shaved the worst of the stubble from his face and changed into riding clothes, but there were faint blue depressions beneath his eyes. The man was tired, and he had good reason to be.

"Why don't you take me where you ride Limerick when you train him?" she suggested as she took her horse's reins and prepared to mount.

Patrick gave her a sharp look. There was something too innocent in the way she spoke. "Did you need something specific from Mick?" he asked, swinging up into the saddle with a grace that came of natural ability honed to perfection.

"Yes, it was specific, but it shouldn't trouble you." She answered his look with a smile. "Patrick, I want to talk to you about the next step in finding Limerick. I've decided to hire a professional investigator. Someone private. I feel certain the horse is close by. I mean to have him back safely at Beltene. Is there anyone you could recommend for the work? I'd ask you to do it, but I know you have your hands full managing the stables and all the men."

Patrick silently cursed his luck. She'd neatly stuck him on the sharp prongs of a hay fork. If he agreed to look for Limerick, then he'd have to let her manage the barn. He knew exactly what she was driving at. She was a cunning woman. And he hadn't missed the amusement sparkling in her green eyes. Dangerously clever and with a bit of humor he'd never suspected before.

"Mick says you're already overworked," Catherine added as she nudged her mare into a trot.

Patrick set Tam to trotting to stay beside her as they left the Beltene gate and headed down the open road.

Before them the green hills dipped and swayed, broken by the neat fences and the vivid flowers that spoke of spring and soil rich with limestone. Small cottages dotted the fields, the traditional peat fires burning as the smoke rose in the chill morning air.

"Mick is a meddling old man. I stay busy, but I'm not

overworked. Before you bought Beltene I did what I do now plus the books."

"And when did you sleep?" Catherine asked.

"When I found a moment." He laughed. "I fell asleep standing up in the barn one day. The men moved some hay to make a soft cushion, and then drew straws to see who would knock me over. Lucky for them I'm not as mean as I sound when I'm rudely awakened."

"It would take a brave man, or a fool, to topple you into the straw," Catherine said. Her laugh was easy, light.

Patrick glanced at her and saw the smile on her lips and in her eyes. His gaze moved down her, taking in her long-limbed grace. Her seat was natural and easy; her hands steady. Her legs, though lean, were strong.

For her part, Catherine noticed that Patrick's hands never lost contact with Tam. His touch was as light as a feather, and the horse seemed to understand what his rider wanted long before Patrick gave any signal that she could see.

"Tell me about 'the touch,'" she said suddenly. "I've heard of it all my life. When I was learning to ride in Dublin, I heard that Thomas Shaw's boy Patrick had 'the touch.' You rode as an underaged jockey when you were barely old enough to go to school, didn't you?"

"We needed a rider."

Catherine saw the look of distress that crossed his face. The past was an open wound with Patrick. It must have been hard for him, forced to give up his childhood and ride like an adult, with all of the pressures of a fully grown man. She almost regretted bringing up 'the touch,' but she wanted to know his explanation for it.

"I've seen the way the horses respond to you. Why is that?" she pressed.

"I don't know for certain." Patrick answered her honestly. "There's a story about a man who was smitten by a beautiful woman. It happened many years ago, when the otherworld and this world were not so far apart."

Catherine let herself fall into the gentle rhythm of his words. If he had a way with animals through his hands, his voice was certainly a powerful weapon on her. "Tell me, please," she said. "I love to hear your stories."

Patrick's grin was quick, boyish. "It will be my pleasure. It was said the man was walking his fields late at night in search of a valuable mare who'd gone missing from his herd. The people of his village warned him to let the mare go. They thought she'd been chosen by the gods as one of their steeds. If so, the man and his farm would be blessed with fertility."

"But he couldn't let the horse go, could he?" Catherine said, anticipating the twist the story would take.

"He could not." Patrick slowed his horse to a walk. They were approaching Mick's cottage. He knew the older man was still at the barn, but he wanted to make sure there was nothing amiss when they passed.

"Wouldn't he rather have the blessing of the gods than one mare?" Catherine knew she was playing into his hands, but she didn't care.

"In most cases, yes. But this mare was the prized possession of his daughter. She was a small chestnut mare with four white stockings and a blaze, trained by the girl to the gentlest touch of silken threads."

"A valuable animal, but certainly not as valuable as the blessing of the gods."

"Perhaps not to some, but this man loved his daughter dearly and couldn't stand to see her suffer. He was determined to find the mare and bring her home, even if he had to go to the otherworld and hunt."

"And if he displeased the gods?" Catherine could see a dark parallel, and she wondered how much of the story Patrick had made up to suit his own purposes.

"Then that was the risk he had to take. His only daughter cried ceaselessly at the loss of her horse. He had to risk everything. So he was walking the fields in the full light of the moon. This was the exact time, thirty days before, when the mare had disappeared. As he topped the last hill of his property, he saw a woman standing beneath a small, stunted tree."

"A stranger," Catherine said, arching an eyebrow.

"She was alone, and she stirred not a finger at his approach. 'Can I help you?' he offered, thinking perhaps she'd lost her way or her horse. There was no sign of how she'd come to be standing in the middle of his pasture.

"'I believe it is I who can help you,' she said. 'You seek a golden mare with a mouth as tender as spun silk.'

"'My daughter's horse,' the man agreed. 'I'd have her back, no matter the cost, if there was any way to do it.'

"'There is a way. But the price is far dearer than you'd imagine.'

"'If it's within my power, I'll pay,' the man said."

"What was the price?" Catherine could visualize the woman, the tree, the approach of the man.

"The man was handsome. A widower, who never thought to love another, a man content to raise his child alone. That was one reason he couldn't stand to see her grieve. She was his only happiness."

"The woman wanted the child, didn't she?" Catherine's voice expressed her outrage.

Patrick chuckled. "No, it wasn't his daughter. It was him that she desired. The woman was the goddess Epona, whose name means Great Mare. She'd been lured from the otherworld by the beauty and spirit of the golden mare and she'd taken her to ride as her own personal steed. But she'd been held on earth by the determination of the man to prevent his daughter from suffering. She'd decided that for a night of passion, to experience the pleasures of human coupling with a man so sensitive and caring, she'd return the mare."

Catherine cast a quick look at Patrick. There was no humor in his eyes. He was deadly serious. She swallowed. Was there really a parallel between the theft of the golden mare and Limerick, or was Patrick merely telling her a tale? "And did the man agree?"

"Indeed, with pleasure and a firm resolve to please. His efforts were so successful, in fact, that he was rewarded thrice-fold. His daughter's mare was returned to the very pasture from which it was taken. He was required to meet the goddess under the same tree each time the moon turned full. And, as a reward for the pleasures he gave Epona, she gave him the ability to bring any horse to his will by the simple touch of his hand upon the horse's neck."

Patrick looked at her. He was surprised by the soft rose color that had crept up her neck and into her cheeks.

"An interesting story," she managed. "How did you come by 'the touch'?"

"The man's name was Patrick Shaw, my great-great-great—back to the days before our time—grandfather. I understand he was eventually hanged for a horse thief, so you wonder how much good 'the touch' did him."

The corners of Patrick's mouth tipped up with mischief. With the story he was mocking himself and inviting her into his past, his world. Catherine's gaze fell to Patrick's hands, and she wondered again what his touch would feel like, just the graze of his fingers along her hip. The flash of desire she felt was unsettling in the extreme.

"How about a canter?" She couldn't meet his gaze, and without waiting for an answer she squeezed her thighs on Mayo's Motion. The mare surged forward, eager to run.

"Catherine!"

She heard the sudden panic in his voice, but she needed a moment to compose herself. The thrill of a run would pull her mind back from thoughts she had no business harboring. Instead of answering, she applied more leg, rose into two point and flattened her back along the horse's neck. Mayo leapt forward.

Hooves thundered behind her and she felt the mare lengthen her stride even more. She grinned to herself as she pulled in rein and allowed the mare to balance on her hands. She was enough of a horsewoman to know that it was up to her to hold the mare steady and encourage her on.

"Catherine!" Patrick pushed Tam faster. He had to catch her. In the fleeting moment before she'd surged ahead of him he'd gotten a clear look at her bridle. There was something odd about the right rein.

When he saw she had no intention of heeding his call, Patrick shifted his weight off Tam's back and gave the gelding the signal to run. If Catherine's reins gave, she could be in serious trouble. Mayo's Motion was a well-trained mare, but she was high-spirited and a handful to manage. If she got her head, there was no telling what the mare might do.

Catherine looked back over her shoulder. Patrick's face was etched with determination. He was leaning into the gelding's flying mane. Her heart caught at the sight of him. He was a graceful man on the ground, but on horseback he was magnificent.

Turning her attention back to the road, she felt her heart slam into her stomach. Not a hundred yards ahead was an old man leading a donkey. The small animal was toiling beneath two heavy baskets of peat. There was no escape for the man to the left or the right, and he stopped in the road, his mouth agape as he saw the horse and rider flying toward him.

Catherine gripped hard with her knees and pulled back. The snap of the right rein almost flipped her backward off the horse.

Free of the restraint, Mayo's Motion snaked her head down and opened up even wider.

Patrick saw the rein give and Mayo's reaction to her newfound freedom. Catherine had no control over the feisty mare.

"Now!" Patrick whispered to Tam. "Now!" he urged. The gelding opened up, pouring on speed. There wasn't time for hesitation. Patrick pushed Tam beside Mayo. He caught one glance of Catherine's frightened but determined face. She was trying to use her weight to stop the mare, but Mayo was intent on nothing more than the glory of the run.

With one long arm, Patrick reached out and grabbed the cheek strap of the bridle. Mayo gave one impatient jerk of her head, then obediently began to slow as Patrick pulled Tam back and kept Mayo's nose pulled toward him.

"Easy girl," Patrick soothed her. In a few strides he had both horses down to a walk and then a stop.

"The rein— Thank you." Catherine gulped air.

They both checked to make sure that the old farmer was none the worse for the experience. His shock had turned to an eager surveying of both horses.

"Nice animals," he offered. "I love to see a fine horse run." He prodded his donkey into a slow walk. Without another word or glance, he left them behind.

"Catherine." Patrick wanted to do nothing more than scoop her off the horse and hold her safely in his arms. For a split second, he'd been afraid she was going to be horribly injured, possibly killed.

"I feel like such a fool." Catherine shook her head. The ride had been reckless. Stupid. She could have injured herself, her horse and an innocent old man. "I lost control. When the rein snapped... I mean, I should have been able to control her."

"She's a spirited animal and always eager to take advantage." He reached over and settled his hand on her thigh. "Are you okay?"

"Thanks to you." She felt her breathing become short, quick. It was just the feel of his hand on her. She couldn't ignore it, nor could she simply pretend it did not affect her.

"Catherine, did you saddle the horses yourself?"

Patrick's question made her look up. His tone was innocent, but she knew him too well. "No. Eamon McShane saddled them both."

Patrick reached across her for the dangling rein. The leather was frayed, broken. "It wasn't cut," he said. He stared at her. "There's no proof that this was deliberate, but then there's no evidence to show it was an accident. McShane is a man who bears watching."

Chapter Seven

The moon was slightly fuller than it had been the night before. Patrick stared at it as he slowly made his way toward the old barn where Limerick waited. Drawing in his breath, Patrick paused. The gray horse seemed to reflect the moonlight. He was as still as a statue, a mythical creature, frozen for a split second by the magic of the moon.

Limerick pawed the ground, and Patrick started forward again.

There was less than a kilometer to go, and Patrick shifted the bag of grain on his back. He'd brought fifty pounds. Not that heavy a load, but he was bone tired and burdened by other items. Only the sight of Limerick, dancing in the moonlight as he watched Patrick approach, relieved his aching muscles and weary mind.

He'd given a lot of thought to the ride he'd shared with Catherine Nelson that morning. The legend he'd made up was a total fabrication. Why? He didn't know. There was no scientific way to explain his relationship with horses. Over the years, he'd been asked that question a million times. He was no closer to an answer now than he'd been when he was a young boy. He had a gift, a power. There were times when he understood so completely what a horse needed or wanted, he'd begun to think that there was the possibility he'd been one in the long distant past.

He gave a low, stuttering whistle, and Limerick called a greeting in return. They'd always shared that—delight in seeing each other.

Along with the feed, Patrick carried a lightweight saddle and a bridle. It was time to put Limerick back to work. Their life together was almost over.

One thing that had become clear to Patrick was Catherine's regard for the horse. She might not know what was best for him, but she didn't mean to deliberately cripple him. She'd been sensible, fun and concerned, during the ride. The action that made Patrick really take notice was when she asked to see Mick's place—to be certain the old man was comfortable. He'd never have suspected that the cold authoritarian who'd first come to Beltene was the same woman. Perhaps he'd been a bit rash in taking Limerick. Maybe he could have talked to her about the injury.

The memory of Kent Ridgeway came back to him and he muttered an oath beneath his breath. The entire thing could have gone a different way if Ridgeway hadn't been around. The man was fatal to horses. He'd ruined more good animals than anyone knew. That had been the determining straw that prompted Patrick to hide Limerick until his leg healed. But Ridgeway had been gone for most of the week. Maybe, with some gentle prodding, Catherine would come around to seeing the man for what he was.

"Hello, fella," Patrick said as he dropped the feed and put the saddle on the low stone wall. His back welcomed the release from the weight, but his heart lifted as the gray stallion threw his head, whinnying, and rushed to the wall to give Patrick a nuzzle.

"Tired of this pasture? Ready for a ride?" Patrick threw the saddle onto Limerick's back and tightened the girth. "I wasn't about to haul brushes and the like up here. You've been a field horse for the past week, so a ride without a bit of grooming won't hurt you. Like all little boys, you like a chance to get dirty, don't you?" He spoke softly to the horse as he bridled him. Limerick took the bit eagerly, blowing out his nostrils in impatience as Patrick made sure the buckles were secure. Before he mounted, Patrick checked Limerick's knee.

Once in the saddle, he took a look at the moon. It was better than half-full, and there was plenty of light. He'd charted a seven-mile course that wound around a small village and stayed on clear paths. There were few rocks and no fences, a good beginning to get the stallion back in peak condition after a week of being laid off.

Tired as he was from a week with little or no sleep, he felt a surge of anticipation at riding Limerick. He was much too tall and heavy to be considered a jockey, but it was Patrick's theory that a horse should learn to carry his weight. Then when the feather-light jockey climbed aboard, it would be as if he carried nothing at all.

Limerick's snort brought Patrick up sharp. The stallion was blowing and sidling away from a black shadow that moved slowly down the stone wall. "That damn cat," he whispered. How was it that Familiar hid away in the Rover and walked all the way up to Limerick's hideout? Twice! It was as if the cat were guarding them—or spying on them.

"Eleanor will skin me if anything happens to you," Patrick said to the cat as he picked up the reins. "You behave yourself and wait here. I'll be back in better than an hour."

EXACTLY WHAT are my options, Einstein? You have the keys. I have to wait here, and you'd better be glad someone did. You've been so busy daydreaming you didn't notice that we were being followed. I couldn't catch a good look at him, but it was a him and he's as stealthy as a wolf. He's been dogging our steps since we left the Rover three miles back. Of course, it wasn't hard with all that grunting you were doing.

That's right, go off on your little joyride. I'll stay here and do the hard work. I want to ambush that rascal who's tailing us. If it's who I think it is, there's going to be trouble later on. Eamon McShane will have the law up here so fast Patrick won't know what hit him.

Why am I doing this? Why am I, a sensible, handsome American cat, involving myself with a wild Irish horse thief and a gray nag with a leg injury? Now that deserves an answer.

Patrick Shaw hasn't as much as checked my teeth or rubbed behind my ears. Sure, sure, he's been busy stealing horses and all. But I ask myself, why am I here, looking out for his back? The only answer I can come up with is that when he does touch me, I know he's kind. And he's Eleanor's friend.

Besides, I think he's being set up to take the blame for something. I don't know what yet, but something serious. If he'd only take Limerick home, then I'd feel much, much better. Instead, he's out playing Lone Ranger and riding along the roads. On a stolen horse. During the middle of the night. When he's liable to break his damn fool neck. These Irishmen have a funny way of entertaining themselves.

So I'll just settle into this cranny by the stone wall and wait to see who comes along. I sense that he's still out there. Not close, but watching. Watching and waiting.

I should have packed a light snack. Had I known the horseman was going to ride off for several miles, I would have. Oh, well, too late to cry over forgotten milk. Mauve promised she'd have a special treat for me in the morning. Some goat's milk delight. Hey, I'm a cultured and well-traveled cat. I'll give any local delicacy a try.

PATRICK'S FINGERS teased the reins as he constantly communicated with the powerful horse. He could detect the slightest difference in Limerick, a shift so subtle that no one else would ever notice it. The week without work had softened rock-solid muscle to solid muscle. It would take only a few days of work to tone him back up.

"Just a trot," Patrick whispered to the horse. Limerick wanted to run. He wanted to fly. And Patrick wanted to let him. The desire was almost irresistible. But it wasn't what Limerick needed.

Trotting, and lots of it. Up and down hills, in small circles along the road, and then possibly a gallop. That's what Limerick had to have.

The seaside town of Clifden suddenly came into view from a high hill. It was a picturesque village, a bit touristy in recent years, but filled with good people he'd known since birth. He pointed Limerick down the hill. He had no intention of going through town, but the road he needed was at the outskirts.

The stallion covered the distance in a few minutes, and Patrick turned him east, along the seacoast. It was wild and rugged country, and the road was little more than two lanes worn smooth through the grass. The landscape was dotted with houses that had been abandoned for one reason or another.

"Hold! Watch who you're near to killing!"

Patrick sat down hard as the stallion lunged to the left to avoid a pile of black rags that had suddenly begun to move on the shoulder of the road.

"Easy, boy," Patrick soothed the agitated horse. The sudden motion, almost under his feet, had greatly upset Limerick.

"Why it's Cuchulain, come to rescue his people and 'rouse their emotions. Aye, riding the gray horse who was known to kill forty warriors with his hooves in a pitched battle. It's high time you showed yourself, my lord."

The old man sounded as if he'd had more than one drink. "Are you injured?" Patrick asked. He ignored the reference to the Irish folk hero, a great warrior who was known for his love of horses and freedom.

"I've been ridden over by a ghost horse and not a hair on my head is out of place." The old man chuckled, but his face was hidden in the shadows cast by a hat and layers of what appeared to be shawls.

"Who are you?" Patrick asked. "Can I help you home?"

"You've helped me already," the man said. "When I tell them that Cuchulain is riding the hills, perhaps they'll listen then. We're Irishmen. We should never forget our history." He tucked his head against the brisk wind.

Patrick considered trying to convince the old man that his near brush with death had not been at the hands of Cuchulain, but he needed to keep Limerick at a constant pace if he was to condition him.

"If you don't need my help, then I'll bid you good night," Patrick said.

"May the gods protect you," the man called. He staggered back and sat down on a large rock. "May the saints protect us both."

"If you're going to find comfort in the history of this land, you'll need the protection of the saints." Patrick spoke more under his breath than to the man. The lessons of history had been bitter ones for his family, especially the ones that involved a free Ireland. He'd lost a sister, his older brother, who was in effect gone, and his family business—all sacrificed for "the cause" as Colin called it.

"Cause, be damned," Patrick said, nudging Limerick into a faster trot. The wind had turned damp and cold. In the short time he'd talked with the old ragman, a heavy mist had blown in from the sea. Patrick tightened his collar and wished for a pair of gloves. He urged Limerick into a gentle canter as they began to climb the road that would give him a view of the Atlantic Ocean.

Limerick's stride lengthened and steadied, and Patrick gave himself to the ride. The road tunneled into dense blackness and there was a savage joy in the way they pounded along, together. Patrick knew he had to let the past go. For the first time he considered leaving Beltene. Once Limerick had been transported to the track, he could go. His last scrap of influence—and protection—over the horse would be gone.

As if he sensed Patrick's thoughts, Limerick crow hopped suddenly. The movement forced Patrick to clamp down with his thighs and pull in rein. Limerick intensified the bucking. He let out a playful squeal.

"And to think I was feeling sorry for you," Patrick said. He rode the rocking bucks, laughing at the stallion. He knew Limerick was only playing. There was no serious intent in the gentle bucks and stiff-legged crow hops.

"You'd best straighten up. If you do this on the track, Catherine will have you to the glue factory."

Tired of the game, Limerick settled back into a gallop. For the last three miles they rode in silence.

MUMBLING CAME FROM the loft in a gentle murmur, as if a conversation was going on just below the actual level of hearing. Catherine paused as she got Mayo's Motion out of the stall and led her to the cross ties.

There were several grooms about, in another wing, but it was barely daylight and she'd come to the barn for another ride. And to see Patrick. Sleep evaded her. No matter how much during the day she could convince herself that Limerick was fine, at night the devils of worry and guilt nagged at her. She was feeling rough and bruised, and the one thing that seemed to soothe her was to see the trainer at work. If he had Limerick, and she felt that he did, then his presence at the barn meant all was well. If anything was wrong with Limerick, Patrick would be with the horse. That much she knew. More troubling was when Patrick would decide to return her horse. The more time that passed, the more anxious she was becoming.

She climbed the ladder to the loft to satisfy her curiosity about who, or what, was making such an interesting noise. Studiously avoiding the door to Patrick's quarters, she walked in the opposite direction toward the hay storage area. The noise was coming from the hay mound where loose hay had been gathered into a pile.

Her gaze fell on the long length of leg, boot-clad, the breeches permanently discolored at the knees from saddle soap. Even before she saw the dark hair, sprinkled with hay, she knew it was Patrick. The big black cat was asleep in his arms. The smile that crossed Catherine's face was amused and tender. It was quite a sight, a grown man curled up in the hay with a cat.

"The past..." Patrick whispered.

Catherine eased down and stroked a purr from Familiar. She didn't stop to analyze her actions; she only knew her heart had begun a faster, racy beat. The cat's green eyes opened, then closed again. "So, I'm not even worth waking up for, am I?" she asked softly.

She felt Patrick's gaze on her before she looked at him. He was wide-awake. There wasn't a trace of sleepiness in his gaze, and she felt suddenly vulnerable.

"Do you find this more comfortable than your bed?" she asked, awkwardly looking down. What was she doing sitting in the hayloft with him? She'd invaded his privacy in a strange way. Even her question was embarrassingly familiar.

"I've slept plenty of nights in the hay." There was no reprimand in his tone, only mild amusement. He was enjoying her discomfort. "How about you, Catherine Nelson? Have you never spent a summer night in the sweet hayloft?"

Catherine knew to get to her feet, to answer him with a smile and a quick retort. But she didn't move. Her mouth went dry and she stared at him. "It isn't summer," she managed. Sunlight filtered in through air laden with dust motes and struck the stubble on his face.

As if he read her mind, he ran a hand over his chin and sighed. "Time for a shower and shave." He pushed up to an elbow, taking a moment to fondle Familiar. "Have I missed breakfast?"

His light remark broke the trance. Catherine got to her feet. "Do you always sleep in your boots?"

"Saves on the wear and tear." He smiled, and it had an amazingly boyish quality. "Actually, I couldn't find my bootjack and I sat down here in the hay to spend a moment with Familiar and I fell asleep. In fact—" he eased the cat onto his lap "—this fellow was acting a little sore last night. Stiff in a back leg, so I decided to check it out. Last year he was involved in a bombing.''

At the look on Catherine's face, Patrick stopped short. ''In America, not here. His owner believes the bombs were directed at her and her husband because of some work they did in putting an animal researcher behind bars.''

Catherine looked down. She'd jumped to a conclusion. She'd heard ''bomb,'' and she'd thought of Patrick's brother and his affiliation with a militant group in Northern Ireland. It wasn't something Patrick ever talked about—he was unreasonably private about such matters. And bigger fool, she'd let him read her thoughts right off her face.

''But, of course, I'm sure you think all Irishmen have a passion for dynamite and a fuse.'' Patrick stood, gently lowering Familiar back into the hay. ''That's one of our national weaknesses, I suppose. Whiskey, song and bombs.''

''Patrick.'' She stood. ''I'm sorry.'' There should have been something else she could say, something more. But the bitter extremities of their backgrounds were laid bare before them. ''Please excuse me,'' she said, heading toward the ladder. No matter that she'd been reared and schooled in Ireland. Her birth and heritage were English. To him, she was British. She was British and she had money. To think that a friendship could ever be built across that abyss was heartbreakingly foolish.

Retreat was the only recourse she had, and she took it, going down to the barn aisle where Mayo's Motion waited patiently in the cross ties. Refusing the offers of the grooms for assistance, she curried the mare, cleaned her hooves, saddled her up and led her into the yard. She couldn't help herself as she cast a look up into the hayloft. Patrick stood there, the cat at his feet. Both of them watched her as she rode into the distance.

MICK DRAINED HIS GLASS and put it down on the bar. ''Tell me again what was said and done,'' he requested, motioning for a refill.

O'Flaherty's was smoky and filled with patrons. It was the hour just before the evening meal when men and women stopped by from the bustle of the day for a quick drink and a chat with their neighbors and friends. Mick shifted onto a stool, taking the weight off his throbbing foot. Patrick hadn't allowed him to accompany him to see the stallion the previous night. Now Mick was hearing the stories of it, though. It stirred a fire in his heart, and it troubled him greatly.

"The old man came in here, babbling about Cuchulain and the mystical horse," the barkeep repeated. "He said the animal was enormous, a chest the width of a brawny man and hooves that sparked fire on the rocks in the road."

"And you're believing this?" Mick said in a mocking voice. "Next you'll be claiming to see St. Patrick running the snakes into the ocean."

"The old beggar was dead serious. His hand was trembling so, I gave him a drink."

Mick hooted. "And now you're out a free drink so you want to keep us all here listening to wild tales and filling your till."

Mick's scorn was not having a detrimental effect on the barkeep's audience. Several men and three women had moved closer to hear the tale.

"How did he know it was Cuchulain?" one woman asked.

"Because he said he was here to remind all Irishmen that freedom is a natural state," the barkeep said. "He urged all of us to remember that."

"Cuchulain," a man said. "It's about time Ireland found herself a national hero. Even one that's been dead for centuries."

There was general laughter, but Mick saw the look of tension that passed from face to face. History and heroes were serious business to most Irishmen. Both could stir a heart to dangerous deeds.

In Mick's mind, he knew who was out on the road late at night riding a big gray horse. Patrick would not be amused to find himself the embodiment of a legend. And Mick would never believe that Patrick was encouraging talk of freedom, not even in jest. Colin Shaw had labeled himself a freedom fighter, and it had cost the Shaw family money, blood, and much, much more.

"Was he as handsome as the legend says?" another woman asked. "If he is, maybe I'll wait out on the road to see him. It might be worth losing a night's sleep to lure him home to my bed."

"He wouldn't want to be riding no horse in the middle of the night if he had an offer from you," a man replied, and was greeted by general laughter up and down the bar.

"I wouldn't put too much stock in the foolish babblings of an old drunk," Mick said. He finished his drink and stood.

"Keep that foot by the fire," the barkeep called to Mick as he saw him prepare to leave.

"Aye, not much else to do on a raw night." Mick pushed his money forward on the counter, picked up his cap and pulled it over his eyes as he stepped into the night. A blast of cold air almost made him turn back inside. He heard someone else follow him out.

"You need a ride, Mick?" a young man who'd been sitting at a table asked. He pulled his hat down lower and cast a glance at the closed door of the bar.

"Do I know you?" Mick questioned. He looked the neatly dressed young man over.

"I went to school with your son, Michael."

"Sure." Mick nodded and suppressed his sigh of relief. It wasn't a long walk to his cottage, but his foot was throbbing, and he was bone tired. Patrick had said another three nights of riding Limerick and he would bring him home. If only their luck would hold another seventy-two hours. "A ride would be nice, indeed."

"The red one," the young man said, pointing to the car.

Mick walked over to it, realizing that the man who'd offered him a ride wasn't a regular in O'Flaherty's. "I'm sorry but I can't recall your name," he said.

"Craig. Craig Murray." The young man stuck out his hand.

Mick took it. The palm was smooth. "Are you sure I'm not taking you out of your way?"

"Not at all." The man slid into the driver's seat and reached across to unlock the door for Mick. "Hop in. Won't take but a minute to drop you home."

Darkness had fallen heavy and thick, and Mick thought about the four-kilometer walk. When he felt better it wouldn't take half an hour, but tonight the wind was kicking up from the ocean, and his foot promised wet weather for sure. Still, he hesitated. There was something about the young man. His face was shadowed by a slight growth of beard, but his skin was smooth, as if he didn't normally allow himself to go ungroomed.

He was wearing a jacket and slacks. Nothing unusual. In fact, as ordinary as clothes could be. That was what was troubling. They were creased, as if they'd just come out of a store.

"Mick?" Craig asked. "Is something wrong?"

"No." Mick slid into the seat and slammed his door. When the motor was cranked, a seat belt slid across his chest and snugged him against the seat. He put his hands on it to hold it back.

"Newfangled things," Craig said. "Cars now have them so you don't have a choice to buckle up or not."

"Nice car." Mick noticed the newness, the expensiveness. It moved away from the curb without a sound.

"So, how are things at Beltene?"

There was a hint of something in Craig's voice. Mick turned to him to ask him what he meant. Before he could say anything at all, a heavy cloth was pressed into his face. A nauseating odor made him choke and gag. Over the edges of the cloth, as he fought to free his mouth and nose, he saw the pleasure in Craig's eyes.

Craig's hands were on the steering wheel and the car continued to move forward. Mick knew then that he'd been ambushed. Someone was in the back seat holding chloroform to his nose. He recognized the odor now, the sweet, sickening smell. He struggled, but the seat belt held him, as did the arms of the man in the back seat.

"My word, he's feisty for an old man," a voice said from the back seat. But the arms that held Mick were strong.

In only a matter of minutes, Mick's struggles ceased and he slipped limply back into the seat.

Chapter Eight

The grain spilled into the feed trough and Patrick stepped back. Eager for a bite, the weanling pushed forward and nosed into the bucket. Very gently, Patrick scratched the little one's neck. He was a beautiful baby with plenty of potential. One of Mick's favorites.

For a moment Patrick's worries about Mick were lost in contemplation of the young horse. As he started back to the barn, the weight of Mick's absence crashed down on him again. Where was the old man? He'd been absent last night when he went to feed and exercise Limerick.

He'd urged Mick to stay home and nurse his foot often enough, but never before had the old man heeded him. Mick's problems kept multiplying. As soon as he finished the morning chores, Patrick decided he'd check up on Mick. He had a terrible feeling that something was wrong.

In a matter of minutes he was striding across the fields toward Mick's. Normally he enjoyed the walk, but not on this day. He entered the cottage without knocking, and it took only a few glances around the house to ascertain that his friend was gone. He checked his watch. It was just after eight. He had a couple hours' worth of chores back at the barn, and then he'd begin to retrace Mick's steps.

THE TEACUP RATTLED in the saucer, but it was the only sign that Catherine gave that Allan's visit was unexpected, and disturbing. He swept into the dining room just as she was finishing breakfast.

"Marmalade." Allan walked to her side, picked up a piece of toast and dropped a spoonful of the orange preserves onto it. "Homemade?"

"I believe Mauve made it." Catherine had to force herself not to show her irritation. Allan had apparently opened the front door and walked in without even knocking. He'd always been a bold man. "What brings you for a visit?"

"I came to see if you'd gotten a ransom note yet. After all, I did leave a considerable sum of money here with you."

"It's in the safe. Safe." Catherine smiled as she rose from the table. "Since I won't be needing it, I'd prefer to return it to you."

"Are you certain?"

She thought she caught a glimmer of distress in Allan's eyes, but his perfect mask covered it too soon for her to be positive. "What are you up to, Allan?"

"Making a profit. Having a good time." He gave her a careless smile and shrugged his shoulders. "You remember, don't you?"

"I do." The thought made her a little sad. Allan's charm was in his boyishness, his enthusiasm for life, but he was rapidly getting to an age where boyishness wasn't cute. "One thing about you, Allan, you're consistently consistent."

"There's something to be said for that." He brightened. "Now why don't we work out the details of our partnership? I'd love to own a piece of that stallion. You know, I have great faith in your ability to make this horse farm pay off. Even though you never cared for the bank, you always had a head for business."

"Thanks." Her smile was still touched with a degree of sadness. "Thanks, but no thanks. Limerick isn't for sale. Not a little piece or a big chunk."

"What if you don't find him?" Allan's sharp question was

softened by another shrug. "I mean, what will you do? Will you lose Beltene?" He searched her face.

"Limerick will race, and he'll win for Beltene." She rose and moved away from the table. What was Allan's big interest in Limerick? Was it possible he was really trying to be a friend? "Let me get your cash, Allan. It was foolish of you to leave it. Help yourself to another piece of toast." She left him in the dining room as she hurried to the safe in her office. The briefcase was still there, just as she'd left it.

Still munching the toast, Allan met her in the hallway. "I don't mean to eat and run, but I do have an appointment."

"In Dublin?"

"No, in Galway." Allan kissed her cheek. "The wine selection leaves something to be desired, but the seafood is excellent. Truly excellent. Maybe you can drive over and have dinner with me one night. For old times' sake."

"Perhaps," Catherine answered. She had no intention of doing so, but she felt no need to coldly state her feelings. Allan was what he was, a handsome man with charming manners. He would not miss her visit; he was far too busy with himself to notice her absence.

Allan hefted the briefcase. "Catherine." His look was serious. "Just keep in mind that there are desperate people out there."

Chill bumps tingled along her arms, more at his expression than at his words. "What are you saying?" She couldn't believe Allan was threatening her. It was so out of character.

"Just a word to the wise. Circumstances can sometimes make people do things they wouldn't ordinarily. You know, desperate measures for desperate times." He smiled, but his eyes were cold. "If you get desperate for some money, you can call on me. If Limerick were my horse, I'd want him home where I could keep an eye on him. You never know what unethical people can do to an innocent animal."

"I'll keep that in mind, Allan. Now if you'll excuse me, I have some errands to run." She opened the front door. She didn't like what Allan implied. As she watched him walk down the sidewalk to the drive, she finally admitted to herself that she didn't like the idea that he was in Connemara at all.

Picking up her purse and keys from the foyer table, she went to her car. She hadn't fibbed about errands. There were several items she needed from the village, and her boots were ready at the repair shop.

Twenty minutes later she loaded her boots into the trunk of the Volvo and walked around to open the driver's door. Her gaze passed down the curving street of the village and stopped on the tall figure of a man paused in front of O'Flaherty's Bar and Grill. It was Patrick Shaw. At first she didn't believe it, but as she stared, she recognized him. His shoulders were stooped, as if he were bone weary, and he stood at the door as if undecided whether to go in or not. She checked her watch. It was eleven. By all rights, Patrick should be at the barn, working.

She got in the car and closed her door, feeling slightly guilty for spying. Seeing Patrick in the village during the morning hours, especially at a bar, was enough to make her look twice. In all of the things she'd heard about Patrick, drinking wasn't one of his weaknesses. If any man ever looked as if he needed a drink, Patrick did.

As she watched, he entered the bar. Instead of driving back to Beltene, as she'd planned, she settled down in her seat and prepared to wait.

INSIDE THE BAR, Patrick checked out the interior. There were two men sitting at a table drinking coffee, newspapers spread before them. The barkeep was washing glasses. In the back there was the sound of someone working in the kitchen.

"What can I do for you?" the barkeep asked.

Patrick took a seat and asked for hot tea. "I'm looking for a friend of mine. An older man, walked with a limp. Mick McGuire."

"Old Mick. He was in here last evening." The barkeep smiled. "He didn't drink enough to go missing from work."

"I'm a friend of his," Patrick repeated, stressing the word friend. "I'm worried about him."

The barkeep put his cloth down and leaned on the bar. "What can I tell you?"

"When did he leave here last night?"

"Sammy was behind the bar, but I was here for a game of darts. There was some talk about this horseman—"

"Horseman?" Patrick's back straightened.

"Some old man had been in saying that Cuchulain was out of his grave and riding the roads on a big gray stallion. He said it was a warning to all Irishmen to remember the past, to remember the warriors, and to remember the time when the Irish controlled their own destiny. A regular rebel, he was, for an old man. Right vigorous when he got to talking. Yeah, whiskey and insurrection took thirty years off him." The barkeep laughed. "Old Mick got wound up a bit, telling everyone it wasn't real. I don't think anyone thought much about it except Mick and the old beggar who started the tale."

Patrick sipped his tea and realized that he hadn't eaten in at least a day. "How about a toasted cheese?"

The barkeep called the order to the back. "Mick drank his drink, talked a bit, and left. He said his foot was troubling him and he had a walk." The barkeep shrugged. "That's all I can remember. Sammy will be back at four if you're wanting to talk with him."

"The old man who saw this Cuchulain, was he here?" A bad feeling was beginning to grow in Patrick's gut. It had to be the same old man he'd run across on the Clifden sea road. How had such an old man made his way to O'Flaherty's? He could have hitched a ride. Even walked it in a night and day. But it was a long stretch for such an old, pitiful man, even if he was fueled by liquor and rebellion.

"I never saw him. Sammy gave him a drink and some food and he was on his way, as far as I know. You could ask around the village. He might be holed up in someone's barn, doing odd jobs. There's not much work to be had in these parts."

"Did you notice if anyone left with Mick?"

The barkeep picked up his cloth and absently dried a few glasses. "I couldn't say for sure. It was a busy time. There were several folks gathered around the bar, talking about Cuchulain and the old stories. I was over at the board." He nodded to the dart board across the room. "To be honest, I was playing for five pounds and my full attention wasn't on what was happening at the bar. There were just a few women and some talk." He laughed. "You know how that kind of thing goes in a bar. Some bawdy humor."

"I do." Patrick accepted the toasted cheese sandwich that the cook brought out from the kitchen. He wasn't hungry, but he had to eat. He felt as if his muscles were bending his bones, he was so tired. "Can you remember if there was anyone here but the regulars?"

"There's always one or two. Folks come to Galway and Clifden and somehow drift in here. We didn't have the traditionals playing last night, so it was more of the local people stopping by after work." His gaze roved around the room. "There were two men I didn't know. A younger man and one close to your age. Well dressed." As he talked, he grew more certain. "They were at a table beside the bar, just beyond where you're sitting. And they were listening to the talk about the horseman. They were interested, leaning forward."

Patrick felt his hopes begin to build. "Irish?"

"Couldn't tell. I didn't hear them talk, but they were comfortable in the bar. You know. They had an idea of what they were about. Not like the tourists staring around and all."

Patrick smiled. "You've a good eye for detail."

"It pays to look at folks. Trouble can start in the beat of a heart. I've learned to try to sniff it out, so I look the people over once or twice."

"Mick left alone, did he?"

"He did as far as I know. Sammy would know more. He

and Mick's son were friendly. He'd take an interest in the old man, you know."

"Do you know where I can find this Sammy?"

"I wouldn't want to find him at ten in the morning. He worked the night and will be sleeping." The barkeep grinned. "But it looks as if you did, too. He lives down past the woolen shop. There's a little lane on the left. Go a bit and there's a house with a red front door. Very neat place, he has. He'll be home. If he's not sociable, Nell will make you welcome."

"Thanks." Patrick finished his sandwich, drank the rest of his tea and left the money on the counter.

When he walked out of the bar he was so intent on his mission that he failed to notice Catherine ducking low in the Volvo. He walked right past her to his vehicle and got in.

FOR A MOMENT Catherine was tempted to follow Patrick. His rugged good looks were honed to sharp angles of worry and fatigue. At the barn he worked hard to hide his problems, but walking down the street he wore them plainly on his face and body. He was headed away from Beltene, as if he were going on an errand. She argued with herself, trying to shake the concern she felt for him. It was certainly none of her business if he stopped in a bar for a cup of coffee or tea or anything else. He wasn't in need of her assistance, wouldn't appreciate her interference. Then why wasn't she on the road to Beltene and the multitude of chores that awaited her?

She got out of the car and walked straight to O'Flaherty's. Pushing open the door, she went in and stopped. Two men were drinking coffee and reading newspapers. The barkeep was drying glasses. An empty plate and a teacup were on the counter where Patrick had obviously been.

"I'm looking for a tall man, dark hair, blue eyes." She smiled. "We were supposed to meet at the post office and I'm late. A bad habit of mine, and one he doesn't tolerate well."

The barkeep smiled. "Everyone knows that women have a tendency to run late. Your friend was here, but he had something else on his mind. If it were me, I'd have been thinking about you instead of old Mick.''

Catherine walked to the bar and took a seat on the stool. ''A cup of tea would be nice.''

''On the way.'' The barkeep busied himself behind the counter for a moment.

''Do you think Patrick will be back this way?''

''If Sammy doesn't take his head off. Sammy's a passionate grump about being awakened. But your friend was intent on talking to him.'' The barkeep pulled a face. ''It's his ears that Sammy will box.''

''What on earth has Mick gotten into now?'' Catherine laughed. ''He can tell a story like nobody else, but he gets himself into some fine jams.''

''I don't think it was his tongue this time. Your friend was looking for him, like maybe he was missing.'' The barkeep frowned. ''Old Mick's not in the best of health. If I'd been thinking, I would have offered him a ride last night. I should have.''

''Missing?'' Catherine tried not to show much interest, but she wasn't very good at pretending. ''For how long?''

''He was in here at five.'' The barkeep slapped the cloth on the bar. ''Now I'll have to worry about old Mick. I should have listened to that crazy talk closer.''

''What talk?'' Catherine felt as if she were spinning in circles.

''Cuchulain.'' The barkeep told her about the old man who'd claimed to see the legendary figure, and Mick's reaction to it.

''Cuchulain. The Irish warrior, the mythological horseman?'' Catherine spoke with a mixture of disbelief and anger. If Patrick Shaw was riding Limerick up and down the roads at night to stir the hearts and minds of the Irish people, he was going to pay a terrible price. She didn't give a damn about the past and old legends and Irish sentiment and history. Limerick was a valuable animal. Riding him along the roads at night was stupid, foolhardy and insane.

"You've been very helpful." She got up and put her money on the counter.

"Are you from around these parts?" the barkeep asked.

"Yes. I am." She spoke with pride and defiance. "My name is Catherine Nelson. From Beltene Farm."

"That's where Mick works." Understanding touched the barkeep's face. "Was Mick at work today?"

"I don't know, but I intend to find out."

"Well, be damned." The barkeep threw his cloth on the counter. "If Mick doesn't show up, let me know. We'll help you hunt for him."

"Thanks." Catherine picked up her purse and left. She was worried about Mick, but that was secondary compared to her anger at Patrick. Every time she was willing to give him credit for decent motivations, she found out something else about him. Stealing Limerick to protect his knee was one thing. Stealing him to ride at night to stir up Irish nationalism was another. Both were wrong, but the latter was so much worse! So much more of a betrayal.

She pointed her car toward Beltene and drove. Well, Patrick would find himself in a pickle when he got home. He'd eventually show up at Mick's cottage again, and when he did, there would be a surprise waiting for him.

PATRICK PUSHED open the door of Mick's small cottage. The dead smell of the peat fire lingered in the room, an odor that tightened Patrick's stomach and made his heart beat faster. His interview with Sammy had yielded no new facts. Mick had left O'Flaherty's after a pint, with the expressed intention of going home. That was the last anyone had seen of him. And now it was twenty-four hours later, with darkness coming on thick, and no sign of the old man. It had taken all of Patrick's concentration to do his chores at the barn and bide his time to return to Mick's. All day he'd held on to the hope that Mick would be here. With the cold and empty cottage as testament, he could no longer deny the fact that Mick had to be in trouble.

"By the saints," Patrick said, slipping into a thick brogue as he eased into the cottage to hunt for clues to what might have happened. He hugged the walls, moving softly, unsure why every signal in his body warned of danger.

There was the sound of something moving outside the house, and Patrick silently cursed the black cat. Familiar had begun to dog his footsteps wherever he went. The cat had a sixth sense about what he was up to, and somehow managed to wiggle his way into the Rover or to follow along, a dark shadow unseen until it was too late.

He crossed the kitchen and stopped, listening once again to the sound of shifting outside. Was it Familiar? He tensed, ready to dive to safety.

The house settled back into silence and Patrick moved forward, quickly looking through the house. There wasn't much of monetary value, but the house was filled with pictures, mostly of horses and the Shaw family. Not a single thing was disturbed. There had not been a fight or struggle in Mick's home. There wasn't the first clue as to what might have happened.

Taking care to close the door softly behind him, he turned toward his vehicle.

"Where's Mick?"

The soft question almost made him jump. He recognized Catherine's voice immediately, and the anger it contained.

"I don't know," he answered.

"Would you like to tell me what's going on? I know it involves one of my employees and my stallion. Have you somehow managed to put both of them in danger?"

The sound of loose rocks shifting forced them into silence. Patrick couldn't be certain where the sound had come from, but standing at the door they were sitting ducks. He took her arm and motioned to the Rover. She had no vehicle. Apparently she'd walked. With a small hesitation, Catherine allowed him to lead her to the Rover.

"Good Lord," Patrick whispered. Familiar sat in the front seat. He was looking out the window, his green eyes glowing in the moonlight.

"Meow," Familiar said, looking into the distance.

To Patrick's complete astonishment, the cat hissed. Not a sound of fear, but of anger. The hair on Familiar's back rose until the cat was puffed to twice his size. Patrick had seen cats cornered by dogs, but he'd never seen such a calculated display of hatred—and directed at something he couldn't see.

"What's wrong with him?" Catherine's voice was barely audible. "I've never seen him act like that."

"Is it Mick?" Patrick didn't even bother to feel silly as he directed the question to the cat. Something had happened to Mick, and Familiar sensed it.

"Meow." Even though he was still outraged, Familiar's answer to Patrick was civil. But when he turned back to look out the Rover's window, another hiss accompanied by a warning growl escaped him.

"Wait here." Pushing Catherine down behind the vehicle, Patrick picked up a tire tool from the back of the vehicle and started off in the direction where Familiar was looking. To his total shock, the cat launched himself out the window and dug into his leg, effectively acting like an anchor.

"Ease off," Patrick said, disentangling the cat's claws from his boots. But Familiar was not so easy to dislodge. He clamped down again. "Let go, cat." Patrick tried to shake him loose, but the cat held.

There was the sound of scuffling in the distance. Patrick stopped fighting the cat and listened. A rock slid, followed by another. It sounded as if someone was throwing stones or toppling the wall that Mick had worked so hard to construct. Anger and fear combined to make Patrick shake Familiar free. He strode toward the sound.

"Who's there?" he demanded of the darkness.

His only answer was the cat. Familiar leapt through the air, landing on Patrick's rear with all four claws digging in. Patrick twisted, trying to free himself from the razor-sharp claws and not lose his balance in the process. The impact of the fifteen-pound cat almost knocked him down.

"Familiar!" Patrick felt his temper slipping. He reached behind him, bending to reach the cat just as the crack of a rifle came through the night. Only inches from where his head had been, the metal top of the Rover ripped from the impact of the bullet.

Catherine's muffled scream came from behind the vehicle.

Patrick dropped flat to his stomach, Familiar still riding the seat of his pants, and crawled to the other side of the Rover. Catherine was crouched down, her head covered by her arms. She wasn't hit—at least, not yet. With one hand, he detached Familiar and put him into the vehicle. When he eased the door open, Catherine got in without any urging on his part. He crept behind the wheel and cranked up. In a matter of seconds he was careering down the narrow road. The back window of the Rover shattered and glass exploded over the front seat. Pulling the cat against his chest, Patrick did the best he could to protect him while at the same time pushing Catherine down below the seat.

"Hang on, this is going to be a rough ride."

The shooters were between him and the main road. If they chose to pursue him, he'd be an easy target. Crouching as low as he could and still see over the wheel, he pushed the pedal to the floor and charged. Hanging around certainly wasn't going to solve any of their problems.

Three more shots rang through the night. Patrick heard metal tear, but he didn't slow. About a hundred yards to his right he saw a flash of the muzzle of the rifle. In the darkness he couldn't detect anything else.

Instead of going to Beltene, he turned toward town.

When the Rover hit the blacktop, Catherine sat up. She took Familiar from Patrick's arms and held him, giving herself a few moments to collect her thoughts before she spoke. She'd never known such fear. Only Patrick's quick actions had saved them. She looked over at him. He was so tense she felt he might explode, but he kept his eyes on the road and his hands on the steering wheel.

"Where are we going?" There were a million questions she needed to ask, but that seemed to be the easiest.

"To Galway. It's time to involve the authorities. Mick is missing, and he hasn't gone visiting his son."

The Rover tore through the night, and Catherine watched the dark shapes of well-known landmarks pass. "I trusted you, Patrick," she said. "Now everything has gotten out of hand. I get the distinct impression that both Mick and Limerick are in danger." She could hear the emotion in her voice and she swallowed angrily. "What's happening here?"

Patrick eased the Rover to a stop on the side of the darkened road. "That's a legitimate question, Catherine. One to which I owe you an answer." He stared into the night.

"If you're thinking that someone has kidnapped Mick in an attempt to find Limerick, I'm afraid you may be right. Don't endanger that old man any further."

Patrick sighed. "That's the question, isn't it? I find myself between a rock and a hard place. I'm sure you know the feeling. If I go to the authorities about Mick, it could put his life in more danger."

"That's the same way I've felt about Limerick."

"How well I know." Patrick tapped the steering wheel as he continued gazing into the night. Suddenly he started the Rover and made a sharp U-turn on the empty road.

"Where are we going now?" Catherine asked.

"Back to Beltene. Give me three hours. There's something I have to do."

"What about Mick?"

Patrick shook his head. "No questions, Catherine. Three hours, and then I'll tell you everything. Is that a deal?"

"Can I really trust you, Patrick?"

The question hung softly in the night, unanswered.

PATRICK MADE the long walk up to Limerick's hideout. Concerns about Mick plagued him. There was only one thing to do. Bring Limerick back to Beltene. Catherine had demonstrated her good faith—and good sense. Now it was time to bring the stallion home and hopefully remove the incentive that had made Mick McGuire a hostage.

Bone weary, he trudged toward the old barn. As he drew close, he glanced around for the horse. Limerick was usually waiting at the fence.

He gave a low whistle, the signal that had been used between them for the three years the stallion had been alive.

Nothing stirred in the pasture.

He walked on, his pace steady. Limerick was sometimes playful. A game of hide-and-seek wasn't beyond his capability.

A small prayer formed in Patrick's brain. "Let him be here. Let him be here." The words were part of his walk. He whistled again.

Nothing.

Patrick climbed the stone wall into the pasture. As soon as he'd discovered Mick missing, he should have known to check Limerick. But in hunting for the old man and doing his chores, he'd had no time. He'd soothed himself with thoughts that no one, no one at all, could find the hideout. The trail was too treacherous, the area too isolated. Limerick had to be there.

The saddle he'd left, in anticipation of the ride, was still on the wall, slightly covered in mist. The bridle hung beside it, untouched. Circling the pasture, Patrick searched everywhere. The decrepit lean-to that had served as Limerick's stable was empty. The pasture was empty.

Limerick was gone.

Chapter Nine

Staring out the window in Catherine Nelson's office, Patrick saw the black cat sleeping on the windowsill. He was stretched in the sun, as if he didn't have a care in the world. Yet Familiar had been at the barn waiting for him when he'd returned from hunting Limerick. The cat had followed him, silent but there, as if he, too, had a stake in what happened to the big gray stallion. It was a pitiful state when he was taking comfort from a big black cat that didn't even live in Ireland.

Mauve brought in a tray of coffee, complete with toast and a rasher of bacon for Patrick.

"You look like you're near to death, Patrick," Mauve said disapprovingly. "You've dropped half a stone in the past ten days. Your skin is as pasty as a corpse, and you look like the devils are eating at your vitals. What's wrong?"

"Too much," he answered, too tired to even try to lie or to take offense at her honesty.

"Miss Catherine will be with you in a few moments. She asked me to see that you had some coffee and something to eat. When she takes a look at you she'll probably ask the coffin maker to take measurements."

"Thanks, Mauve." But the cook's remarks earned a slight grin. Patrick reluctantly took the seat that Mauve indicated and watched her pour the coffee. The caffeine would help ease his pounding headache, he knew. That would be something.

Nothing would cure the fact that both Mick and Limerick were gone. Both without a trace—that he could find. He had every intention of going back to the hideout in the next hour or two. He'd take several of the best men from the barn. Men who knew how to track a horse through river and bog. Because whoever had spirited Limerick away had not gone down the road. They'd taken him toward the Twelve Bens, the magnificent mountain range, where only the locals knew the safe paths. The bogs were extremely treacherous for those who didn't know the way.

"Patrick."

Catherine Nelson's voice was businesslike, but there was a hint of something else. Pleasure? Anticipation? Patrick groaned silently.

He stood and turned to face her. Before she could say anything else, he told her. "Limerick is gone."

"It would seem we're back to square one." Catherine smiled. "So when will he be coming back?"

Patrick realized that she knew he'd taken the horse. She'd known all along—or at least for the best part of the time. Yet she'd done nothing. Why not? What had possessed her to trust him with an animal as important to her future as Limerick? It was something that required a great deal of thought, and time was the one thing he didn't have.

"Catherine, he's gone. I've lost him." He watched reality dawn on her, and he realized the depths of shame and guilt he was capable of feeling.

"How is he gone? What do you mean?"

"Someone took him yesterday. Probably during the early evening hours. When I went to ride him, he was gone."

Catherine walked very slowly to her desk and sank into the cushioned chair. Nothing had prepared her for this. She'd come into the room anticipating a bit of a negotiating session with Patrick—she'd consent to his racing schedule and he'd agree to bring the stallion home. Nothing had prepared her for this blow.

''He was safe and well taken care of.'' Patrick forced himself to look at her pale face, at the way her green eyes widened with distress. This was his doing. This was his fault. He'd taken an action that had resulted in a terrible turn of events. Not to mention the fact that his best friend, a man who was like a second father to him, was also missing and might be in terrible danger.

''What happened?'' Catherine picked up the pen on her desk and pulled a pad toward her. She would make notes. Once the facts were written down, they would be easier to understand. She'd lulled herself into an acceptance of Limerick's disappearance because she'd been certain that Patrick had him and would take care of him. Now what?

''He was about twenty-two kilometers from here, tucked away in an old barn and pasture that was my mother's sister's place years ago. No one knew about that place. I planned to ride him once more tonight and bring him home tomorrow. He was healed. I was merely putting the last bit of conditioning on him so he could go to the track next week for you.''

Catherine's eyes were glazed with the shock of the news. ''Am I supposed to believe this?'' she asked quietly.

Her words were more effective than a slap. Without a doubt, Patrick knew that his word was no longer good coin with her. She had every right to feel that way about him. Hadn't he lied to her once before? Hadn't he managed to lose her horse and possibly her future? Yes, he wasn't exactly the kind of man in which she should put her trust.

''I intend to get him back.'' What else could he say?

''And how do you propose to do that?'' The glazed look was disappearing from her eyes. What was left was flinty jade. Hard, cold, angry and afraid.

Patrick saw and understood each of those emotions. ''I'll begin by tracking him from the hideout. Perhaps it would be best if you called the authorities.''

''It's a little late for that.'' Catherine was shaking with rage, a great deal of it self-directed. ''How would I explain to the authorities that I'd allowed my head trainer to steal the horse and keep him for over a week? Should I ask them to call my father and explain that I'd made a small mistake in judgment? That I'd known the man who'd taken Limerick all along, but that I'd dragged my feet about reporting him? That I could have had the stallion back at Beltene, safe and sound, if only I'd taken the action that anyone with two brain cells would have taken!''

Patrick accepted the truth of her words. For whatever reasons, she hadn't called the authorities. She'd known he had the horse, and she'd trusted his judgment. Now she'd suffer because of it.

''Whatever can be done to get him back, I will do. Mick is missing, too.'' He saw her blanch even more. Her skin was so white, almost translucent. If he touched her, she'd probably bruise. But God, how he wanted to touch her. If he could only put his fingers on her cheek, she'd know how sorry he was, how worried about Mick and Limerick.

''Are Mick and Limerick together?''

''I don't know.'' She'd get the truth from him from now on, no matter what the cost. ''Mick was taken the night before. I've been everywhere looking for him. There's a chance he might have been...forced to tell where Limerick was. Catherine, they would have had to hurt him badly to make him tell.''

At the look that crossed her face, Patrick started forward to steady her.

''Stay away,'' she said, leaning back in her chair, away from him.

Her words stopped him short. He was helpless to give her even the smallest comfort.

''What can I do?'' she asked slowly, looking out the window instead of at him. ''What should I do?''

From the first day that Catherine Nelson had appeared at Beltene as the new owner, Patrick had wished to see her knocked down from her high horse. She'd been so arrogant, so cold. He'd laughed with the others and made bets on how long it would take to put a little muck on her breeches. Now he saw her, completely vulnerable, unable to decide what course of action to take. He felt no satisfaction, only shame. He had forced this on her.

"Let me look for them. I've thought about it, and I believe the two disappearances are related. Maybe I can find something, some clue that will help me locate them. I've some contacts in the border patrol. The horse won't go north. Maybe I can make sure he doesn't go across the water, either."

"Patrick, who do you think took him?" The question was sincere and filled with dread. "Will they hurt him?"

They looked at each other, taking each other's measure. "I don't want to make this any worse, but I'm not going to lie to you again. Whoever took the horse may be completely ruthless. They've taken an old man, with no regard for his...way of life."

"Who would want to hurt me that much?" Catherine's eyes beseeched him to come up with a plausible answer. "I've never hurt anyone. Even at the bank I always argued for more time for people who were trying to pay their loans. Daddy said I was a hopeless soft touch. That's why he finally agreed to buy Beltene for me. He realized how unhappy I was at the bank. Who would want to hurt me this much?"

Patrick cleared his throat. "It may not be you, Catherine. Whoever took Limerick knows I took the horse. They've stolen him from my care, not yours. Therefore I'm responsible since I stole him first. This could be directed at me."

"Who?"

It was a simple question, but one without an answer. "I have enemies. Maybe more than my share. I've been a hard man to some, and I haven't walked away when I felt a wrong needed to be righted."

"Especially when a horse was involved." There was the faintest touch of humor at Catherine's mouth. "I want you to tell me one thing. Honestly. Were you riding Limerick and pretending to be Cuchulain?"

"Honestly, no. I was riding on the Clifden seacoast road and I ran into an old man who called me Cuchulain. It was foolishness. I didn't pay it any attention, but when I went looking for Mick I discovered it was a topic of conversation in O'Flaherty's."

"You didn't take the horse for that reason?"

"It may be hard for you to believe, but I have no interest in stirring violence. I've lost my family to the troubles. It's cost me my home and my heritage. My brother can give his speeches and rally the mobs. I've no use for that silly rhetoric. I love the past, the stories and legends, but the past is the past. Ireland must move forward."

Catherine stood. "I won't say that I believe you, but I don't disbelieve you. When you get ready to search for Limerick, please notify me. I'm going with you."

Patrick started to argue then stopped. She had a right to go. God knows, he wouldn't trust Limerick's return to the same idiot who'd lost him. "I'll send one of the men up to get you," he said. "It should be about forty minutes."

"I'll be ready." She wavered slightly, as if standing made her dizzy. Regaining her balance, she walked to the door and opened it for Patrick.

The sharp shrill of the telephone froze them both. Patrick waited while Catherine ran to answer it. Both were thinking it could be a call about the horse. They'd played with the idea of ransom, but now it was a reality. Patrick watched the clear emotions on Catherine's face. He saw alarm.

"No, it would be best if you stayed in England." She looked briefly at Patrick and then away. "I'm busy, Kent. No, Limerick is fine." She twisted the telephone cord. "I'm perfectly fine, I don't care what you think." There was another pause. "I need some time to myself. If you care about me, give me that." She replaced the receiver.

"Kent is coming, I'm afraid. He's in England, but he said he'd be here in the next day or two. I tried to discourage him, but he started getting suspicious."

Of all the people in the world, Ridgeway was the last one Patrick wanted to see. But there was a certain justice in it, he had to admit. Kent might have crippled horses left and right, but he'd never lost a stallion like Limerick. He'd never allowed a horse in his care to vanish into the night without a trace. Bitterness made his voice sound harsher than he intended.

"If we haven't found anything in twenty-four hours, I want you to call the police," Patrick said. "Mick's life might depend on it."

"And if I call them and they kill him or the horse because I did... That's what I think about."

"It's a knot." Patrick strode through the open door and down the hall. He couldn't get outside soon enough. It was as if the walls were inching down on him, drawing in closer and closer. He had to get into the sunshine and the fresh air.

Bursting out the front door, he stood nearly panting on the portal. The two things he loved most in his life, an old man and a gray horse, were in danger. He had to think of a plan. A good one.

So, Ice Queen and the Lone Ranger are going to team up, at least until the horse is found. That makes me feel better. There's something between those two that they don't recognize. Every time they're in a room together it makes the hair on my back bristle. Electricity. It's the old yin and yang principle, and not even two such iron-willed creatures can hold out against the forces of nature forever.

The important thing is that Patrick told her the truth. He came clean, even though it nearly killed him to admit he lost Limerick. That tells me something about his character, and I'm beginning to see why Eleanor and Peter are so taken with this man. He's got a core to him, a solid core.

But that doesn't have a thing to do with Limerick or Mick. What clues can I put together? Well, they were both abducted at night. Mick from a bar and Limerick from his hideout.

It's crossed my mind that a few of the grooms might get

together to show Catherine Nelson who really runs Beltene, but they wouldn't hurt Mick in the process.

No, this is an outsider. Someone who has nothing to lose by taking Mick and the horse. The question in my mind, since I know someone followed Patrick to the hideout, is this—why did they need to take Mick if they already knew where Limerick was? Unless they thought it might keep Patrick silent. Wrong! Man, this is getting complicated. I need a bite of brain food. Fish. That's what my little mama always told me when I was a kitten with teeth as sharp as needles. Eat plenty of fish to help develop my brain. And even though I'm a fully grown cat, I'd never want to disobey my loving mama.

Meow, Mauve, I'm coming your way.

This would be a great vacation if Mauve ran the place and everyone else was gone. No mystery. No disappearing acts. Just good food and a nap in the warm sunshine. Maybe even time for a postcard to Cassandra and Adam back in Tennessee. I miss that little mountain witch. And Adam wasn't bad, for a suit-wearing kind of guy.

My, my, what's the hubbub in the kitchen? Mauve has her daughter Bridget almost ready to cry. I'll do a little purr and distraction maneuver. It always startles them so when a cat demonstrates a talent for diversion. They forget what they were about. I wonder if that short-circuited thinking is a by-product of walking on two legs. It's long been my theory that humanoids don't get enough blood to their brains. Charming creatures, but not always real bright.

Ah, Mauve. Meow! Meow!

THE CAT WALKING nonchalantly along the kitchen counter made Mauve pause in midsentence. Familiar had always been so well-behaved in the house. ''Scat, cat,'' she said, waving her hands at him. ''Get off my clean counter, you four-legged satan.''

Familiar did a dodge and weave, leaping completely over a

bowl of chicken and making tracks through the remains of flour for a pie crust.

"My land!" Mauve grabbed a dish towel and flapped it at the cat. "The creature has been possessed! Get out of here!" She flapped the towel and waved her other hand, calling loudly for help.

Bridget leaned forward on her stool, entranced by the sight of her mother driven to extremes by the beautiful black cat that leapt from counter to counter, never breaking a thing but never allowing Mauve to touch him.

"Look, Mama, he's on top of the refrigerator!" Bridget was delighted. "Here, kitty." She held out her arms and to her surprise, Familiar leapt into them. The weight of the fifteen-pound cat almost toppled her from the stool, but she locked her feet around the bottom bar and managed to stay upright.

"Meow," Familiar offered, nuzzling her chin with his whiskers.

"He likes me." Bridget stroked the cat's head, and when Mauve approached with the broom in hand as a weapon, Bridget put herself between the cat and her mother. "He's fine now. I have him."

"That little rascal," Mauve said, panting. "I let him in and fed him and now he runs the house. He even sleeps in Miss Catherine's bed. He's moved in here like he's a lost lord. Next thing you know he'll be writing the dinner menus."

The black cat looked at her and blinked.

"Look at the devil. He's thinking that's an excellent idea! I swear that cat is smarter than all of your brothers rolled up together."

Bridget laughed, and some of the tension left her shoulders.

Mauve sighed and went to her daughter. She brushed the bangs out of the twelve-year-old's face. "I didn't mean to scare you, but you have to tell Miss Catherine what you saw. Every bit of it. And you shouldn't have laid out from school. Life is hard enough. If you don't get your education, you'll wind up cooking and cleaning in a house that's not your own."

"Yes, Mother." Bridget tucked her chin. A salty tear rolled into Familiar's fur and in a moment he turned to lick the tears from Bridget's cheeks.

"Aye, you're a conniving devil, you are," Mauve said, stroking the cat's head as she hugged her daughter.

"He came to my rescue," Bridget said. "He was protecting me."

"From your own mother?" Mauve laughed. "Well, maybe you did need a bit of protection. Next time you skip school, I promise you that you'll be punished. Now enough said about that. Let's tell Miss Catherine. I heard Limerick is well and truly gone this time. Maybe what you saw will help."

"It was just a—"

"We'll tell her together." Mauve started to tell her daughter to leave the cat, but Familiar had the run of the entire house. Why not bring him along?

Mauve and Bridget found Catherine in her office. She was staring out the window and hadn't answered the light tap on the door.

"Are you ill?" Mauve asked. The entire farm was looking peaked. Maybe they all needed a dose of tonic. And she'd missed seeing old Mick. He had to be deathly ill to miss work.

"Sick at heart." Catherine turned to face the door. "Hello, Bridget, I didn't realize you were home from school today." Catherine had developed a real fondness for Mauve and her children. Bridget was the only girl, and the boys were wild and rambunctious as young colts, but they were all honest and well-mannered children.

"I skipped school. Today and day before." Bridget looked at her mother and then back at Catherine. "That's when I saw the man."

"What man?" Catherine was careful not to show too much interest. If the little girl thought it was very important, she might get frightened or confused.

"He was staring at the house. And he put something in the mailbox. A letter or card. I didn't look." She gave her mother a glance. "Mama says we should never look at another's mail. I just saw him put it in the box."

"What did he look like?" Catherine knew who the man was, or at least, what he was doing. She'd received four notes telling her that Limerick was safe. The last had been the day before. And none of the notes had borne postage. They'd all been hand delivered, but she'd assumed it was someone from the barn, someone protecting Patrick and not wanting her to worry. Someone who was trying to make sure their job was secure.

"He was tall. Light-colored hair, I think, but he was wearing one of those wool hats that matched his tweed jacket. Very smart, he was. Wool slacks and all."

Definitely not one of the stable hands. The dress code for a working farm was a far cry from wool slacks. The man sounded as if he didn't work outdoors.

"What did he do?" Catherine asked.

"He looked up and down the lane, like he was expecting someone. Or maybe looking to be sure no one was coming." Bridget thought. "That's it. He was more making sure no one was coming because he'd sort of been hiding behind one of the trees. Then he hurried down the drive and put the letter in the post box. He was very quick, then gone."

"Did you happen to see what he was driving?"

Bridget's forehead wrinkled. "That's strange, but there wasn't a car, as far as I could see. He went back to the road and climbed the wall. He was in the pasture, and I thought that was odd, but I was waiting for Emily and I heard her coming so I forgot about him and started whistling to her."

"Where were you?" Catherine asked.

Bridget threw her mother a pleading look.

"She was in the fir tree in the side yard. The tree she's been told again and again not to climb."

Catherine suppressed her smile. She was too old to climb trees, but to a young girl or boy, the fir would be almost irresistible. It rose high and straight with limbs easily accessible.

"Then you had a good view and the man had no car?"

"I didn't see one, or hear one. I'm sure I would have heard it. Emily and I like to watch for cars, trying to tell if it's someone we know by the way they sound. Like old Mr. Bailey's truck makes a chug-a-chug sound. We know him from miles away."

"So you didn't hear anything?"

"Nothing."

"Would you recognize the man again if you saw him?" Catherine smiled to keep Bridget from seeing how urgent the question was.

"I'd know his clothes." Bridget looked up at her mother. "I don't know if I'd know him or not. It was mostly his clothes I looked at."

"You did fine, Bridget," Catherine said. "You're a good girl to tell your mother. This information could help us find Limerick and Mick."

"Mick? What's with Mick?" Mauve was instantly interested.

"I'm afraid he's missing." Catherine tiredly sat back in her chair. "He's disappeared and we're worried. I don't want the news to go any farther. You have to keep the secret, too, Bridget. You can't tell anyone. Mick's life could be endangered, so we have to keep this to ourselves."

"I won't talk. But who would hurt old Mick? He gives all the children candy and sings songs for us. He's very nice."

"He is, indeed," Mauve said. "It's that horse, isn't it?"

"Very likely." Catherine stood and began to pace. She was exhausted but she couldn't settle down to think.

"I heard that Cuchulain was out riding the seacoast road," Mauve said. "I figured it was Limerick with that damn fool Patrick on his back. I wondered what on earth he was up to. If Patrick can find the horse, he'll bring him back."

"I'm expecting Kent Ridgeway for dinner tonight. Would you plan something a bit heavier than I usually request."

"Yes, ma'am." Mauve touched Bridget's shoulder, signaling the child they were getting ready to go. "It's none of my affair, but I thought Patrick had taken the horse all along. To protect him, you know. If Patrick has lost the horse, maybe you should give him a chance to get him back."

"The gossip runs rampant through this household, doesn't it?" Catherine couldn't help the frosty tone in her voice. She was afraid, and now everyone knew what a fool she'd been to trust Patrick. "I've given Patrick a chance. I don't know that I can afford another one."

"I don't know that you can't," Mauve said as she turned her little girl toward the door and left.

Chapter Ten

Head throbbing and body aching, Catherine paced the room. The intensive search of the area around the hideout where Limerick had been hidden had revealed nothing new. She and Patrick, along with four men, had gone over the area with extreme care, but they had only confirmed what Patrick already knew. Whoever had taken Limerick had taken him into the bogs and high country. The thief was either a fool or someone who knew the local landscape very well.

There was nothing she'd learned to help her with the decision she faced. What to do about Patrick?

She held two sets of notes in her hands. The first note, cut from newspapers and magazines, was Patrick's creation. He'd told her that he'd sent it in an effort to keep her from going to the authorities. Since he'd intended to return Limerick, he'd wanted to keep her away from the police. He'd also tried to keep her from looking foolish by reporting a horse stolen that turned up later—if she could believe him on that count. If she dared to believe him.

There was a low fire burning in the library fireplace, and she tossed Patrick's note into it. In a second the flames curled the edges, then pulled the ash in toward the center. In less than a minute, the note was gone.

The other notes, four of them, she held in her hand. They were handwritten, sealed with the wax and the horse head crest. She'd assumed those notes had come from the barn, at Patrick's behest, to reassure her that Limerick was fine.

Her assumption was incorrect.

Dreadfully incorrect.

No one in the barn had penned the notes. Or at least no one whom Patrick had encouraged. Patrick had been upset when he saw them. Extremely upset.

"The paper is expensive. The writing shows a great deal of schooling."

That was all he'd said, but the line of his mouth was compressed, doubly worried.

The tension between the two of them was almost unbearable. Catherine couldn't bring herself to completely trust Patrick or what he said. Yet she wanted to. Even after everything he'd done, she wanted to believe him. It was a sickness with her. When was she going to learn?

"Miss Catherine, Mr. Ridgeway is here." Mauve eased into the room, careful to close the door behind her. "I know you aren't feeling well this morning. Would you like me to show him in here and bring some tea?"

"Make it something a bit stronger than tea," Kent said as he strode into the room, pushing Mauve forward as he swung the door wide. "You look beautiful, Cat. A bit pale, but that color green is magnificent with your eyes."

"Some brandy for Mr. Ridgeway would be nice, Mauve." Catherine kept her seat and tucked the envelopes into the cushion behind her. Kent would be more than willing to help her. He'd offered repeatedly. But it wasn't his problem, it was hers. And she intended to keep Limerick's second disappearance a secret from him if she could. The last time she'd trusted him, he'd told Allan Emory. Or at least told Allan enough so that he figured it out.

Allan!

The name was like a revelation, a treasure forgotten and then found. He fit perfectly the description of the person Bridget had seen, right down to the tweed coat. And he was lurking around the Great Southern Hotel in Galway, not thirty kilometers away.

But what would Allan have to do with the matter? He was a gambler and a fortune hunter, but he wasn't a horse thief.

"Since you go into a trance when I talk about how lovely you are, why don't we talk about Limerick? I think it's completely foolish that you didn't attempt to find out who took him, but since you haven't scratched him from the race, I assume that he's back, I guess it's a moot issue. When will he be ready to go to the track? There's a big race this Saturday in Kildare. I know he's on the schedule to run. Fifth race, a match against King's Quest."

"Yes, he is." Catherine's mind was poring over Allan and his possible involvement with Limerick's disappearance, but she took in the fact that Kent's smile was smug. What was Kent saying? "I bought King's Quest yesterday. It should be an interesting race."

"You bought King's Quest?" She finally understood what Kent was up to, but she didn't believe it. King's Quest had never been for sale. He was a horse that David Trussell had brought along himself, a privately owned and trained horse much like Limerick.

"I thought it might be fun if we raced against each other. You've always impressed me with your competitive spirit, Cat. I thought it would add a little spice." He smiled.

"I'm not certain Limerick will be fit to race. He's under the weather. I hate to admit it, but Patrick was right about that knee. We should have rested it more." Catherine knew she was talking in circles, but she had to get Limerick out of that race without arousing Kent's suspicions.

"Rot!" Kent stepped aside. Mauve had returned with a silver tray with one teacup and a snifter of brandy. She set it down and stepped back to the door, a frown on her face as she listened to Ridgeway talk. "Shaw will be the ruination of you. I wouldn't put it past him to put a nail in the horse's hoof to make him limp just to win his point with you."

"I believe I can tell the difference between a sore foot and a knee injury," Catherine said. She had to hold on to her temper, and she noted the cook was doing the same. Mauve's face looked like a thundercloud as she left the room. Catherine had to remember, the objective was to get Kent away from Beltene before he became suspicious about whether Limerick was actually there or not. If she'd been hesitant to broadcast the horse's disappearance at first, now she was convinced that she had to keep it quiet. Limerick was at stake, but so was an elderly man.

Kent had already proven that he couldn't be trusted to keep his mouth shut.

"I didn't mean to question your judgment when it comes to an injury," Kent said gently. "It's just that Shaw is a slick devil. He's capable of pulling the wool over anyone's eyes. He has that Irish charm and the complete ability to feed you a line a kilometer long."

"Thanks for the warning." Catherine picked up her cup of tea. "I made the decision to rest Limerick. He's too valuable to the future of Beltene to risk in a match race. Not even for the pleasure of beating your horse."

"Then you've forgotten the terms of the race?" Kent looked startled.

"What terms?"

"The winner of the match has the option to buy the defeated horse, for the amount of the purse. Thirty thousand pounds, which is a lot less than I paid for King's Quest. So if Limerick wins, you could be in an excellent position to have another stud at your farm."

"It's a match race, not a claim race." Catherine forced herself to stay calm. "I'd never agree to a claim race. Not in a million years."

"But you did. I saw the contract." Kent looked genuinely puzzled. "I thought it was curious, knowing that Limerick was the horse you considered to be the future of Beltene, but then I thought what an absolute stroke of genius it was. I was dazzled by your confidence in the horse and your willingness to risk him and everything. That takes guts, Catherine. Real guts. I'm proud of you."

Kent's words were like projectiles pinging into her soul. She'd never voluntarily agreed to a race where she risked Limerick. How had this happened? She remembered signing the racing forms to set up the match with the blood-bay stallion called King's Quest. He was a good match for Limerick, and she'd viewed it as a fair and equal test of Limerick's heart and ability. But the terms she'd agreed to were for a match, one horse against another. Nothing more.

She'd never agree to a type of claim race where the loser was sold.

"If you're the competition, you don't have to claim, do you?" Catherine asked Kent suddenly. "I mean, you could simply decide not to invoke the claim clause, right?"

"Getting cold feet?" he teased.

"Merely trying to understand my options." She answered him with a lighthearted smile. Her heart was pounding so hard she thought he might hear, but she'd learned at the bank never to let a competitor smell blood. And Kent, no matter what his professed feelings for her were, was a predator.

"I don't know if I have to claim the loser, but I do know that there isn't a scratch clause."

"If Limerick is still unsound, would you consider a rematch in, say, two weeks? Give me a chance to top him up. After all, a true sportsman wouldn't want to run against an injured horse."

"I might consider. On one condition." He swallowed the last of his brandy.

"What might that be?" Catherine kept it light, coy. Kent was playing with her and enjoying every minute of it. He was a risk-taker, a man who loved the thrill of putting everything on the line. She'd watched him come alive more than once at the track when he had his money and his reputation riding on a horse that was in a dead heat and almost up to the wire. She simply could not let him suspect how thin the ice she walked on was. "What is your single condition?"

"That I judge whether he's fit or not."

It wasn't an unreasonable request. Actually, it was exactly the request she'd make if the positions were reversed. The only trouble was that Limerick wasn't around to be checked.

"That's agreeable." She'd just have to brazen it out. "How about giving me three days to try to work him into condition? That'll still give you time to reschedule the race if he isn't in peak condition. I wouldn't ask you to do this except he was out of my care for almost a week."

Kent smiled. "That's fair," he said. "You drive a hard bargain, Catherine Nelson. I'm beginning to see that you learned a lot from your father."

"Enough." Catherine returned her cup to the tray. "I'm going up to County Mayo to look at some prospects. I'll be gone for a couple of days. Maybe we could meet here in three days to check out Limerick, if I still feel he's not in condition. Patrick may be able to work a miracle."

Kent's irritation was immediate. "I didn't realize you were leaving Beltene. It's a long drive here and I'd hoped to spend some time with you. I want to look over those two-year-olds. I'll take them to Wicklow on your word. I've never known the Nelson family to default on a debt."

"I'm sorry, Kent. You didn't give me a chance to tell you my travel plans, and the opportunity to pick up a very nice mare or two is one I can't pass up." She saw his next request coming and had to avoid it. "I'd ask you to come with me, but I've made arrangements to take Patrick. The two of you mix like oil and water."

"You could leave your employee at home," Kent said pointedly. "I believe I can give you the proper advice on horse purchasing."

"I could do that, but as you say, he is my employee. You—" she smiled and lifted one eyebrow "—are my competition. Now who would you trust?"

"Touché," Kent agreed. He tugged at his top lip with his teeth. "What about those two-year-olds?"

"Your offer is kind and generous, but I don't want to get in a position of running Beltene in the red, especially not until Limerick is on the track and making some money and a name for himself."

"I trust your word." Kent came toward her. "Let me do that for you, Catherine."

"Maybe in a few months. When I'm in a better position, it won't seem like I'm obligating myself to you." He was terribly generous to offer to train the animals with no guarantee of pay. She felt guilty at her lack of trust in him.

"You could pay me back now. Get rid of Shaw. Put him on the road and get him out of your life. As long as he's here, Beltene will run under a cloud. The men still look to him as boss and owner. They know you've paid good money for the place, but to them, Beltene is still the Shaw farm and Patrick calls the shots."

"The men are getting used to me." Catherine started to get up but she remembered the notes tucked into the cushion of her chair. She had to stay put, but damn, Kent was making her antsy.

"Patrick will always have their allegiance. Let him go. It's the best thing for both of you, Cat. How do you think it is for him to come to work to the place that used to belong to him? Every little change you make, even if it's an improvement, is like a slap in his face."

"He seems to be living with it." Catherine shrugged. "If he's unhappy here, he can move on. There's nothing stopping him."

"Except he can't free himself from the past. He suffers from the Irishman's disease, a bulldog tenacity to cling to events and traditions that no longer apply to their lives. It's pitiful. And dangerous."

"Tradition is a hard master, for all of us." Catherine couldn't help the anger in her voice. It wasn't fair that Kent accused Patrick of the very traits that he so lovingly manicured in himself—the tradition of Wicklow, the winning tradition, the rituals of the true sportsman. Kent acted as if the Ridgeway name and money bought him a right to such fancies that others did not have.

She'd grown up in a world where such attitudes were second nature. In fact, she'd never noticed them before; they'd been so much a part of her life. Now, though, there was a distinct difference. As far as family and financial status, she was Kent's equal. Socially, yes, without question. Buffered by the mountains and mountains of money the Nelson name symbolized, she might even be Kent's social superior. Once she'd stepped into the role of horse breeder, she hit the gender wall. As a woman, she'd never be Kent's equal. At least, not in his opinion. It was a galling revelation.

"I see by your tone and your expression that I've angered you." Kent was more amused than distressed. "You are a volatile woman, Catherine. I find that exciting."

"I find the idea of—" She stopped herself. She was about to say that a book up against the side of his head would really be amusing. "A match race between Limerick and King's Quest will be irresistible. I'll look forward to it. Either Saturday, or two weeks from Saturday, if we can arrange the track."

"Yes," Kent said. "I think I'll stroll over to the barn and see that big gray devil, if you don't mind?" He watched her carefully.

"Patrick has taken him to the upper pasture where he can graze without smelling or hearing the other horses."

"And you left him unattended, after he'd been stolen once?"

"Someone is with him." Catherine itched to stand up and pace the room, but she couldn't without revealing her stash of notes.

"When are you leaving for County Mayo?"

"In a few hours." She looked at her watch and frowned.

"I have a lot to do before I go." It wasn't subtle, but then, she was tired of the game.

"I'll head back to Dublin." Kent watched her. "Is something going on here, Catherine? I've never seen you look so tired or act so stiff."

"Beltene is a lot of work. Probably more than I bargained for." She had to get a grip on her impatience. Kent was getting ready to sniff around for trouble. "I'm upset with myself for thinking it was going to be easier than it is. And I've made some bad decisions. It's part of learning, but I really can't afford to tutor myself by bad example."

"The bank is a world, for all of its complexity, with less risks than the horse world." Kent straightened his expensive jacket. "I don't know that it's a woman's world, but I believe if any woman can survive it, you can, Catherine."

Rather than argue the point, Catherine smiled. "Thanks for the compliment. I hope you're right."

"I'll call you Wednesday. If I have to come here, you have to pay for the ticket. I'm tired of running the roads."

"Agreed. I hope Limerick is fit and ready, but if he isn't, I'll gladly pay for your trip so you can see him for yourself."

"I'll tell you, if he comes to live at Wicklow, he'll learn not to bite the hand that feeds him."

Catherine had forgotten how the horse had snatched at Kent's arm. Obviously, Kent hadn't forgotten. She didn't respond.

"We'll talk soon." Kent bent and kissed her cheek, then left the room without looking back. As soon as Catherine heard the front door close, she stood, gathered her notes and stuffed them into the top desk drawer. Someone had to go to the track at Kildare and find a copy of the racing agreement she'd signed. Allegedly signed, she reminded herself. Never, ever, in a million years would she have agreed to such a crazy arrangement.

Yet the paperwork was there. Kent had seen it. Which meant

that not only had someone stolen Limerick, they'd arranged it so that she'd lose him without a prayer of getting him back.

Going to the file cabinet in her office, she pulled the file on the Saturday race she'd set up for Limerick. The edges of the papers were slightly askew. She knew instantly that someone had been in her files. The racing agreement with David Trussell and King's Quest was the first document. Scanning it quickly, Catherine saw that it was, indeed, a claim agreement allowing the loser to be purchased by the winner for the price of the purse. Thirty thousand pounds, for a horse worth more than a million.

The last page showed her signature in black duplicate. Even as she studied the long scrawl of her name, she knew it looked authentic. It couldn't be, but it looked it.

Limerick's registration information was all in order. The document was exactly as she remembered it to be—except for the claim clause.

Because of the nature of the race, it was basically an agreement between herself and David Trussell. That meant that she had a copy of the contract, Trussell had one, and the track had a complementary copy. In all probability, Trussell had sent his agreement with the horse to Kent.

Whoever had switched contracts had had access to either Trussell's or Kent's records, her records, and the track.

Someone had methodically set out to ruin her. Someone who knew her business inside and out. There had been no secret about her race with King's Quest, but neither had it been advertised. Both horses were unknowns. It wasn't as if two record winners had been pitted against each other. So someone had been on the lookout for the race, and they'd gone to the trouble of switching documents, adding the one clause that would be her ruination. She couldn't race Limerick because she couldn't produce him. If she didn't race him, he went up for sale to the owner of King's Quest.

By some fluke of fate, that now happened to be Kent Ridgeway. Or was it merely coincidence? Kent knew more about her personal business than almost anyone except her grooms and trainers.

She picked up the four notes. Expensive paper, well-schooled hand, sealing wax with a horse head crest. Surely Kent wouldn't be so obvious. Was it possible someone was framing him?

"Oh!" She got up and paced the room. It was completely maddening. Her thoughts went 'round and 'round in circles. Who was lying about whom and for what purpose? It only seemed that everyone was suspect.

She had to get the track records and destroy that agreement and Kent's copy. Both had to be replaced with the original agreement.

Kent would certainly recognize the change, but if he didn't have a document, he couldn't prove anything.

Pounding in her temples signaled the beginning of a fierce headache. She had no intention of going to County Mayo for horses. No, she was going to Kildare and then Wicklow Stables. The simplest thing would be to drive and take the ferry across to England, she thought. She picked up the notes from the desk drawer, looking at them once more. Kent? Allan? Who? The possibilities were endless. It was even conceivable that Patrick still had the stallion and was using all of this as a ruse to throw her off his trail. He, too, could benefit. If she lost Limerick, then there was a very good chance she'd lose Beltene. The farm would go back on the market, not to mention that it would be cursed with a reputation for bad luck. Patrick might be able to get it back.

If he was working on that premise, then he, too, could be guilty of stealing Limerick.

Catherine walked out of the office and down the hallway, slapping the notes in her palm. But would Patrick risk Limerick in a claim race? Only if he knew the gray stallion would win.

Had Patrick had time to switch the papers around?

Maybe Mick wasn't missing, after all. The trainer was old

and walked with a slight limp, but he was wily and plenty smart. It was possible the old man had been traveling around the country slipping racing papers in and out of offices.

"If there's a way to find out, I intend to get to the bottom of this, and then someone is going to be in deep, deep trouble," Catherine said, speaking softly as she walked up the stairs to her room. She had a bit of packing to do, and an adventure in mind. It just so happened that the Kildare track might be the best place to find out the scoop on several of the suspects on her list. For the first time that day, she smiled, and there was a hint of pleasure in it.

OKAY, so Ice Queen is up to something. She's putting some things into an overnighter, which means she intends to be gone for at least twenty-four hours.

That business about the race comes out of the blue. Catherine would never risk Limerick. Someone's been very busy forging her signature on papers, and making a few switcharoos.

Now let's see, she's packing jeans and a shirt that looks like she salvaged it from...in Ireland, I don't know what the term would be. Let's just say it's pretty worn and threadbare. Brogans and socks. She's going somewhere dressed as an urchin á la Charles Dickens. It looks like a great costume, but I've learned one thing about humans. When they begin trying to look like someone they're not, trouble generally follows.

Catherine is going to the track. There's no way to stop her, so I guess I'd better go along. And Mauve was going to make my favorite seafood casserole tonight! I wonder where Catherine will be eating.

Maybe I should go and alert Patrick so he can follow along, too. He may not know it yet, but he'd never forgive himself if he let something happen to the green-eyed lady.

And Limerick and Mick. Why do I get the idea that Kent wasn't all that surprised by the fact that he didn't get to see the horse? It was almost as if he was testing, probing to see how Catherine would respond to his questions.

If I'm reading too much into this, then take away my birthday. In the meantime, I'm going to find a comfortable little nook in Catherine's car. She can go gallivanting around all over the country if she wants, but she isn't going alone.

Chapter Eleven

Catherine tossed the overnight bag onto the floorboard of the Volvo and slid behind the wheel. The car door jammed and she pulled harder to close it. It wouldn't budge. She looked up to find Patrick's blue gaze searing into her.

"Going somewhere?" he asked. His hand was on the door and he held it firmly, his expression wary. He took in her shabby clothes. "Costume party?"

"I'm going to Kildare," Catherine said. "Something's come up." The urge to take action made her impatient. "Let me go."

"I thought we'd agreed to work together. We both know dangerous people are involved in this."

"Something's come up," she repeated. "I have to go." She met the challenge of his gaze. "This is something I have to do."

Patrick took in the determined square of her jaw, and the troubled emotions in her eyes. "Every instinct I have tells me you're about to walk into serious trouble, Catherine Nelson. I won't let you do that." His hand covered hers on the steering wheel. "I won't sit back and let you put yourself in danger." His fingers covered her hand, an offer of help and security. "We're together, remember?"

"Kent has purchased King's Quest from David Trussell."

"I never thought Davey would sell that stallion. That's the

last of the line for him. I doubt he'll train another." Patrick sighed. It was difficult to watch; more and more of his father's contemporaries were being forced out of the business. Still, he didn't see why Catherine should be so hell-bent to get to Kildare. "How did Ridgeway manage to finagle the horse from Davey?"

"I don't think he sold willingly. A claim race agreement has turned up. Winner has the option to buy the loser for the price of the purse."

"What kind of damn fool would sign that paper? Limerick would win hands down. Trussell's not senile." Understanding dawned in Patrick's face. "He didn't sign it, and you didn't, either, did you?"

"Not on your life. Limerick would win, no doubt about it, but I'd never risk Limerick for a silly race and the chance to buy an inferior stud. King's Quest is a wonderful horse, but he's not Limerick."

"You're going for the agreement." Patrick pushed his hat back from his forehead, revealing blue eyes that held pride, admiration and concern. "How?"

"I have a plan." She didn't want to discuss the details. "I have to do this alone." She wouldn't allow Patrick to put himself at risk.

Before she could think, Patrick walked around the car and slid into the passenger seat. "Whatever it is you're up to, I don't like the looks of it. I'll go along."

"I'm capable of taking care of myself." She was desperate and she knew it. Patrick would try to stop her. "You have to stay here, to watch the horses."

"I can always quit." He leaned back against the seat. "If you press me, I will. Then I can go wherever I want."

"Men! You're always trying to push me into one corner or another." She slammed her door and started the car.

"I know better than to ask." Patrick leaned back deeper into the seat. "Just wake me when we get to Kildare. Or when you get ready to tell me what you're planning."

"Buckle your seat belt," Catherine answered. She spun gravel as she turned the car around in the drive and headed toward the main road.

With her foot heavily pressed on the accelerator, Catherine pulled into the beautifully maintained track near Kildare in just over two and a half hours. Exhausted, Patrick continued to sleep. The drive had given her a chance to streamline her plan.

The track was a big place. She could ditch Patrick easily enough. If he continued to sleep soundly, it wouldn't take any effort at all. She gave one final glance at his tired face, the stubble of his beard evident in the sunlight. The door opened with only a quiet click. She was slipping out of the car when she caught the glow of Familiar's golden eyes tucked beneath a jacket on the back seat.

"Cat!" She was shocked and upset. "What are you doing here?"

"Meow." Familiar came out from under the jacket. He gave Patrick a curious look, then slapped him on the jaw with a paw, claws carefully sheathed.

"Hey!" Patrick's eyes opened wide.

"Familiar!" To Catherine he looked like nothing more than a naughty child caught in a prank.

"Meow." He jumped into the driver seat where he could put his paws on the window and rub against her arm.

"So we're a threesome." Patrick hadn't moved, but he was taking in the situation. He gave Catherine a sleepy grin. "Any woman should be flattered to work with such accomplices as a sleepy horse trainer and a stowaway black cat."

"You're bad enough, Patrick. I won't be worried to death about Familiar." She opened the door to roll up the window. Familiar made a bold leap, sailing past her and landing a good three yards away.

"Meow!" Tail straight in the air, he started toward the stable area.

"Hey, they won't let cats in there," Catherine called after him. The spectator stands were almost empty, but from long experience, Catherine knew the stable area would be a beehive of activity. Even though no races were scheduled for that day, the riders who breezed the horses for their daily exercise, the owners, the jockeys, bookmakers and gawkers, would all be about.

The racetrack was an exciting place, usually. Today it seemed like a frenetic place of sinister possibilities. And now she had the cat to worry about and Patrick to shake.

"Familiar, you'd better stay right with me," she said. Maybe no one would notice the cat. He had a way of hiding in the shadows when he wanted to. She'd caught him several times in her office or bedroom, curled inconspicuously in some soft corner, but always alert. Always watching and listening.

"What's the plan, Catherine?" Patrick's tone was lazy, amused, as he got out of the car.

"I'm going around the stables and see what gossip I can pick up." To that purpose she'd worn her oldest jeans, a long-sleeve cotton shirt and her muck boots from the barn. With an expert motion she hurriedly braided her hair and tucked it up in a denim cap.

"You look like a street urchin. A tall street urchin," Patrick said.

"My intentions exactly." She grinned at him. If she could just get away, then he wouldn't be able to stop her. "Can you help me?"

"I'm afraid my face is too well known around the track for much subversive activity."

"No one will recognize me in this getup."

"And what is it you hope to find out?"

"Someone forged my name to those papers. We both know that there are no secrets on a racetrack."

He nodded. "I'll take a more direct approach. There are a few of the men here who can be trusted. I'll speak with them."

"Thank you, Patrick." Catherine was sincere, and relieved. "Let's meet in an hour. Back here at the car."

He nodded, then glanced down at the cat. "So, Familiar has made his choice. He's going with you."

Catherine wasn't about to argue. "We'll be fine," she agreed.

With several backward glances at Catherine and the cat, Patrick headed toward the area where several trainers had gathered. His best bet at gathering information would be from the men who knew him.

When he was out of earshot, Catherine turned to the cat. "Stay out of the stalls and out of the way," she warned Familiar as they set off.

Elegant horses walked by while trainers or grooms moved them from one place to another. Once the spectator portion of the track was left behind, the scene was total bustle. Watching for her moment, Catherine joined the flow of traffic, blending in with all the other track employees.

She'd been there less than three minutes when she heard a familiar voice. As a ruse to stop and listen, Catherine bent to tie her shoe.

"Sold to that British trainer, Kent Ridgeway. He's one fine horse. I never thought old Trussell would let him go."

The man speaking was Theodore Pope, a retired trainer and one of the biggest bookies in Ireland. He made the rounds, lining up his bets only on very special races. When Theodore Pope took bets, the stakes were high, the profits fantasy material and the losses staggering. There were always more losers than winners.

Catherine moved over slightly to stand by a stall door, acting as if she were inspecting the gelding inside. Out of the corner of her eye she saw Familiar stretching near the stable door. He was as calm as if he'd lived at the track his entire life.

"Trussell didn't want to let him go. Was mostly forced, if what I hear is true. There's a crazy claim agreement against the loser."

The man speaking was one of the hundreds of trainers who

came and went along the racing circuit. Catherine cast a look over her shoulder and couldn't put a name to his face, but she knew him. He'd been around ever since she was a little girl and would come to the track with her father.

"Well, if he didn't like the agreement, why did he sign it? Why would he risk losing his stallion?" Pope demanded. "This sounds like someone's trying to queer the race."

"Not me." The man shook his head. "Makes no difference to me who runs and who wins. It's just talk along the track. That's why Kent Ridgeway was able to buy King's Quest. Or at least, that's the gossip. Trussell is getting old. He's been up and down like a yo-yo. When he found out the terms of the racing contract he'd signed, he decided to sell Quest, take the money he could get up front and be gone. I heard he got double the claiming purse." The man chuckled. "He's put the word out about that redheaded woman. He says Catherine Nelson switched the papers on him. Says he signed one agreement and that then the other one with the claiming clause showed up."

"You don't say?" Pope's eyes were gleaming with interest at learning information that might prove valuable.

"That's what Trussell's saying, and he won't back down. He'd say it and spit in the devil's eye. If it's true, that Nelson woman is stone. Takes her advantage no matter what the cost to others. There's even talk her family cheated the Shaws out of Beltene."

Catherine cast another glance at Pope and the talkative man. They were leaning closer, whispering to one another. Her face was burning with suppressed anger and shame. To have people saying those things about her! It took all of her willpower not to march over and set Pope and his crony straight.

It was significant that talk about the odd circumstances of the race was already covering the track. That put a different light on things. She should have known that Kent's ego wouldn't allow him to keep quiet. And now Trussell was roasting her over the coals. Not that she blamed him. He'd been duped as well as she had. If he was mad now, he was going to be furious when he discovered that they'd both been taken in a con of some sort.

She pulled her cap lower. One single question niggled at her. How often was it that a man was willing to risk an expensive horse for the sake of one race? Kent had paid better than one-hundred-and-twenty-thousand American dollars for King's Quest. It was the kind of gesture Kent loved. Risk was like oxygen to his blood. But it was a risk weighted to loss, and Kent knew that. He'd seen Limerick.

Catherine considered her options. If she got the paperwork from the track, she might be able to get out of the claim race. But it would always throw doubt on Limerick, and on her own ethics, especially since Trussell was bandying her name about as if she were little more than a common thief. If Limerick didn't run this race and win, his potential as a breeding stallion might suffer. Hers undoubtedly would. And Beltene needed a winning season of purses and a good breeding season next spring.

She made her decision then. She'd destroy the papers with the claiming clause and let Limerick run the match race, just as she'd originally proposed. It was all the more important that she got those papers from the track and from Kent.

As she watched, Pope and the unknown trainer went their separate ways. She called softly to get Familiar's attention and then drifted back into the crowd, wandering past the stalls to watch the grooms and trainers getting horses ready for a breeze along the track or walking them cool after an exercise session.

The animals were magnificent, but as she looked at them she couldn't help but think of Limerick, and Patrick. There was definitely something about the big gray stallion that was different from the other horses she saw. His chest was a bit broader. More room for heart and lung, Patrick would say. There was also something else, something harder to define. A look in his eyes, an attitude of eagerness—whenever Patrick approached him.

There was something about all of the horses that Patrick worked. As she stood and watched, a trainer went into a stall to bring out a young stallion. The horse rolled his eyes and held back.

Never, ever, in all of her time at Beltene had she seen a horse react to Patrick in that fashion. They waited for him, heads over the stall.

They *liked* to work with him. That was the elusive difference. Not muscle or tone or agility, although there was that, too, but an eagerness to work. They waited for a chance to run. Limerick was that extremely rare combination of athletic perfection and heart. Because of Patrick's handling? She couldn't answer that question yet.

It was a sight she never tired of, the glistening animals in the peak of condition moving so gracefully through the crowds. Jockeys, with their saddles tucked over their arms, were moving back and forth looking for the mounts they were to work. Some of the better known jockeys were standing together in a group discussing either the last races or the ones upcoming.

In past times, Catherine would have stopped to talk with the ones she knew. Not today. Part of the reason for her outfit was to disguise who she was. There were several other questions she needed answers to.

She saw a groom she remembered and hurried forward. "Have you seen Mr. Ridgeway today? I was to meet him for a job interview." She tried her best to imitate the accents she'd heard. She was a bit too proper, but she did a passable job of assuming a less privileged dialect.

"Ridgeway's over on the left," the groom said. "He doesn't hire no women."

"Not even as hot walkers?" Catherine was shocked. Kent had a little chauvinist blood in him. She'd seen it before. But most men from wealthy and powerful families did. They'd had generations of women meeting their needs while they went out and brought home the money. But not to hire women hot walkers? A lot of trainers preferred female walkers because they had a more calming influence on the horses. After a day at the track, the horses needed as much soothing as they could get.

"Won't hire women here for any reason. Says a woman's place is in the bedroom or the kitchen." The groom grinned, aware of the touch of red that flushed Catherine's neck and revealed her displeasure.

"Well, tell him he missed a good worker." She turned away and eased back into the flow of traffic. She'd never intended to talk to Kent, she just wanted to know where he was—and that he was occupied. Now she had to find his setup at the track.

Out of curiosity she stopped by the stall where King's Quest stood. He was a magnificent animal. Inch for inch he was as big as Limerick, with the same wide chest, sloping shoulder and lean-muscled body. It would be a match race to make the history books. The thought made her smile, but it quickly faded. If Limerick was found and able to race.

In the distance she spotted Kent. He was talking with a group of trainers. They all wore his colors, even though they wouldn't be racing. That was Kent. He had an eye for showmanship and detail that made his stables noticeable—and profitable. Owners with horses to train liked the flash and dazzle. They liked to come to the barn area and see their horses groomed and ridden by a jockey in silks, even if it was an expensive extra that was costing them plenty. This was a lesson she could learn from Kent.

As Kent turned her way, she ducked instinctively. Of all the people at the track, Kent would be the one who recognized her if he saw her. She hid behind several tall men, using their bodies to shield her as she slipped past Kent toward the entrance to the track offices. Glancing down, she saw that Familiar was right at her heels. Behind her there was no sign of Patrick. Now was her chance. She pushed the door open and slipped inside.

Before she could close the door, she felt a hand on her shoulder. "What is it you're about, Catherine Nelson?"

She turned around into Patrick's chest. He slipped into the hallway with her, crowding her against the wall. With one hand, he lifted her chin and studied her face. "You're going to steal that agreement."

"Someone forged my name," she answered hotly. "I never signed any such agreement. I don't see where it's theft to take something that someone fabricated."

"And Trussell's copy, which Ridgeway now probably holds? What of it?"

Catherine looked down at the ground, unable to meet Patrick's eyes.

"Sweet saints," Patrick whispered. "You were going to steal it, too!"

Before Catherine could look up, she felt Patrick's hands return to her shoulders. He grabbed her roughly, pulling her forward. Her head snapped up to see the look of amusement in his eyes just as his lips came down to hers.

It was a joyful, spontaneous kiss that held approval, relief and acceptance. Catherine felt all of those things, and something more. What might have been a quick, friendly kiss held longer than it should have.

Patrick drew back, slowly. The merriment in his eyes had faded. He hadn't intended to kiss her. In fact, he felt somewhat like giving her a good lecture for trying such desperate measures. But the fact was that she had tried them. She'd intended to steal the papers from Ridgeway, not trust him by asking for them. It showed a degree of good sense he'd been afraid she didn't have.

"Patrick?" His name was a question.

Instead of answering her, he dropped his lips to hers again. This time they met softly, each assessing the other. His fingers traced the line of her cheekbone, resting at her temple.

Catherine opened her mouth to him, inviting, as she lifted her arms around his neck. In all the maddening events that had churned around her, she'd finally found a degree of steadiness. Nothing else that was happening to her made sense, and her strong feelings for Patrick were the most nonsensical of all, but she couldn't deny them. In his arms, she felt that she could overcome everything else.

Patrick pulled her tighter against him. He could feel her ribs against his forearms, her breasts pushed against his chest. The desire to have her was overwhelming. His hands moved up her back, and he felt her respond, pressing closer still to him as her tongue teased his. Desire pulsed through him, heavy and sweet.

Catherine moved against him, wanting as much of him as possible. His touch and body and kisses fed a hunger she never knew she had. Or at least, had never acknowledged. All along she'd teased herself with half-dream fantasies of Patrick. But those she'd hidden from herself when she was fully awake. Now she could no longer bury her emotions. Patrick wasn't some gauzy dream figure. He was a man who moved her to the core of her being.

Patrick pulled back suddenly. "Ouch!" Both of the cat's front fangs had been sunk into his shin. He looked down to see a fuzzed-out Familiar, back arched, eyeing the corridor to their left.

"This way!" The voice coming from the corridor was Kent Ridgeway's. There was no mistaking it. And he was approaching them.

Patrick grabbed Catherine's hand and pulled her after him as he sprinted down the hallway. He looked back only once, to make sure Familiar was with them. The cat was at their heels.

"Here." Catherine saw the door marked Ladies and pulled Patrick in with her, holding the door long enough for Familiar to scoot inside, also. She was panting, her chest heaving up and down. She saw Patrick watching her and felt a flare of desire so intense that she almost moaned.

"We have to get you out of here," Patrick said. "You're

too well known, Catherine. With everything that's happened, you can't be seen here, especially if those papers go missing. The reputation of Beltene now rests with you. Any scandal or smudge could ruin the farm."

"I know." She stared at him as she spoke. She did know. Patrick was absolutely correct. "What are we going to do?" With careful control, she checked the desire she felt for Patrick. Another place, another time...

We. Patrick had heard her say it. It was amazing how one single little pronoun could make a sentence so significant. "We're going to take care of this," Patrick said, reaching out to her.

"How?" Catherine didn't sound very reassured, but she took his hand and let him pull her into his arms. "I didn't have a plan. I was just going to see what I could do here, and based on that, drive over to Wicklow and see if I could find the contract in Kent's office."

"Maybe not such a bad idea." Patrick lifted the cap from her head. The braid had loosened and he shook out her hair. His fingers curled in it, lifting the silky red mass and letting the slight perfume intoxicate him. He'd dreamed of her hair, of lying in the hayloft with her beside him, that mass of red hair flung over his chest and shoulder. Her creamy skin exposed to the soft light that filtered into the old barn.

"You want me to go to Wicklow?"

"Kent was going to train some two-year-olds for you, wasn't he?"

"Yes." Catherine hesitated. "I've been rethinking that, though. I've implied that I can't afford to do that."

"But he doesn't know for certain that you aren't. Couldn't you tell him you'd changed your mind and wanted to be sure he had enough space for you?"

"I could. But he thinks I'm north buying breeding stock. And that Limerick is back at Beltene."

"Good." Patrick thought. He didn't know Kent's role in forcing David Trussell to sell King's Quest. He had much the same opinion of the trainer that Catherine had—Ridgeway loved a risk, a gamble, and he had the money to support his vice. The idea of a claiming race with stakes as high as Limerick would really appeal to him. Win or lose, it would build the reputation of high-stakes player that he loved to cultivate. It could be that he stumbled into a situation someone else had created. Or it could be that he'd manipulated circumstances—and forged documents—to suit himself.

"Catherine, if Ridgeway is behind the forgeries, he's completely unethical. He's capable of anything."

"Of taking Limerick? Of killing him?" Catherine tensed her fingers into the muscles at Patrick's back. The gesture was involuntary, but he reacted to it.

"Don't give up on Limerick. I promised I'd get him back and I will. Now I'll take care of the documents here at the track. I know one of the employees in the office. I'll stand a lot better shot at getting them than you. We don't have much time, though. Can you manage Wicklow?"

"Kent's here at the track. I can drive there now and be at the stables when they open tomorrow. With luck, I can check Kent's files before he even goes home. It'll be tricky, but it won't be that dangerous." She looked up at him and nodded. "I can do it."

"If he catches you at it, it could be extremely dangerous," Patrick warned her. "But there's no other way. Now let's get you out of here and back to the car."

GOOD GRIEF! These two have the finesse of a couple of alley cats, no slur intended on my fellow creatures. I mean, they shoot daggers at each other for months, and then fall on each other like love-starved fiends in a washroom while trying to pull off a heist. A poorly planned burglary at that!

Lucky for them, one of us kept his wits about him or Kent Ridgeway would have caught them red-handed, or hot-lipped as the case may be. I know, I know, my puns are going downhill faster than a greased sled.

So, we're off to Wicklow soon. I've always wanted to see England. Wicklow's in the northwestern part of the country and a light-year from the bustle of London, Big Ben and all of that, but still, the English countryside has inspired many a novel. Eleanor has given me quite a taste for good fiction. She reads aloud to me and Dr. Doolittle. I'm particularly fond of the English mystery writers. As a lot, they seem to have such a fine eye for detail, the sort of thing an alert feline might observe. At any rate, I pick up a few tips here and there from the best of them. Perhaps I'll pen a line or two someday.

The allure of England aside, I'd like to know how Ridgeway's luck is running on the track. Why do I get the feeling that maybe he's losing money faster than it's coming in? Perhaps he's bleeding like a stuck pig, as those colorful Tennesseeans like to say.

I keep going over the area of the hideout in my mind. That horse was ridden away. That's what's so strange. Not that Limerick wasn't ridable. Far from it. But whoever rode him took him without a saddle or bridle. Unless they brought their own. But just for the sake of argument, think about who could ride him through treacherous terrain without benefit of a bridle. That limits the list of suspects to a very select few.

And Mick? I know someone was watching the hideout. They didn't need Mick to tell them where the horse was. So why take him? The only conclusion I can come to is that they are using his disappearance to make sure that Patrick doesn't do anything rash. It's all too much.

Hey! Watch your step, me bucko! Take your hands off me! Patrick! So, it's back to the car for me and Catherine. Then off to Merry Old England. If you'd give me a chance, I could walk. But no, I'm going to be suffocated in your jacket. Oh well, I'll just go limp and relax. As one of the highest lifeforms, which cats are, I've learned a great degree of wisdom, especially when it comes to humanoids who think they're the superior race. All a smart cat has to do is give the impression that they yield to the humans' demands. A small—and some-

times annoying—price, but so easy to do once the rudiments are learned.

I'll demonstrate. Just a little purr, to make Patrick think I'm very happy and content curled up in his warm jacket as he hauls me to the car. He thinks he has won me over.

That's fine. I don't mind going to England—a new adventure and all. I'm more than a little curious about Wicklow. And why Kent Ridgeway would risk a fortune on a horse he knows can't beat Limerick. Ridgeway is playing another angle, and it's a darn good thing these two humanoids have me to look out for them. They hardly have sense enough to dodge bullets.

Chapter Twelve

Wicklow was something out of a storybook. As much as Catherine had heard about it, she wasn't prepared for the reality. One look and she felt all of her doubts about Kent were unjustified. With so much at stake, why would he want to risk everything by involving himself in something illegal? It didn't make sense.

Turning into the long, tree-lined drive, she followed the neat signs that directed her toward the stable office. On either side were lush pastures. Mares grazed while their foals ran and bucked, playing the games that would develop muscle, wind and heart. The land surrounding Wicklow was much gentler than that of Connemara. At Wicklow, it was as if the very earth accommodated the horse. In contrast, Beltene wore the face of stubborn survival, carved out of rock and limestone, rugged and enduring.

"Stay put," she ordered Familiar as she got out of the car.

She didn't give the cat a chance to back talk. She got out and slammed the door before he could escape.

"Can I help you?"

The man who confronted Catherine was middle-aged and perfectly groomed. He stepped forward helpfully, as if he thought she might be lost. After spending the night in a bed and breakfast not twenty miles up the road, Catherine had dressed in an expensive business suit, stockings, heels and as much of the Nelson family jewelry as she could wear with any degree of comfort and taste.

"I'm Catherine Nelson. Kent is going to train some two-year-olds for me and I wanted to surprise him." She smiled and brushed her long hair back from her face, revealing the Nelson rubies at her ears. "He isn't expecting me, but I think he'll be glad to see me."

"I'm terribly sorry. Mr. Ridgeway is away." The man frowned. "He isn't expected back until tomorrow. I'm afraid he's in Dublin on business."

"Oh, dear." Catherine looked crestfallen. "I should have thought. It's just that I spoke with him yesterday morning and I understood he was coming straight back to Wicklow."

"You're from Beltene, aren't you? The new owner." The man held out his hand. "Cecil Baxter, the farm manager. Maybe I can help you."

Catherine took his hand in a firm handshake. "Kent is doing a favor for me, Mr. Baxter. To be honest, I wanted to make sure that I'm not putting him in a bad position. I know how busy Wicklow is, and I don't want to burden him with these extra horses. He's agreed to take them on because...well, as a personal favor."

"I see." Cecil motioned her toward the office door. "Come in and we'll have some tea. You look tired."

"It's been a...difficult trip."

She followed him into the stone office, her footsteps absorbed by plush carpeting. Everything was modern, new, immaculate. A well-groomed secretary sat at a desk with a headphone on, while another girl was ordering files.

Cecil led her through a solid door and into his private office. "How many horses were you thinking of sending us?" He pulled out a chair for her at a table.

"Four, maybe six. It all depends." She fluttered her hands. "I'm rather new in this business. Kent has been so helpful to me. I'm just sorry he isn't here."

"I can call him."

"No!" Catherine cleared her throat. "I mean, I wouldn't want to distract him from whatever he's doing. I didn't make the proper arrangements. If he'll be back tomorrow, I can wait until then."

"Perhaps you'd like to see the facilities?" Cecil picked up the telephone on his desk and ordered tea. "Meg will bring it in a few moments. We'll just chat a bit. If I can tell you anything about Wicklow, I'll be glad to do so. You're making a wise decision to send your horses here. As a new farm owner, you need to establish yourself with a winning season. I know the Beltene horses. Excellent stock. They just lack training and exposure." He smiled broadly.

Gritting her teeth at the insult, Catherine smiled. "I believe you're absolutely correct." She wanted him out of the room long enough for her to search for the racing contract. But she didn't know how to go about removing him. It was obvious he was going to stick to her while she was there. Her apparent affluence had caught his attention—too well. Sudden inspiration struck.

"I've forgotten my papers in the front seat of the car. Would you excuse me for a moment?" She rose. "I'll be right back."

Before Cecil could protest, she made a swift exit. As soon as she got to the car she spoke to Familiar. "Make an escape now, and do your best," she whispered as she reached for the cat and put him on the edge of the seat. "I hope you're as smart as I think you are."

Familiar eyed the area. He took in the trees lining the parking lot, the stone walls perfectly edged and even, the stone building that was the office and the dark shadow of the barn behind. His eyes lingered on the slanted roof of the barn. It was an enormous building, stretching east and west with one wing extending south.

With perfect grace, he sprang forward and ran toward the open window of a stall in the barn.

"Mr. Baxter! Mr. Baxter!" Catherine ran back into the office. She fled past the receptionist, who looked up too late to do anything more than make a garbled noise. "My cat has run into your barn. You have to help me catch him."

"Cat!" Baxter stood. He was perfectly composed, but a small pulse beat at his neck. "What cat?"

"I had my cat in the car with me and he got out when I opened the front door."

"You brought a cat here from Ireland?" Baxter was incredulous. "How did you get him through customs?"

"I, uh, hid him. I didn't mean to stay here and I didn't think it would hurt." Catherine looked suitably miserable. "It was stupid, but I wasn't thinking. You see, he'd hidden in the car before I left Beltene. By the time I discovered him, I was halfway to Kildare. I couldn't turn around then. I simply didn't have the time. I only meant to come here, speak to Kent and go home."

Baxter said nothing, but his look confirmed the thought that he agreed with her. She didn't think, but probably because she couldn't. She was a bird. A rich bird, but a bird nonetheless.

"Where did he go?" he asked.

"The barn."

He picked up the receiver of his telephone and pressed one button. "Meg, call some of the grooms together. We have to catch a stray cat in the southern wing of the barn." When he looked up at Catherine, his face was composed.

"I'm terribly sorry." Catherine stood in the center of his office wringing her hands. "What can I do? I—" She broke down into tears.

"Have a cup of tea," Baxter said, rising to the occasion. "We'll catch him. Don't worry. We'll get him safely."

"Oh, thank you." Sinking into a chair, Catherine pulled a tissue from her purse. In a final move, she turned the purse upside down, spilling the contents over the floor. "Oh, damn! Look what I've done. I'm such a fool, such a clumsy fool. My father always said I was fumble-fingered."

"I'll see to the cat," Baxter said. To his immense relief, Lucy brought in a tea tray. He nodded for her to leave it and get out of the room. As soon as she was gone, he spoke to Catherine. "Have a cup of tea and pull yourself together." He tried not to stare at the tubes of lipstick, the change and pens and paper clips that were all over the floor of his office.

"I'm such a fool!" Catherine sobbed.

"A cup of tea will soothe you," Baxter said softly. "I'll find that cat and return shortly." He left before she could say anything more.

Catherine wasted no time gathering her belongings and stuffing them into her purse. Then she went to the files. Her fingers moved quickly through the alphabetical listings until she came to King's Quest. Inside the file was the stallion's registration papers, photographs, his lineage and the racing agreement. The yellow pages of the document were identical to her own. The original had to be at the track, and she could only pray that Patrick would be successful in his attempt to retrieve it.

She pulled the papers from the file, stuffed them in the pocket of her skirt and returned to the floor, pretending to search for her lipsticks. There was something else in the file drawer she'd seen, but she was afraid to risk looking at it. She'd gotten what she came for, and she didn't want to push her luck. Still... She reached for the cabinet to pull herself to her feet.

"Mr. Baxter said you'd spilled your purse." Meg, the young secretary, stood in the doorway. She was obviously miffed by the uproar Catherine had created at Wicklow.

"I have it now," Catherine told her. She walked forward on her knees, pulled her last lipstick from under a chair and finally got to her feet. All of her things were bulging out of her purse. "This has just been a disaster. Maybe I should go help them with that cat."

"He seems to be eluding them." Meg frowned. "Shouldn't you keep him on a leash or something?"

"I shouldn't have brought him with me," Catherine agreed in her most contrite voice. "It was very foolish of me. The truth is, he was in the car and I was halfway here before I noticed. I couldn't just throw him out on the side of the road, you know."

"I should hope not." Meg was offended by the mere suggestion. "Perhaps in the future you might check your car before you decided on a cross-country trip."

"Of course." Catherine forced her voice to sound meek and repentant, but her green eyes snapped with displeasure. The secretary was something else, quite a little bossy thing. Catherine took in the tight red dress, the high heels, the rounded hips. Looking up at Meg's face, she saw the perfect skin and big blue eyes, all framed by blond hair. So, that was the way of it. Meg could afford to act arrogant. She was sleeping with the boss.

"Shall I pour your tea?" Meg asked, implying that Catherine would undoubtedly wreck the china.

"That would be lovely," Catherine answered. "I'll bet you're quite expert at performing the little services that make the day go by so pleasantly for Kent." She spoke in the most innocent of voices, but the other woman did not misread her intentions.

She paused, teapot in midair, and really looked at Catherine. "Is there anything else I can get you?" The condescending note was gone from her voice. In its place was a calm, pleasant, professional voice.

"Nothing." Catherine picked up the fine china. "I'll take my cup of tea to the barn and help look for Familiar. I'm certain Kent won't mind. After all, he's dragged enough of my china and crystal about Beltene while inspecting horses there." She refilled her cup, stirred in another sugar and got up. Meg made no peep of protest.

Catherine wasn't certain, but she saw a door that looked as if it might lead to the barn. Teacup in hand, she opened it and walked into another office. Two men were sitting at desks, bent over papers. She nodded, walked past them to another door. Opening it, she smelled leather and hay, liniment and horse.

"Familiar!" She walked into the barn, aware that several

grooms had paused to look at her. She was ridiculously overdressed and overjeweled. But Wicklow wasn't Beltene, and she realized she didn't really care what Kent's grooms and trainers thought of her. The papers in her pocket told her well enough that she'd have no business with Wicklow in the future.

"Is it your cat?" one short man asked irritably.

"Yes, I'm afraid he is." Catherine had resumed her regular tone. There was no need to sound hysterical or foolish now. She'd gotten what she'd come for, and it had been easier than she'd ever dreamed. If she'd only had a little more time she might have found out many interesting things.

"If it were mine, I'd sight it down the end of a barrel. That blasted creature's been running right under our feet." He shook his head. "It's like he's playing a game with us."

"Kitty, kitty." Catherine called innocently. She wondered how much Familiar was enjoying himself. In all likelihood, he was having a blast making fools of all the humans who were chasing him.

"There he goes!" The cry went up at the end of the barn, and Catherine saw a small back figure dashing her way.

"Familiar!" She opened her arms wide and he sailed into the safety of them. "What a good kitty!" She kissed his head. "He knows who loves him."

Sweat was dripping off the tip of Cecil's nose when he ran up to her. His immaculate wool pants bore traces of hay. "He was in the loft, running above the horses' heads. We were afraid he'd drop into a stall."

"He's quick. The horses would never have stepped on him."

"It wasn't the cat I was worried about," Cecil said dryly. "He could have spooked one of the horses and caused an accident. We don't allow any animals in our barns. That's one thing you can rest assured about here at Wicklow."

"Oh, no companion animals?" Catherine looked around. "That's too bad."

"We simply can't allow it. The men have no time for such."

"Certainly." Catherine held Familiar lightly in her arms, teacup dangling off one finger. She waggled it at Cecil, releasing it into his care. "The tea was delicious, and thank Meg for all of her help. I guess maybe I'd better not stay around for a tour of the facilities. I'll go to my hotel and call Kent tomorrow. Maybe he'll have time to see me then."

"I'm certain he will." Cecil was regaining his posture and dignity. He'd wiped his face with a clean linen handkerchief and he brushed the tiny bits of hay from his pants.

Holding Familiar against her chest, she saw a barn door that would lead to the parking lot. She took it, bending once to kiss Familiar's head. "Quite the little rascal, aren't you?" she whispered. "You did an excellent job."

Once she'd driven out of Wicklow she stopped and checked the time. It was midmorning. She could make it home by early evening, maybe sooner, depending on the ferry to Dublin. She'd crossed once without any trouble with Familiar. Would she be so lucky twice? The black cat was asleep on the front seat beside her. Reaching out, she stroked under his chin and was rewarded with a rich purr.

"Ah, Familiar, I wonder if Mauve wasn't right. It would seem you've bewitched the lot of us at Beltene. Especially me and Patrick Shaw."

Opening one green eye, Familiar gave her a look. "Meow," he said sleepily. He closed his eye and returned to a nap.

"NO ONE'S BEEN there for several days," Timmy said slowly. He raised his voice as he continued talking into the phone. "Patrick, is there something wrong here? It isn't like old Mick to take off for a few days' visit during the middle of the spring training."

"His foot's been gnawing at him and making him sore to live with," Patrick said, forcing a bit of lightness into his tone. "I told him a few days off it would help. He didn't want to leave but I made him."

"Well, there's no sign that he's back. Maybe he finally took some good advice and went to visit Michael and Kate."

"That must be it. Thanks for checking his cottage."

"How much longer will you be away?" Timmy asked.

"Another day, possibly two." Patrick heard the nervousness in the jockey's voice. "What's going on at Beltene?"

"Nothing really."

"My eye. Spit it out, Timmy. What is it?"

"McShane. He's trying to say you left him in charge. Miss Nelson is gone and most of the men are doing their jobs, ignoring Eamon. But he's talking about calling the authorities about Limerick. He says now's the time to do it while you're away and there's no one to threaten him."

Patrick was silent. He felt balanced on a wire, in a position where any little puff of wind could blow him over. Eamon McShane could supply that push. Once the authorities were called in, Patrick would never get Limerick back. It was a gut feeling he had. Not to mention Mick. At the thought of the old man, held against his will, Patrick felt impotent rage begin to build.

"Tell McShane if he calls anyone, I'll come home and personally break his neck."

"Patrick..." Timmy didn't finish. He could hear the fury in the other man's voice. He'd seen Patrick mad only once before, long ago. Patrick had caught one of the grooms flogging a young horse who wouldn't obey him. The groom had managed to survive with only a broken arm, but no one at Beltene had since forgotten the Shaw rules about mistreatment of the horses. Patrick's voice was as angry now as it had been back then.

"Tell him, Timmy. He's been telling everyone I beat him up once. I didn't. If I decide to put a hand on him, he won't be walking around to tell about it."

"It might be best not to speak of it," Timmy said hesitantly. "Talk like that can get a man in trouble."

"If it's trouble McShane wants, I'm the man to give it to

him. Tell him. And tell him this time Peg won't stop me. I'm sorry for her, true enough, married to the likes of him. But pity won't hold me back this time. Tell him all of that."

"I will." Timmy had no desire to argue with Patrick. Not in the black mood he was in. "Take care, Patrick," Timmy cautioned.

"And you." Patrick returned the telephone to its cradle with a short curse as he paced the small room he'd taken near the track in Kildare. He'd asked Timmy to check Mick's cottage on the hopes Mick had somehow magically returned. The lie Patrick had given Timmy was that old Mick had gone to visit his son in Belfast to rest his injured foot.

Even though Patrick knew it wasn't plausible that Mick had returned, he couldn't stop himself from checking to see if the old man was home. But Mick's cottage had remained vacant. There was no sign that anyone had been around, Timmy said. Mick had vanished.

Patrick paced the floor and tried to imagine what Catherine was doing. With any luck on her side, she'd be on her way back to Kildare. Back to him. Joy at the prospect surged through him, only adding to his sense of restriction. All he could do was pace and wait.

He could only hope that Catherine's search would prove more useful than his. There was no document at the Kildare track reflecting a claim race between Limerick and King's Quest. There was a racing agreement signed by Catherine and David Trussell, the two owners, for a match race. But it was only a brief form. The contract was missing, a fact that Patrick wasn't sure was favorable or not.

It had taken every bit of his considerable charm to get one of the young secretaries to call up the files on her computer. When she couldn't find it electronically, he'd begged her to look manually. Zip. That was the end result. That and the fact that he'd felt like a heel for using the girl. Had there been another way, he would have taken it. Unfortunately, the security in the office at Kildare was a bit more professional than he'd anticipated. It was a good thing he'd stopped Catherine from her harebrained scheme of trying to break into the office and steal the document. She would have been caught for sure.

Something else that disturbed him was the gossip floating around the track about Catherine. There were some harsh rumors being spread regarding the race with King's Quest and the bad position David Trussell had been pushed into. Track sympathies were running hard against Catherine Nelson, new owner of Beltene Farm.

Patrick sat down on the narrow bed and tried to put the chaos of his life in order. Limerick. Whenever he closed his eyes he saw the stallion arching his neck eagerly toward him. Who had taken the horse? And why?

The worst of it was that no ransom note had arrived. Deep in his heart, Patrick knew that whoever had taken Limerick was up to something other than money. If it was a simple case of horsenapping, then Catherine would have heard the ransom demands by now. The very fact that kidnappers were still holding Mick spoke of other motives.

He got up and paced the small room. Eight strides in either direction in the cramped space. He'd been cast into limbo, unable to do anything to help. The only two facts he had were that Mick was taken and Limerick had been ridden into the treacherous bogs.

And ridden was the key word. Someone had ridden the horse away.

That was perplexing. Patrick could ride him easily. Timmy managed him on the track. Other than that, no one else had ever been on his back. Limerick loved a good run, but would he willingly accept a strange rider?

Even more troubling was old Mick. Someone had known that the old man would be able to tell where Limerick was hidden. So it had to be someone who knew Patrick and Mick had taken the stallion in the first place. At the barn, only Jack had discovered their plan, and he would never do anything to injure Mick. No, it had to be someone else.

The finger of guilt pointed toward Beltene Farm and some of the hands there. All of them were men and boys Patrick had known for years or handpicked himself. The exception was McShane. He was the bad apple in the barrel, but McShane knew nothing. He suspected a great deal, but he had no facts.

He was exactly the kind of man who would kidnap an old man and force him to talk. At the thought of what Mick would have endured before he told where Limerick was, Patrick clenched his fist. He drew it back and aimed it at the wall but held himself in check. Smashing walls wouldn't undo anything. It would only prove he was out of control, and of all times he needed every ounce of intelligence and power, it was now.

Mick needed him.

Limerick relied on him.

Catherine had even put her faith in his ability to get the horse and Mick back safely. And, by God, he was going to do it. He knew exactly the next step that had to be taken. He couldn't find Mick and Limerick. He hadn't the first idea where to look. But he could find David Trussell and find out the truth of the racing agreement.

The thought that perhaps Trussell, an old man who felt cheated out of the end of his life, might be involved in Limerick's disappearance blossomed in Patrick's mind. Trussell and Mick were old friends. Long-time friends. Trussell could have met Mick at O'Flaherty's, offered a drink, and taken him without a struggle. Mick wouldn't have been the wiser until it was too late. And Trussell might be holding Limerick just long enough to cause a forfeiture of the race, so that Catherine would lose the horse to Kent Ridgeway. Not a perfect solution but a biblical justice—eye for an eye and all of that. Yes, it was a scenario that might appeal to Trussell.

For the thousandth time Patrick glanced at his watch. Catherine knew where to find him. They'd settled it all before she'd left for Wicklow. He'd simply have to endure the waiting, and as soon as she arrived, they would head for Castlerock, the

Trussell farm. It was across the country, north of Beltene on the Dingle Peninsula. It was spectacular countryside, as rugged as County Galway. And, like the country, David Trussell was a hard man, capable of stealing Limerick and holding Mick.

Patrick had the exhilarating feeling that at last he was on a hot trail.

Chapter Thirteen

"David said to tell you it's not personal, man, but he has nothing to say to anyone from Beltene." Stephen Trussell stood beside the gate to the inner stable yard at Castlerock, one hand resting on the latch in an unconscious gesture of defensiveness. He shot a look of hatred toward the Volvo where Catherine sat.

Patrick assessed the young man who spoke to him, hat pulled low over his eyes, face stubbly and clothes unkempt. It was David Trussell's nephew, one of the last Trussells to remain on what had once been one of the most prestigious breeding and racing stables in western Ireland.

"Is your uncle forgetting that the Shaws and Trussells go back in time together?"

"He's not forgetting. He's just hurting something fierce about King's Quest." Stephen Trussell shook his head. "That horse was his heart, his hope for the future."

Patrick sighed. "That's what I've come to talk to him about."

"Talk to that redheaded devil who sent you here." He jerked his head toward the car. "She's the one tricked him out of the horse. He can't see enough to read anymore and she put the wrong papers on the table. Trusting fool that he is, he signed them and gave away his last dream." As he spoke,

Stephen's face grew white with anger. "There's a special place in hell for the likes of her."

"If that was the way it happened, you have a right to hate her." Patrick took a few seconds to try to figure out the best way to tell Stephen what he had come to tell him. "I had some sore feelings toward Catherine Nelson myself, as you can imagine. Beltene has been in the Shaw family for generations."

"And how did she trick you?" The young man was eager to learn the details. They would be fuel to feed his anger. "And how is it you're traveling the country with her?"

"Wasn't any tricking involved. She bought the farm fairly. If there was any fault, it was from my family. Da' had taken out some loans against it."

"Yeah. Colin." Stephen shook his head. "Uncle Davey talked about the troubles you had. He could see the road Colin was taking, but there was no way to get him on another track. He admired Colin in a way, and pitied him in another. He said the time for rebels had come and gone in Ireland. When Colin was in prison, we thought it was done. That he'd be there long enough to grow up a bit. Then when he escaped..."

"It nearly killed my da'." Patrick said it simply enough. He'd trained himself not to let the hot, boiling emotions rise. Colin, his older brother, drew so many conflicting things from him. In most recent years, resentment was the primary emotion, mixed with a good portion of anger. Colin had jumped from one bad incident to another, breaking his parents' hearts and costing a fortune in legal fees. Beltene had eventually been sacrificed to Colin's wild dreams of Irish independence. But there had been a time when Colin was the hero every young boy worshiped, especially a younger brother. He was a man who believed in a cause, and was willing to fight for it. Storybook stuff. Until their sister was killed.

"Where is the boy now?" Stephen asked.

Colin's whereabouts was anyone's guess. There were rumors that he'd gone to America, or to Australia. Or that he was building up a paramilitary organization in the rugged terrain of the north. All Patrick knew was that Colin had failed to show up for his own father's funeral two years back. There had been no note, no call. That his brother was in hiding was a fact—he was an escaped convict. But in Patrick's mind, not even that excused his lack of concern for his family.

"I have no idea where he is." Patrick spoke softly, calling up his rigid control once again. "I hear he might be in Boston. I hope he's doing well."

"Just hope he never comes back here. If he can start his own life, it'll be best for everyone."

"True." Patrick looked around at what had once been a thriving farm. The barn roof had sloped on one end, showing a desperate need for repair. The stable yards themselves were dirty. There was a general air of neglect about the place, and Patrick felt his heart twist. If he hadn't sold Beltene to the Nelson family, it would have grown to look this way. He didn't have the money to keep it up. If he'd been able to race Limerick, he might have made it. But that was water under the bridge. Now, at least, Beltene was well kept. The farm showed signs of love and money.

"Looks sad, doesn't it? Unc' Davey won't let go. But I'll tell you, he won't last much longer. His heart."

"Is he sick?"

"Nah. Not medical sick. Just he's lost his will. King's Quest was it. He'd hung on and hung on because he saw potential in that horse. The race with Limerick was to be the beginning of a new era for Castlerock." Stephen snorted. "King's Quest has potential. No doubt about him. He could have rallied the troops here at Castlerock. Now Unc' Davey's given up and all of the help except me has moved on."

"I need to talk to him. Whether he wants to hear it or not, Catherine Nelson didn't cheat him. The papers calling for a claim are forgeries. Catherine wants to tell him that herself."

"Be off with you." Stephen looked amused and angered. "Unc' Davey's not going to cause a stink. She can rest easy.

He sold the horse to that Ridgeway character. I think that cost my uncle as much as anything could have. Ridgeway.'' Stephen sneered. ''Might as well have sold him by the pound to the meat packers.''

''Maybe not.'' Patrick understood Stephen's desperate anger. It was heartbreaking to see a good horse go to a home where he would likely be ruined. ''Just think this through. If Catherine has been tricked, also, then the papers can be proven to be false. David may be able to get King's Quest home.''

''From Ridgeway? How? Even if the papers are false, it doesn't invalidate the contract with Ridgeway. He has the horse and his papers.''

Patrick hesitated. ''It would if Ridgeway initiated the fraud. Or if he knew about it. Catherine is willing to tell the truth. She was tricked, too.''

Stephen's face opened with the first hint of hope. ''That's true.'' His eyes shifted to Patrick's. ''If it could be proven.''

''We need to talk to David.''

Stephen hesitated. ''He's gone down, Patrick. He doesn't care to see anyone.'' Sorrow moved across Stephen's face. ''It's heartbreaking to look at him, and the old man knows it. He doesn't want pity so he hides away where no one can see him.''

''Maybe I can give him hope.''

Stephen looked around the stable yard. ''This place needs hope, and a lot more.'' He sighed, weighing both sides. ''Come on, then. He's in the office. Sitting and staring out the window, more than likely. Just don't act like you're sorry for him. He'll go into a rage. And there's no guarantee about what he'll say to Ms. Nelson.''

Patrick laughed. It held neither humor nor bitterness. ''That's what we're left with, isn't it? Pride.''

''If Colin were around, he could probably recruit.'' Stephen looked back over his shoulder. ''I hope you can give Unc' Davey more than hope. That might just be the thing that finishes him off if it's pulled out from under him one more time.''

Patrick took those words to heart as he went to the car and opened the door for Catherine. "It's touchy," he told her softly. "Let me do the talking." He looked at Familiar, curled on the back seat. "And you stay put. No shenanigans from you," he warned as he carefully closed the door.

Together they followed Stephen into the barn. The place had gone down fast. The stalls, once neatly cleaned and filled with fine animals, were empty and dirty. The barn aisle was cluttered with tools and pieces of equipment that had never been put away. Several puddles indicated there were chronic leaks in the roof, and the air itself was musty, old and forlorn.

"Good Lord, Stephen," Patrick said with disapproval.

"There's no money, Patrick. He put away the funds he got for King's Quest. He won't say where and he won't spend them."

Patrick's heart sparked. "Then he still has hope himself, the old devil. He knows he's been tricked. He's hoping to get King's Quest back."

"Maybe. He knows he's been had, that's true enough. But he hasn't a clue what to do about it."

The thought that David Trussell might be behind the theft of Limerick and the disappearance of old Mick returned to Patrick like the bitter aftertaste of bad food. It was possible. Anything was possible. But David Trussell had always been a man of honor. He might shoot Catherine if he discovered she'd cheated him, but he wouldn't steal from her. Or at least, that was how he'd once been. They were about to discover if time had changed him.

When Stephen opened the door of the barn, Patrick saw the anger ignite in David's eyes.

"Get her out of here," David said. His knuckles whitened as he gripped the desk.

"Give us a chance," Patrick said before the older trainer could say more. "I think you and Catherine Nelson have both been duped. She didn't trick you, David. You have my word on it."

Catherine felt the old man's look as if it were a physical blow. Though it cost her to do so, she straightened her back and refused to look away from him. There was plenty she wanted to say, but Patrick had asked her to hold her tongue.

The anger was slow to die in David Trussell's eyes. When it had fallen to glowing embers, he sighed. "I don't know what to believe. If it wasn't her, who was it?"

"I'm not certain. Do you have the agreement?"

"Ridgeway took it."

Patrick nodded. "I thought as much. I checked the track and there isn't one filed there."

David sat up straight. "Then it isn't valid."

"Want to make any bets that one will appear before the race date?"

David Trussell stood. He was a tall man, still lean and muscular even though he was in his late sixties. "Are you certain Ms. Nelson doesn't have all the copies?"

"I'm positive." Patrick put his hand on Catherine's shoulder, a gesture of friendship and support. By word and deed he was demonstrating his bond to her. "Catherine is no cheater. You have my word on it."

"And how can you be so certain of the family that put you out of your own farm?"

Patrick's hand tightened, restraining her. "Because there's a clause in there that doesn't allow for a scratch unless both parties agree." His voice was soft.

"Don't you think I know that, man?" David pounded the desk top. "If I'd had a chance to scratch, I would have pulled King's Quest from that cockamamy agreement and he'd still be here. I'd still have a future. That clause means nothing to her!" He glared at her.

"Four months ago, I might have agreed with you. But now...I know for certain that Catherine stands to lose far more than you by the terms of that agreement." Patrick waited until he saw the interest build and grow in the older man. "Limerick's been stolen. If he isn't there to race, and if Ridgeway won't agree to a delay, Catherine will lose him. And believe me, David, Limerick is as much to Beltene as King's Quest was to Castlerock. The heart and future."

"The stallion's gone?" David was incredulous. "How? What were you doing when they took him? This isn't possible. I thought you and that old reprobate Mick never left his side."

"It's worse than that. Mick has disappeared without a trace or word. I'd stolen Limerick myself in an effort to force Catherine to rest his bad knee. I hid him out in the bogs, very isolated. Only Mick and I knew where he was. Someone stole him from me."

Catherine couldn't help herself. Her hand moved up Patrick's back, stroking a soothing path. He was a man of great pride, and it had cost him to admit that he'd lost Limerick. And he'd done it for her. No one had ever given her so much.

David sat. "This is the damnedest tale I've heard." He motioned to Patrick, Catherine and Stephen to take a seat. "What's going on here?"

"I wish to hell I knew, but somehow I think Kent Ridgeway is behind it, or at least behind part of it. He stands to gain too much. He's got King's Quest, and if this goes off as it looks like it's going to, he'll have ownership of Limerick, too," Patrick said.

"But the horse is stolen."

"Want to bet that Limerick will suddenly reappear shortly after the race deadline?" There was anger in Patrick's voice. "I can see it now. Ridgeway at the track with your horse waiting for Limerick to show. When he doesn't, Ridgeway will make a suitable fuss and declare Catherine in default. By the terms of the racing contract, which will conveniently be found in the correct place in the office, he'll own Limerick."

"All without risking a single thing," Stephen said. "It's genius."

"And Patrick gets the blame." David was seeing his way to the heart of the issue.

The three men looked at each other, then at Catherine.

"Let's drive the snake out into the open," Stephen said.

"How?" David asked.

"This could take a bit of planning and a lot of luck, but that's why we came here. If anyone can help us, you can."

The sound of a dog barking interrupted the three men. Stephen walked to the window and craned his neck. "Fancy car. Nicely dressed gent." He waited. "Well, well, the snakes are indeed crawling. It's O'Day."

"Come to pick the carcass," David said bitterly. "Can't even wait for it to quit twitching."

Patrick and Catherine said nothing. Benjamin O'Day was a horse trader, of sorts. He specialized in foreclosure sales on horses and then resold them as hunters or breeding stock. He had no particular concern about what happened to the animals that passed through his hands, nor about the people who once owned them or now purchased them. He made no guarantees on his "products," and rumors abounded that his tactics were often less than ethical. Yet he was highly regarded by the hunt set.

There was a knock on the office door. David reached down to the side of his chair and let his fingers grip the handle of the cane. "Open the door, Stephen, and I'll give him the beating he deserves. Five years ago he'd know better than to put foot on Castlerock. Damn vulture."

"Wait." Patrick spoke softly. "O'Day makes the rounds. He could prove useful to us."

Stephen nodded at his uncle. "Let him in," David said with a bit of rancor. "I can always beat him when we're ready to throw him out."

Patrick smiled. It was as close to the old spirit as he'd seen in David Trussell. Maybe the old man wasn't buried under bitterness and disappointment. It only made Patrick more determined to help him. Beltene was gone, sold. But Castlerock could maybe be redeemed.

Ben O'Day hadn't expected to see all three men and Catherine Nelson sitting in the office. He nodded at all as he stepped into the room. His tweed coat was immaculate, his slacks pressed with a razor-sharp crease. "Well, Ms. Nelson, Patrick, I hope you haven't already beaten me out of the best of Castlerock stock."

"We're not buying," Patrick said easily. "In fact, David was asking about some of the Beltene brood mares. We're here to sell."

"I thought you sold your stud to Wicklow." O'Day looked at David for confirmation.

No one said anything.

"What's going on here?" O'Day demanded. "It's like a conspiracy. You act like you're plotting the overthrow of the government." He laughed sharply. "Has the talk of Cuchulain ridin' in the mists gotten to all of you? Dreamin' the dream is a speciality of the Shaw family, but I had no idea it had wormed into the Trussell brain. And you, Ms. Nelson, a good ways out of your heritage, I'd say."

O'Day's words were dangerously inflamatory. Patrick clenched his fists at his side, but he didn't move.

"What talk of Cuchulain?" Stephen asked. He looked at his uncle, who shrugged.

"I hear the old legend has risen from the grave and taken to ridin' the Clifden seacoast road late at night calling for a free Ireland." O'Day grinned. "The women are abuzz."

"Go on," Stephen said with a snort. "I've heard that you used some mighty crude methods of cheating folks out of their stock, but this is beyond the worst I've heard."

"I've never cheated anyone." O'Day's eyes were hard. "Ms. Nelson has no doubt enjoyed my efforts on some of her Dublin hunts. It's a hard business, boys."

"Where did you hear about Cuchulain?" Patrick asked. There wasn't a hint of emotion in his soft voice. Only the slight thickening of his brogue attested to his emotional state.

"Oh, it's all over Connemara. Folks are talking left and right. It seems the old legend put in an appearance night before last and scared the hell out of a family whose car had broken down. They were walking home and heard the thunder of hooves. Out of the mist rode the warrior. He called for a free Ireland and urged the family to take up arms and fight."

Stephen and his uncle were grinning, but Patrick's face had gone dead still. "When was this?"

"Two nights back." O'Day's face grew cagey. "Why so interested?"

"I've heard the talk. In a way it concerns me."

"With your family history, I'd say so. Since you've lost your farm, maybe revolutionary work wouldn't be such a bad idea. Of course, it would be difficult working for a legend." O'Day chuckled at his wit. "You'd have to sit out in the mist on the sea road and wait for him to ride up and give you instructions." He laughed out loud. "I can see it now. 'Gather all the sea horses and leprechauns and arm yourselves. The battle approaches.'"

"Your history is as twisted as your sense of humor," Patrick said easily.

"There are folks who wouldn't appreciate your talk," David added. "Irish history is a very real thing to them."

"Those who live in the past, die in the past. It's the future that bears consideration. And that's what I'm here about. Now what horses would you like to see go to good homes?"

"David has promised me first choice on his stock, if he decides to sell any," Patrick said. "I'll give you a call once we've made a determination."

"I came with money in my pocket." O'Day stood. "By the way, Patrick, I'll see you at the track Saturday. I hear half the kingdom is riding on the outcome of the race between Limerick and King's Quest. The odds makers are having a time of it, two unknowns racing. If Kent Ridgeway hadn't gone around telling the terms of the agreement, the race probably would have drawn little notice. To risk Limerick! That's a bold move on your part, Ms. Nelson."

"Catherine is something of a gambler." Patrick smiled. "In

fact, I hear it's Catherine dressed up like Cuchulain who's riding the countryside. She likes a bit of adventure in her life." He grinned at her.

O'Day's face showed shock. "Now that would be a turn, wouldn't it? I did hear it was a big gray stallion. A fiery devil. That family, the Adamses, said the horse cleared a four foot stone wall from a standstill and took off across the pastures without a misstep. As you know, that's rocky terrain. A horse is likely to break a leg. But, I suppose if it's a legendary horse, the gift of the gods to Cuchulain, then it's hardly worth a worry about a few stones."

"Hardly." Patrick had to force the word through his teeth. He stood. "I have to be going, David, Stephen. I'll be in touch." He looked at O'Day. "Don't go counting which horses you want here, Benjie. Castlerock is still solid."

"Believe it or not, Shaw, I came because I didn't want to wait until the nags were starving with their ribs showing and their feet gone to ruin. I can give David a fair price now, and take the animals before they go down. I came when I could have waited."

Patrick stared at the man. "Put your money on Limerick. He'll win that race."

O'Day put his hand on Patrick's arm, holding him at the door another moment. "How come the gray hasn't been worked, Patrick? There's talk that he's injured."

"He had a sore knee two weeks ago, but he's fine. A bit of rest, a little work. He'll be ready to run. And though King's Quest is a very fine animal, Limerick will beat him."

"Spoken like a man who believes." O'Day removed his hand and looked back to Catherine. "You'd best get your animal to the track where he can be seen. That would quell a lot of rumors, you know."

"Have you ever considered the fact that those are exactly the rumors we don't want to squelch?" Patrick countered. "There's a lot more to horse racing than running the horse."

HOME AGAIN, home again, Molly Magee. I never thought I would feel this way, but I'm delighted to see the rooftop of the barn at Beltene. I've been doing a lot of thinking about future travel modes. I'm ready for the old, ''Beam me over, Scottie.'' There's such a lot of wasted time sitting in a luxury car, coasting along the highways. But I do have a better idea of the countryside here. The Emerald Isle. I know why they call it that. There's a ruggedness to this land, especially the western coast, that haunts a person—or a cat, for that matter. Not an inch of land untended, uncared for. Up around the hideout, where Limerick was staying, there's wild land. The bogs, with the rocks and heather. No one has claimed that, and maybe never will. Leave it to the sheep and the occasional traveler. But in the cultivated areas, there is regard for each square foot.

Catherine has been too quiet on the entire drive back. I watch her face and see her feelings play across her features. It's Patrick. What is she to do about him? He got her into this mess by stealing Limerick in the first place. He's been a thorn in her side from the first day she bought Beltene. And yet she finds herself drawn to him. A quandary, to be sure. No matter what she ultimately wants, if Patrick doesn't find that horse, he'll be gone.

And Patrick, driving so silently. Responsibility rests heavy on his shoulders, for Limerick and Mick. If he hadn't taken the stallion, then Mick would never have been put into danger. At least, that's how he thinks.

My problem is that whoever took Limerick—because someone was surely tailing us to the hideout—didn't have to take Mick. That's the part of this that doesn't make a bit of sense.

Ah, the car finally stops and we're home. Hmm, what's that I smell? Fresh garlic in butter? Thank goodness the preparations have just begun. I have to do some work before I eat. I've left it up to these humans long enough. So far the only thing Catherine and Patrick have discovered is their mutual desire. Harrumph! I could see that from the first. There are none so bllnd as those with two eyes—and two legs.

See, when I first met Clotilde, that little beauty who pines for my return to the capital city, it was love at first sight. I do admit, she was a bit on the coy side at first. Her eyes said yes, but her claws said beg a little, mister. But it was a game. We knew how it would end. And now I'm her devoted slave. My adventures take me around the globe, but she sits in the window of her posh town house and waits for my return. Let all the passing cats admire the fine arch of her back leg as she cleans herself, the perfection of her whiskers, especially the way they pucker when she's slightly distressed. That little edging of black along the tips of her ears. Ah, Clotilde, the calico of my dreams. I can't think about her too much, or I'll get homesick. And there's work to do here.

Someone is going to have to figure out where Limerick is. That race deadline is approaching fast. No one has to tell me that Limerick should run. In order to save Beltene, he'll have to run. Okay, everybody out. Well, Patrick is going to be the gentleman and carry Catherine's bags. I hope they consider dinner before they fall all over each other. I guess it's up to me to scope out the area.

Time for a prowl around the premises. There's bound to be some clues that everyone has overlooked. I want all of this resolved before Eleanor and Peter come to claim me. They'd never forgive me if I left a mystery only partially resolved.

Ah, the barn. There's McShane. At least his face has healed. Too bad the same can't be said for his bad heart. I wonder what drives him to be so bitter. And so furtive. He's looking around as if he were going to commit a crime. There he goes into the barn. I guess I'd better put it in gear if I'm going to keep up. He's walking like the devil's got a pitchfork in his backside.

Why am I not surprised? He's going straight to the loft. To Patrick's quarters. That's excellent, since I wanted to get into

Patrick's abode myself. Good old Eamon can open the door for me.

That's the ticket. He never even saw me slide past his leg. Now that we're here, I'm going to duck under the bed and see what happens. Once, when Clotilde took a fancy to a dandified Himalayan, I wished for a more flamboyant hide. Once and only once. Black is chic, and also very practical in the line of work that I do. As it happens, even Clotilde came to her senses about that.

Patrick! Ever heard of a dust mop? Jeez, there's enough dust and puff balls under this bed to make an asthmatic go into a fatal attack.

Ah, old Eamon isn't wasting any time. He's going to the telephone. Pretty strange, to break into someone's home simply to use the phone. Five digits, which means the call is local.

"Hello, it's me. Yes, I'm calling from his quarters. That will link him directly. I saw them go up to the big house, yes. How's the old man? Good. I'll be in touch." The telephone clicked back down on the receiver.

There he goes, leaving as stealthily as he came. And not even a look around. My first conclusion is that it was Mick he was talking about. The old man—that makes me a bit nervous. I wouldn't trust McShane with a pet rock.

The coast is clear for me to do a little investigating on my own, but first things first. A little nudge and the phone rocks out of the cradle, then that amazing redial button. One ringy-dingy. Two ringy-dingy. Three ringy-ding...

"Hello. Who's there? McShane, is that you again?"

A little paw on the switch hook to break the connection. I've heard everything I need to hear. I know that voice. Ah, yes, the cultured and cultivated tones of Mr. Allan Emory. Five digits would give us Galway, but not Dublin.

So, Allan and Eamon are in cahoots. And Allan knows something about "the old man." Now, how to convey all of this info to Patrick? I mean, big sigh, I do all the work and even then I can't relax.

Not to worry, I'll mull over this matter while I check out what Mauve is making in the kitchen. I've always considered garlic to be one of the better brain foods. Indeed, where would the world be without da Vinci? Galileo? Both garlic eaters from the get-go.

Chapter Fourteen

"Let me make you something hot to drink," Mauve said as she followed Catherine into her office. "I hope you won't hold it against me if I speak my piece, but you look like warmed-over death."

Catherine smiled despite herself. "If I didn't already feel bad, that description would make me take to my bed. I will have a cup of tea, though. I'm very tired."

"I was worried sick about you until I figured Patrick was with you. What's wrong, Catherine?" Mauve was curious, but she was also concerned.

"Too many things." On the long drive home, both she and Patrick had been worn down by worries over Mick and Limerick. Even Familiar had been unduly quiet. Patrick had left her, saying he wanted to check on Mick's cottage. Though he hadn't stated it specifically, Catherine had known he needed a little time alone. "Maybe things will look better after some sleep."

Mauve shook her head. Taking a step forward, she hesitated. "What's going on here, Miss Catherine? Mick's disappeared. Patrick's acting like he's killed his mother. You look like you haven't slept in days. That strange man leaving messages on the front yard. What's wrong here?"

Catherine sighed as she went to Mauve. "It would be better if I didn't tell you. The less you know, the better."

"Has someone hurt Mick?" Mauve's eyes widened with that possibility. "He's an old man. I'm worried about him."

"I wish I could tell you something more, but it's best that I don't. Where Mick is concerned, I don't really know anything to tell you."

"There was a message for you while you were gone." Mauve went to the secretary and picked up an envelope. "Bridget didn't see anyone leave this, but it was by the front door, like the others. Looks to be the same paper and hand."

Catherine opened it slowly. The message was brief. "The old man is safe, but not forever. Where's the horse? Expect my call tonight." Cold dread clutched at her spine. For a second she stared blankly at the message, forcing herself to betray nothing to the cook. Whatever was going on, she wasn't going to embroil another innocent person in her troubles.

Without showing any emotion, she folded the note and returned it to the envelope. "I think you're right. I believe it did come from the same person who sent the others. When did you find it?"

"Just before you drove up. I went to see if the paper had come. It was almost propped against the door. No one saw it delivered. I've asked everyone around the house. Sonny was working in the front flower beds for several hours this morning. He didn't see a soul."

"Whoever is doing this is very, very clever."

"Miss Catherine, if you asked the men in the barn to help you, they would. All you have to do is ask."

Catherine smiled. "You know, the irony is that I believe they would. I didn't exactly win their hearts, did I?"

"Well, it's a hard situation. Being a woman and all, you had to come in tough, or so you thought."

"Being a banker's daughter, I thought I had to come in very tough."

"A bit of softness sometimes works the best, especially with men. My mother always told me if you couldn't cook for a man then you'd better know how to soften him up. First line of attack is the stomach, the second is the heart.''

Catherine and Mauve laughed together. ''I'll keep that in mind. And thanks. I'm going to have a talk with the men. Maybe it isn't too late to get things off on the right foot.''

''You'll find they're a right agreeable lot, with the exception of a few.'' Mauve was practically beaming. ''I knew when I said I'd cook for you that it would be all right. Everyone thought I was crazy, that you'd be too hard to please. But you've proven them wrong in more ways than one.''

''Thank you, Mauve.'' Catherine felt the sting of tears. If nothing else, she'd won the heart of Mauve McBride, and that was no small accomplishment. Mauve was nobody's fool.

Once she was alone in her office, Catherine took out the four messages saying that Limerick was okay. The latest note, a threat regarding Mick's life, was in the same hand. It had not been sealed with wax. Apparently the formalities were over. It was also the first solid piece of evidence should she decide to call in the authorities. The note was a threat against Mick's safety if not his very life. Up until this time, there had been no way that she could prove Mick had been kidnapped.

Well, she had only to wait for a call of some sort. Only to wait. It was one of the hardest things she could imagine doing.

As much as she dreaded it, she decided to go to the barn. The men must think her a fool. She'd puffed and blustered, and her horse was still missing. She'd accomplished nothing except endangering the life of one of her employees.

She couldn't ignore the possibility that someone at the barn had seen something that might help her find Mick before it was too late. If she had to crawl and beg, then she would. Pride was too expensive; she couldn't afford it for the time being.

The day was growing short and she picked up a heavy jacket and slipped into it. She checked the window seat for Familiar, but he wasn't in sight. Had she imagined that he'd come in with her? She distinctly remembered him jumping out of the car and sniffing around like a dog. Who knew with that cat?

Instead of going out the front, she cut through the kitchen, her mouth literally watering at the scent of the meal Mauve was preparing. If she knew Familiar, the cat would be parked somewhere nearby.

She saw the tip of his tail as he sat patiently waiting in one of the kitchen chairs. He'd invaded Mauve's kitchen just as he had the rest of the house—all with total complicity on the part of the humans involved.

"I'm going to the barn for a few moments," she said to Mauve.

"Would you take these over to the men?" Mauve held out a platter of cookies.

Catherine hesitated. Never in a million years would she have considered handing out cookies at the bank. She took the tray. She knew exactly what Mauve was doing. Beltene wasn't a bank. She might be the owner, but what harm would it do to pass out a few cookies? It was a gesture the men would see and understand. The first step in her program to start over.

"What a wonderful idea, Mauve. I'll tell everyone you baked the biscuits and I'm merely delivering them."

"Good girl," Mauve agreed. "Dinner will be ready by the time you're back."

"I'm starved," she said, pushing the door open with her free hand. "And I know Familiar is famished. But then, isn't he always?"

The cat looked up at her and very slowly, carefully yawned, as if to say that a human's sense of humor was beyond redemption. Then he hopped to the floor and followed her out the door.

"Get her back in time to eat," Mauve called to the cat. "You seem to be the only one around here who understands the importance of a good meal."

Catherine had made it across the road and was standing at the front door of the barn when she heard the vehicle approaching. Patrick pulled up beside her, his blue gaze moving over the picture she presented. He took in the tray, the cookies and the cat at her heels.

"Did you find anything?" Catherine knew the question was useless.

He shook his head and got out of the Rover. "So Mauve's up to patching things with the men." Picking up a cookie, he forced a smile. "She knows how to do it, too. Sandies, my favorite kind of biscuit."

Catherine's heart was pumping so hard she used both hands to hold the tray. Patrick's face was stubbled with beard and the lines around his eyes were worn deeper than she'd ever seen them. But there was a light in his eyes that kindled something warm inside her.

"You're going to make a right good farm owner, Catherine," Patrick said slowly. "You have good instincts."

"So we can both sink together." There wasn't any bitterness in her voice, just acceptance. "I'm to get a call tonight about Mick. I got a note threatening to hurt him if I didn't tell where Limerick is."

"Mick hasn't broken, or at least he didn't tell them until..." Patrick stopped talking. "This could prove more interesting, or dangerous, than I thought. We've two sets of thieves. One has Mick and one has the horse."

"Two?" Catherine had followed his thinking. "They're working at loggerheads against each other." She filled him in on the similarities between the handwritten notes.

"So, whoever wrote the notes knew where Limerick was in the first place and wanted him to stay there. They probably had intentions of snatching him from the hideout. That's why they kept sending those reassuring notes, to prohibit you from doing anything. Someone got there before them, though."

"And since I thought you had the horse and the notes were from you, I completely accepted the situation."

"And now that Limerick's been stolen from the hideout, the party who wrote the notes is left out in the cold. So they snatched Mick, but now Mick doesn't know where Limerick is.''

Catherine lowered the tray of cookies onto the hood of the Rover and leaned against the warm vehicle. ''This is like a spider's web. The deeper we look, the more entangled we become. It isn't just Limerick, now it's Mick and David Trussell and Kent and you and two other factions. Where will all of this end?''

She looked so beset with anxiety that Patrick didn't think. He put his arm around her and drew her into the solid safety of his chest. ''It will end with Mick and Limerick returned safely. The rest doesn't really matter, or at least not that much. There's criminal activity here, enough to keep the authorities properly busy for months. But that can be their worry. We've only to look out for the ones we love.''

''You do love that old man, don't you?'' Catherine spoke into the warmth of his jacket. He smelled of horses and hay and maleness.

''Mick's been like a second father to me, except he never put the pressure on me that my own father did. Sort of best friend and father.''

''And I've no doubt you love that horse.''

''No matter what else you think of me in the long run, Catherine, you have to know that I would never have deliberately endangered Limerick.''

Something in his voice made her slowly push back and look at him. ''Is Limerick in some kind of danger? Have you learned something I need to know?''

''All the way back I've been thinking. Something about what O'Day said kept troubling me.''

''Benjie said someone saw the horse and rider two nights ago, on the Clifden road...''

''Exactly where I was seen by that old man. But it's the time. Two nights ago. Limerick's been gone longer than that.''

''Someone's gotten the time confused is all.'' Catherine didn't understand why Patrick was hanging so stubbornly to the topic. No harm had been done except a few ghost stories had been spawned. There were tales of banshees and walking spirits aplenty in Ireland. One more wouldn't hurt.

"Except Benjie said he was seen by an entire family, and that he entreated them to take up arms for freedom, then jumped a stone wall and rode across a treacherous field toward the bogs."

Catherine visualized it all. The gray horse thundering up out of the mists, the call for freedom by a cloaked rider, and the horse pounding over the wall and disappearing into the mists and the bog.

"Highly impressive story. Someone's already embellishing the dickens out of your ride."

"Possibly."

"But what?" she pressed. He was looking past her, into the barn, as if some answer would come from there. She lifted her hands to his shoulders and felt the tension in him. There was something else going on with Patrick Shaw, something that had him strung tighter than high *C* on a concert harp.

"What is it?" she asked again.

"I'd like to go and find that family."

"The ones who saw Cuchulain?"

He nodded. "You see, if O'Day had his story straight, then the horse might very well have been Limerick." He finally looked at her, his blue eyes tormented by the possibilities he'd uncovered. "If it was Limerick, God help me, Catherine, it might be my fault. By accidentally starting that business with Cuchulain, I might have given some people the perfect opportunity to capitalize on it."

Catherine swallowed. Her throat was unaccountably dry. "You think Limerick's been taken by rebels, by someone who deliberately plans to use him to ignite the passions of the people."

"Passions and fears. That's the one thing I never considered when I hid him away in the bogs. And there's more." He forced himself to continue. "When my father died and my older brother didn't come home or even send word, I let it be known that if he ever returned again, I'd turn him in myself. I created some bad blood with Colin's mates. They might think it amusing to put me in a bad situation.''

''If they have Limerick, they won't care if they hurt or maim him.'' Catherine knew it, she only said it aloud hoping that Patrick would contradict her.

''They wouldn't deliberately injure him, I don't believe. But horse care was never high on the list of requirements they had for membership in their little club.'' Patrick couldn't help the bitterness. ''I mean, Colin destroyed our family, why should one horse more or less matter to his friends?''

''Patrick, what can I do?''

''The worst of it is that you're involved. It will give them double pleasure, you see. You're an outsider. You don't belong here.''

''So the blade cuts two ways. Vengeance and revenge.'' She felt the tears building and she had to divert them. She'd be willing to lose Limerick, to let him go without a fight, if she could only believe whoever had him would take care of him.

''They would never have taken Mick, so I didn't even consider such a thing until I learned that whoever had Mick didn't have the horse. This is far more serious than I'd ever expected.''

''What are we to do? What can we do?''

''Talk to the Adamses first. Then we can stake out the seacoast road. If it's Limerick, he'll respond to me.'' Patrick grinned. ''I bred and raised that stallion. There are a few tricks left that no one could anticipate.''

Patrick's smile touched the cold, brittle part of her heart that had been frozen with fear. There was something special between Patrick and Limerick. Catherine accepted the full measure of what that meant. If anyone could save the stallion, it would be Patrick. She had to trust him and allow him to do whatever he planned to do.

''I'll go with you,'' she said. ''I can help.'' At the consternation that crossed his face, she reached up and touched his chest. ''Patrick, I need to help, and I won't interfere.''

''Okay,'' he agreed. ''Let's deliver these biscuits and grab a bite ourselves. We'll wait until you get your phone call, and then we'll travel to Clifden. Maybe you could arrange a different vehicle, one that no one would recognize as yours or mine.''

''I can do that.'' Mauve would gladly trade. She picked up the tray of cookies. ''Shall we? As a team.''

''Why not?'' Patrick took her arm and led her into the barn. He saw the startled looks on the faces of grooms, trainers and jockeys as they noticed the obvious bond between new owner and old.

''So, you finally figured how to hang on to the farm?'' Eamon McShane said, stepping out to confront them.

''Have a biscuit, McShane,'' Catherine said. ''A bit of sugar might sweeten up your attitude.''

''Well said, Miss Catherine,'' Jack said. He gave Patrick a wink.

There was applause and several whistles of approval. Catherine felt herself flush with pleasure. Well, she'd wanted to be accepted by her employees. Perhaps she was on the way.

''We've a bit of a problem here,'' Patrick said. He spoke clearly, but his tone was soft so that people stopped working and drifted around them. Catherine passed the cookies around until Timmy took the tray from her. It was his way of showing that he accepted her position, and didn't mind. She gave him a grateful smile.

''As you know, Limerick is gone. We've begun to believe that his plight might be dangerous. There's been no ransom, no request for money or anything else. He's scheduled to race Saturday. That's three days from now. He has to run, and we have to get him back. Now, has anyone seen a stranger on the premises, someone who might have been over at Catherine's house to deliver envelopes or letters? Someone lurking about, watching?'' Patrick kept his gaze on McShane. The assistant trainer looked down at the ground. If he wasn't guilty of something he surely acted as if he were.

As if he felt Patrick's stare, McShane suddenly looked up. "Ask Patrick what he did with the horse. Everyone knows he took him. Him and Mick, and now that old codger's cut and run, leaving his work shuffed off on everyone else."

"We're concerned about Mick," Catherine said softly. "He was last seen at O'Flaherty's bar."

"He's not been home," Timmy volunteered. "Patrick said he was with his son."

A murmur moved swiftly through the gathering of men. "Old Mick would never have left here voluntarily. I said that myself," Sean said. "This was his life. If he's missing this long, something bad's fallen on him."

"I'm afraid he's been kidnapped," Patrick said. As he watched, McShane twitched. Patrick had to clench his fists to keep from jumping the other man and pounding the truth out of him.

"Well, we've got to figure how to get him back," Jack said. He gave Patrick a puzzled glance. "Mick is one of us. We can't forget about him. Not even for a horse, Patrick," he added softly.

"We've no intention of forgetting him," Catherine assured him. "Now you all know the truth. Limerick's truly been stolen, and Mick has been kidnapped. Think hard. I've had five messages delivered to my house, all anonymously. The last one was a threat aimed at Mick. We've got to figure this out and be quick about it."

"This isn't a game about Limerick's knee," Patrick said. He met the question in Jack's eyes. "I did take Limerick in the beginning. I wanted to rest his leg, and I wasn't certain Catherine would listen to me. What I did was wrong, maybe, but I'd no intention of keeping the horse."

"That's a fine tale. You've taken him once, what's to make us believe this isn't part of your plan to keep him for yourself?" McShane's voice was ugly.

"There are reasons. Plenty. If I had him, he'd be back in time to race Saturday, you can be sure of that. But as long as Catherine's sure, I don't have to worry about your doubts, McShane. In fact, I'm worried about your honesty. I get the distinct impression—"

"Let's not make this personal," Catherine interjected. Her fingers on Patrick's forearm, light as her touch was, stopped him.

Patrick recovered himself. "Keep a sharp watch, and let me or Catherine know if you remember or see anything."

"We will," the men answered in chorus.

Catherine twined her arm with Patrick's as they left the barn. "Keep walking," she said, moving toward the main house.

"Why?" Patrick did as she requested but he looked down at her. Her face was pale, but her eyes were glittering.

"McShane is trouble. I can smell it all over him. I want to make him believe we're as united a front as we can possibly be."

Patrick's arms closed around her. "If it's united you want to show, then let's give them a real look." His lips claimed hers. What began as a teasing kiss deepened. Drawing back, he smiled. "This isn't a game of pretend, though, Catherine. In all of this madness, I can't stop myself from thinking about you."

Catherine needed no explanation. She understood. Taking his hand, she led him away from the barn to a private spot sheltered by darkness and trees. This time, she was the initiator. When she was dizzy with the sensations of Patrick's kiss, she pulled away. Leaning her head against his chest, she sighed. "Would we have ever found our way here without Limerick and Mick and all of this tragedy?"

"We're a stubborn pair," Patrick said, his fingers weaving through her hair. "A mule-headed team, I'd say. Perhaps it took a mighty kick in the butt to wake us up to what we felt for one another. But there's no doubt now what I'm feeling."

He kissed the top of her head. "But I'll not speak of it until this is all settled between us. If Limerick is injured..."

Catherine squeezed him tight. "Hush!" she demanded. She knew what he was about to say. If Limerick was injured, he'd assume the blame and the responsibility. He'd also leave. That was something she didn't want to hear. "Mauve will be ready to skin me if I don't get home for dinner," Catherine said quickly.

"Does that mean you're inviting me to the big house to eat?" Patrick couldn't help teasing her, even with things as bad as they were. They needed some lightness between them, even if it was just a few moments of banter.

"For dinner, that's correct. And to wait for that phone call. I need your help, Patrick." She took his hand. "It's a difficult thing for me to admit, that I need you. But I do."

"I've a feeling that we both need each other a great deal." Patrick's fingers closed on hers as they walked through the darkness to the house.

By the time Catherine and Patrick sat down at the table for dinner, Familiar had already sampled the feast and was reclining on an antique chair near the table. One front paw outstretched, he purred with contentment and gave Mauve a ripply meow whenever she came near him.

"That devil knows how to live," Mauve said, balancing a tray with one hand and petting the cat with the other. "I'll bring your coffee."

Catherine glanced at her watch. She'd been too nervous to really enjoy the food. It was drawing close to eight. When would the call come?

"You can't rush it," Patrick said, picking up her hand and kissing her palm. "They'll call. Mick is of no value to them. What they want is the horse."

"What will we tell them...?"

The telephone in the hallway shrilled. Catherine clutched her napkin and remained frozen at the table. Rising swiftly, Patrick went to the phone.

"The Nelson residence."

"Patrick?" Mick's voice sounded foggy, confused. "Is that you? Patrick, they have me and they want the horse. No matter what they say, don't tell them—"

There was a break and a new voice came on the line.

"The old man can't take much more of what we've been giving him. If you want him back alive, you'd better hand over the horse."

Patrick studied the inflection in the man's voice. No matter how hard he tried to sound tough, there was something else there, a core of educated pronunciation.

"Perhaps you'd better speak to Miss Nelson." Patrick signaled her to the phone.

"Don't hurt him," Catherine said before the caller had a chance to say anything. She felt Patrick's fingers squeeze her shoulder tightly.

"Let them talk," he whispered to her.

"We don't want to hurt him anymore," the caller said. "It's the horse. A fair exchange, I'd say."

"What can you hope to accomplish? Even if you have him he'd be valueless to you."

There was a pause. "The horse. We have to have him by tomorrow. If not, the old man suffers."

"We don't have Limerick," Catherine said. "You're a little late on the thieving front. Someone has already taken him."

"Don't play me for a fool!"

"Check the barn! Check the hideout where Limerick was. Mick knew about it. Tell him to tell you. The horse is gone."

"This isn't a game. We get the horse or the old man will suffer."

Patrick took the phone from Catherine's hand. "She's telling the truth. Limerick's been stolen. Check wherever you'd like."

"You've got him hidden until the race Saturday. You think you're going to trick everyone."

"It's a fact. Let Mick go and we'll forget about this. This

is my warning to you. If that old man is hurt in any little way, I'll hunt you down. You'll suffer tenfold anything you do to him. That's a promise." Patrick returned the receiver to the cradle.

"Did he believe you?" Catherine asked.

"I can't be certain." It was a definite gamble, and Mick was the stakes. "Mick sounded good enough. A bit confused, as if they'd been giving him something to keep him calm. If that's the worst of it, he'll come out of this fine." He didn't mention the fact that the kidnappers might not want to leave the one witness who could identify them.

But Catherine was no fool. "Mick knows who they are. They won't forget that."

"If they don't hurt him, then they have nothing to worry about. That man understood what I was saying. I gave him a way out where he can return Mick and go on about his business." Patrick turned Catherine's face to the light. "Are you okay?"

She nodded, blinking back tears. "I'm worried about Mick and Limerick. I feel so helpless."

"Was there anything about that voice that you recognized?"

"He was trying to change his voice. He was trying to sound like he'd grown up on the streets, but he hadn't. He was educated."

"My thoughts exactly." Patrick frowned. "I keep going back to Ridgeway with this."

"And to think, I invited him in here. I showed him Limerick." Catherine shook her head and walked back into the dining room where Mauve had cleared the table and left coffee. "What a fool I've been."

"We've no proof that Ridgeway has Limerick or Mick," Patrick reminded her. Light from the chandelier glittered on her bowed head. Her shoulders were slumped, her posture reflecting dejection.

Unable to resist, Patrick moved behind her, circling her with his arms. "You did what you thought was right, Catherine.

There was no malice. How do you think I feel about the horse? I stole him, and I lost him. My only excuse is that I did what I thought was right. If anything happens to him, or Mick, I'm to blame."

Catherine turned in his arms. "There's no point in either of us blaming ourselves." She leaned her head against his shoulder. "Oh, Patrick, if we could only go back to a month ago."

He kissed the top of her head, remembering the way she'd ignited in his arms at the racetrack. Gently he released her. "Drink your coffee and grab a jacket."

"To Clifden?" she asked.

"To find the ghost of Cuchulain."

Chapter Fifteen

Sitting in front of the fire in the Adamses' home, Patrick watched Catherine accept the cup of tea that Mrs. Adams offered. Before them a fire flickered in the quiet house. The children were in bed asleep. The two women smiled at each other, a shy offer of friendship. Patrick was momentarily struck by the openness that Catherine exhibited. How had he ever thought her cold and arrogant?

"It gave us a bit of a scare," Ralph Adams said. "Tamara and me and the three children were walking home. There'd been a flat on the car and, of course, the spare was flat, too. The fog was thick and it was chilly, but not too bitter for a walk. It seemed the quickest way to manage."

Patrick sipped his tea. "Where were you exactly?" he asked.

"Not far from here. The sharp curve about a mile back. Right at the bend."

It was exactly the point where Patrick had nearly run over the old man. "And this was two nights ago?"

"Exactly." Ralph looked at his wife.

"We'd been to visit my sister, Beatrice. It's our regular Sunday outing," Tamara said. "We'd stayed longer than we planned." She shook her head. "I won't be traveling that road at night again. I must have had ten years scared off my life."

"He came out of the mist?" Patrick said encouragingly.

"There was the thunder of hooves," Tamara said. She'd sat down on the edge of a chair and her eyes were sparkling as she recalled the event. "I gathered up the baby and held him in my arms. I couldn't be certain what was happening. It was those hooves striking the ground. In the gray mist and all, the first thing I saw were the sparks flying on the pavement. I swear to you I thought old Lucifer himself was coming up the road, clanging his tail behind him."

"The children must have been terrified," Catherine murmured.

"No more than us," Tamara said. "The horse was enormous, a big gray animal with nostrils flaring. The man astride was hidden in a black cloak, but he rode bareback. That much I remember. I thought, 'How can he stay with that big animal without even a saddle?'"

Patrick lowered his cup. Only Catherine saw the way his fingers clutched the delicate handle of the china. "And a bridle? Did he ride with a bridle?"

Tamara furrowed her brow. "I can't rightly say. He had reins, but it could have been a halter. I didn't pay that much attention to what was in the horse's mouth. I was more taken by the man. His shoulders were broad, his legs long and hugging the sides of that dancing horse." She cast a glance at her own husband, a man of average height who'd begun to accumulate a stomach. "No harm in looking, Ralph, especially since it was a ghost." She smiled at him, a smile full of affection.

"He was a big man," Ralph agreed. "It was dark, but even in the broad light of day he could have passed for a god. And that voice."

"What about it?" Patrick felt his excitement grow.

"The purest Irish I've ever heard. He spoke in Gaelic, as if he'd never been taught another tongue."

Patrick felt as if he'd been slapped. He realized then how much he'd wanted the rider to be English, to be Kent Ridgeway. That way, at least, he'd find pleasure in dealing with Ridgeway on a one-to-one basis.

"Who speaks Gaelic?" Catherine asked. "I know it's taught in the schools, but does anyone really speak it?"

"A few scholars, some young people who're interested in preserving the language. Some of the older people." Tamara skirted the obvious—the political groups who wanted Gaelic as the official language. She smiled at Patrick and continued talking.

"I remember the story about Cuchulain's birth. He was born at the same time as twin horses. The horses were given to him as gifts, and they'd been blessed by the ancient ones, the gods. One was black and the other gray. It was the gray that he rode into battle as a young man." When she saw recognition of the tale in Patrick's eyes, she turned to Catherine. "It was said that when Cuchulain was injured, his horse felled forty of the enemy with his hooves."

"And what happened to the horse?" Catherine's pulse beat in the temple at her forehead.

"He was killed in the battle, but he saved his master."

THE FOG had been building as Catherine drove Mauve's compact up the Clifden road toward the Adamses' house. On the way down, her headlights couldn't even penetrate the thick, swirling mass of moisture.

"Bad night to be out," Catherine said. She was trying to think of anything to say. Patrick was silent as a stone in the passenger's seat. Tamara Adams had brought all of his worst fears to the forefront.

"When you get to the curve, stop," Patrick said.

Catherine didn't argue. There was nothing Patrick could see in the fog, but what would it hurt to stop and look?

She concentrated on her driving as she eased along in the fog. Images danced in front of the lights, tempting her to apply her brakes too fast. They were only slivers of fog, shifting and dancing on the wind that blew from the Atlantic.

At the curve, Catherine pulled far to the left and got out. The fog immediately touched her face, a moist greeting with a sinister promise in it. She felt beads of moisture spike her eyelashes and she blinked them away.

Patrick got out and from the pocket of his jacket withdrew a flashlight. He searched along the side of the road, looking for an imprint in the soft ground.

Leaning against the fender of the car, Catherine watched, wisely saying nothing. What good would it do to find a hoof-print? Would it prove it was Limerick? Maybe, maybe not. Either way, the outcome didn't look good.

"Patrick, why would someone want to stir up things now? I mean, Tamara said Cuchulain was trying to rouse them to fight for freedom. This isn't the north."

"You don't have to be born in Belfast to have a hope for Irish freedom," Patrick said. His voice was tense. "It's not a subject I'm fond of discussing. I know Mauve has told you about Colin and my sister, about how she sneaked out of the house and caught the train to Belfast to stop her older brother from getting killed." There was a pause before Patrick's voice came out of the fog, slightly distorted by the moisture in the air. "She was only thirteen. She tracked him to the city, and then to the place where he was supposed to be. Only it was a trap. No one ever claimed the bomb that was hidden in the building, but it didn't matter to us. What mattered was my sister died."

"Mauve told me," Catherine said gently. Her hands splayed across the fender of the car. She wanted to go to him, to hold him and help ease the pain he still suffered. But now was not the time to offer solace to Patrick Shaw. The angry sound of his strides let her know that he needed action, not sympathy.

"I would think they'd ask for money if they had Limerick. What I could scrape together would buy them a lot of things."

"What? Bombs? Guns? That's great, so there can be more and more killing."

Catherine bit her lip. Patrick was an enigma. She didn't

know where or how he stood on the issue of independence, but it seemed he wanted peace for his country, and for himself.

She was about to suggest that they get back in the car and return to Beltene. They could come back in the daylight when the fog had lifted. It was useless to try to track now.

"Here it is!" Patrick's light shone toward her out of the gray fog. "Come here, Catherine."

She walked toward the light, placing each foot carefully. There were loose rocks everywhere. She tried not to think of Limerick galloping through them in the darkness. One false step and he would break a leg. Then whoever had him would surely put him down. Horsenappers weren't interested in getting vet care for an injured animal.

As she approached the light, she felt Patrick's hand on her elbow. He led her forward and then directed her to kneel. In the cone of light, there was a perfect print.

"See that notch, a double nick on the left side. That's Limerick. I made the shoe myself. I always mark the shoes so that if we come across one in pasture, we'll know who it belongs to. That's Limerick's, all right."

Catherine stood slowly. "So he was here." She felt empty, drained of everything. "What now?"

"Leave me here, Catherine. He was here two nights ago, he might come back."

"The rider might be armed." Catherine felt Patrick's desperation, but she wasn't going to let him do anything stupid.

"I won't need a weapon."

"Spoken like a hero, but one that's likely to be dead." She shook her head, then realized he couldn't see the gesture. "No way, Patrick. I'm not leaving you here. We'll come back tomorrow. Bring a few men who can help you track. Maybe you can follow the prints. They go up into the bogs and the Twelve Bens. You know the mountains better than anyone, but it's something we should do in the daytime."

"Listen." Patrick's hands came out of the fog and gripped her shoulders.

"What?" The fog was like a thick blanket, muffling all sounds. Even the wind seemed to moan and hiss around her.

"Listen," Patrick said again, his hands tightening on her shoulders as he moved her toward the car. "Get inside," he said. "Lock the door."

"What is it?" Catherine balked. Patrick was scaring her. She couldn't hear anything, but there was something in the night. He sensed it if he didn't hear it. Catherine had grown to develop great respect for Patrick's senses.

"It's a horse, I think. Now get in the car and wait."

Catherine allowed him to push her toward the driver's door. When he opened it, she folded into the seat and cleared the way for him to softly close the door.

"Lock it," he ordered.

She did, and rolled down the window. In the distance there was the sound of hooves on asphalt. The animal was large and moving fast. Catherine drew in her breath. Patrick disappeared into the fog as he stepped away from the car.

"Patrick!" She called his name softly and cursed when he didn't answer. He didn't have a gun or even a tire tool. He was completely unarmed, and there was no telling what the horseman carried.

Opening the door softly, she slipped out. She left it ajar to avoid making a noise. Taking off in the direction she thought Patrick had gone, she went after him.

The pounding of the hooves grew louder, more intense. In the fog they sounded like thunder, like rocks being hurled against the earth by an angry god. As she listened, Catherine knew the horse was traveling at ultimate speed. She took a deep breath and moved forward until she was at the edge of the road.

Her eyes strained to find Patrick, but there was nothing but the swirling fog and the sounds of the hoofbeats. They were on top of her, coming from all directions. In a moment of panic, Catherine realized she had no idea what direction they were coming from. They were pounding down on her, and she didn't know which way held safety.

Out of the fog she saw the spark of metal striking asphalt. It was only ten yards away. The horse was coming from the north. Before she could make a move, there was the sound of a curse as the rider hauled back and the horse reared. Looking up, Catherine saw nothing but a huge horse, hooves pawing the fog as they started to crash down on her head.

The rider yelled something in a language Catherine could not understand. She knew it was Gaelic, but she'd never learned to speak it. He was nothing but a large shadow leaning over the side of the horse, his features hidden by a black cloak.

"Limerick," Catherine breathed, holding up her hands to ward off his hooves. It was indeed her stallion. The horse twisted in midair in a valiant effort to avoid her.

The force that struck her side was like a wall. She was swept off her feet and pushed into the ditch. Her shoulder crashed against a sharp rock and she cried out in pain. Then there was the sound of a horse's scream and the rapid dance of hooves upon pavement.

"Damn you," a strange voice called out. "You're a bloody fool, Patrick Shaw." The hooves danced and the horse screamed again. "Gallop, you beast!" the rider commanded, and there was the sound of the horse fleeing down the road.

"Patrick!" Catherine crawled to the road. She knew then that Patrick had seen her danger and had pushed her to safety—with no regard for his own life. "Patrick!"

She found him at the side of the road. As she ran her hands over him she found a pool of sticky blood beside his head.

"Patrick." She kept her voice calm. "It's okay. I'll get you to a doctor." She felt his neck. His carotid artery pulsed at a funereal pace. "Shock," Catherine said to herself. She had to get blankets and keep him from getting cold.

Reluctant to leave him, she got up and went to the car. Even after she pulled on the headlights, she could barely make out his form on the side of the road, but at least she'd be able to check his wounds. From the back seat she took a jacket and several articles of clothing that belonged to Mauve's children. Rushing back to Patrick, she staunched the flow of blood from a gash in the side of his head.

He moaned softly, a sign Catherine took to be good. She put the jacket over him and lifted his hand. Pressing it against her lips, she talked to him, telling him that he was going to be fine, that everything would work out.

When he tried to stir, Catherine forced him to be still. "Take it easy," she warned. "Head injury."

"It was Limerick," he whispered, forcing his eyes open. "He knew me. He tried to avoid me. I almost had the bastard. I had his leg and he was coming off."

"You almost got yourself killed," Catherine added.

"We have to get home." Patrick forced himself to sit up. Dizziness struck and he braced himself with both hands behind him. "Now. We have to get back."

"We have to go to the hospital. And no arguments."

"To the barn, Catherine. We can get torches and follow the tracks."

"He went down the road," Catherine admitted. "Hell-for-leather." She almost flinched as she thought of Limerick's beautiful clean legs pounding on the pavement.

"But not for long." Patrick pushed himself to his feet. "Not for long. The horse is here, in Connemara, and I'll have him by Saturday." Weaving slightly, he went to the car. "Drive me, please," he called out to her. "Damn the fog, drive me home."

AT PATRICK'S insistence Catherine drove to the barn. He had no intention of staying in her home for the night. He wanted his loft. How he was going to get up the stairs was another matter, though. During the tedious drive home, he'd drifted in and out of awareness.

"Quiet, now," Patrick ordered as he stumbled out of the car.

As quietly as she could, Catherine made her way to his side. Together they lurched toward the stairs that were little better than a ladder. Catherine had no idea how Patrick would negotiate them. She hadn't counted on his total stubbornness. Step by step, he worked his way up, weaving a couple of times to the point where Catherine feared he would topple over backward and to his death. At the top, he wisely crawled a few paces before standing and staggering into his loft apartment.

Following closely behind him, Catherine stopped at the door. He'd not invited her in, but he wasn't in any condition to issue invitations. Looking around, she wondered if he'd feel that she'd invaded his private domain. The loft was definitely a man's abode. There were touches of home—a braided rug, several very nice drawings on the wall, all of horses, and a beautiful quilt on the big bed. Curled in the center of the bed was Familiar. He watched them with his lazy yet alert gaze.

Although there was no hearth, there was a rocker beside a good lamp and a stack of books. Patrick made his way to the sturdy rocker and sank into it. Groaning softly, he let his head recline and touch the back of the chair. "I feel like someone hit me in the head with a hammer."

In the better light of the room, Catherine went to examine his injury. The gash was at least three inches long, and in places it was deep, but it was not too serious. "You need stitches," she said.

"No time for that," Patrick answered. "If I go to hospital, they'll give me drugs and want to keep me for observation."

"Not a bad idea." Catherine went to the bathroom and returned with antiseptic and cotton. It looked as if one of the horse's iron shoes had clipped the side of his head in a glancing blow. There was the possibility of concussion, internal bleeding, a clot that might suddenly break loose. The horrors were endless, and only a hospital could run the proper tests. But she knew Patrick well enough to know she'd have to knock him in the head again to get him to a doctor. Besides, his speech was clear and his pupils dilating properly. He'd have a headache—a big one—but she didn't think he'd die.

"Clean it out and get me some aspirin, please." He added the last as he squinted up at her.

"Men," Catherine muttered as she applied the antiseptic. Patrick flinched, but he grasped the arms of the rocker and held steady. Feeling every stroke of the cotton, Catherine forced herself to thoroughly clean the wound. "I can try taping the edges," she suggested. "If that doesn't work, you're going to have a nasty scar."

"Get the tape," Patrick answered. His voice was worn out, drained.

Catherine finished dressing the wound as well as she could. She'd cut his thick black hair away from the gash and now she picked up the pieces of it.

On the bed, Familiar stretched long and luxuriously. He hopped to the floor and promptly dug his claws into Catherine's foot.

"Hey!" She tried to shake him loose, but he held tenaciously. When she bent down to unhook him, he grabbed her hand. "Familiar!" she cried, holding steady so as not to set his claws more firmly in her.

"I think he's trying to tell you something," Patrick said. In the rocker, his eyes were barely open. "He's rather adamant."

"Okay, what?" Catherine stopped resisting and allowed herself to be maneuvered across the room by the cat. When he had her beside the telephone, he let her go and flipped the receiver off the hook with one deft movement.

"So who should I call? The doctor?" Catherine asked. "I agree completely, but Patrick will shoot both of us."

Familiar pulled the receiver down to him and deftly pressed the redial button with his paw. Bemused, Catherine lifted the receiver to her ear as she heard the digits being pressed. The phone began to ring. Four, five, six, seven times. She was almost ready to put it down. It was well after midnight.

On the ninth ring, it was answered. The voice that spoke was heavy with sleep. "Hello?"

Catherine caught the hint of something. She *knew* that voice. Who was it?

"Hello?" The man was more fully awake, and growing angry. "It's nearly one o'clock. Who's calling?"

"I've seen the gray stallion." Catherine lisped the words in a guttural tone. "He's on the road tonight. How much for his location?"

"Who is this?" There was a sudden caginess in the man's voice.

Catherine swallowed a gasp. She knew who she was talking to. How could she have forgotten he was in the area? How had she failed to consider that Allan Emory might be involved in everything that was happening at Beltene? He was also a man who knew too much of her business.

"Who is this?" Allan was growing angry.

Catherine replaced the receiver slowly, depressing the hook before she eased it back into the cradle. As soon as the connection was broken, she picked up the phone and pressed redial. Before it could ring, she hung up and went through the process again. When she'd memorized the pattern of beeps, she matched them to the numbers on the phone.

Galway.

The call had been made to somewhere in Galway, and she had the number. She had only to figure out where.

She gave Patrick a hopeful look, but he was dozing in the chair. She hated to wake him, but... Why would he be calling Allan in Galway? She concentrated on watching his chest rise and fall as he sprawled in the rocker. The answer to that question was crucial. Her answer. No matter what Patrick said, she had to decide whether she trusted him. Why had he called Allan? Or did he place the call? He'd been gone for two days. Someone else could have slipped into the loft apartment and used the phone.

On a hunch, she went to the apartment door. Slight scratches around the lock gave her the answer.

She turned back to survey the room one more time. Familiar, who'd been sitting on the foot of the bed, jumped to the floor and dashed across the room to the telephone. One quick movement of his front paw flipped a pen to the floor. That was quickly followed by a pad.

"I suppose you want me to leave Patrick a note," she said softly. "Probably not a bad idea, as long as you stay here and watch him for me."

"Meow," Familiar said agreeably.

"But first..." Catherine dialed directory assistance. Speaking as softly as possible, she explained that her child had gone to visit a friend but that he'd left only a phone number, no name or address. Since no one was answering the phone, Catherine was justifiably worried. Would the operator possibly give her the address so she could check on her son? She smiled as she listened to the operator's crisp answer.

After hanging up the phone, she lifted the pen to paper.

Gone to Galway. Allan Emory is involved and I have to find him. Someone used your telephone to call 55575. It's a long story, but with Familiar's help I made the connection. It's Andrew Bessler?—never heard of him—at One Robby's Lane. Once I find Allan, I'll know more.

She signed her name.

"Take care of him," Catherine said to the cat as she put the notepad in a prominent place by the telephone.

She took one last look at Patrick to make sure his breathing was steady and unlabored. She wanted to move him to the bed, but it was a physical impossibility. Sighing, she settled for giving Familiar a scratch under his chin.

As she left the loft she tried not to think about the fact that she'd never really known Allan. She'd thought she knew him—she'd almost married him. But there had always been a dark and controlling side. Now she was about to find out how deep that side went.

Chapter Sixteen

What's a cat to do? Catherine has decided to run off to Galway, alone, to talk to that unsavory Allan Emory. Women! No matter how much of a jerk he's been, she only wants to see the good side of him. I get the impression he'd sell his mother down the river for top dollar. There's no telling what he might do to Catherine if he gets hold of her and feels cornered.

And Patrick? He's out like a champ. I can see where he's been clouted on the head, but as thick as his skull is, I'm shocked to see it made an impression. It must have been a wallop.

So, should I go with the broad, or hang out with the comatose horse trainer? That's hardly a choice. Both of them need me to take care of them. I suppose it's a matter of degree. Whose need is greater?

Catherine can certainly get into more trouble, but if I'm with her, I can't help Patrick find her. If I'm with him, I can't help her when she gets in a jam. And somebody needs to be organizing a hunt for Limerick.

SINCE MAUVE had long since gone home for the night, Catherine pointed the cook's car toward Galway and stepped on the gas. It wasn't a long drive, but it was long enough that she felt the pressure of time.

Speeding into the city, Catherine crossed Galway Bay and

picked up the main highway that led south from the city. There were probably shortcuts, but Catherine didn't know them. And she'd never heard of Andrew Bessler. No matter how she searched her memory there was no way she could connect the name.

Driving through the heart of the city, she took the highway out of town. In only a few moments the lights became more scattered, moving further back from the road and appearing more infrequently. It was beautiful land by day, marked with stone walls and green pastures that gave it the quality of a patchwork quilt. Now darkness hid all of the familiar landmarks.

The foolhardiness of her actions made her grip the wheel of the car tighter. Panic was a deadly element, and she couldn't allow it to get a toehold. She could manage Allan. He might be a crook and a womanizer, but he wasn't violent. Who had been talking with him from Patrick's loft, though? She didn't have a shred of proof, but she was willing to bet it was Eamon McShane.

She almost stopped the car when she realized that she'd left Patrick alone, sleeping, without protection. But Familiar had stayed behind with him. That was some consolation. The cat was an extraordinary creature. As the wheels rolled over the miles, Catherine tried to remember all of the times she'd been around Familiar. He could hide in plain view when he chose to, yet he had a knack for always turning up at just the right moment to avert trouble. If his owners didn't come back for him, he certainly had a home at Beltene—for as long as she owned it. Which wouldn't be much longer if she didn't find Limerick.

She came back to the problem at hand. Robby's Lane was the turn she sought, and she found it, a narrow paved road bordered by flowering shrubs that grew at least eight feet high. In the dark night, the narrow road was a cave of blackness. Catherine made the turn and tried to keep her skin from rippling with unease.

Her foot automatically eased off the accelerator as the headlights picked up the stone front of a small cottage. With her breath shallow and light, she stopped the car. Darkness swooped down around her as she switched off the headlights and stepped into the night. There wasn't a sound at the house.

It was after three in the morning. What would these people think when she banged on their door? What if it hadn't been Allan's voice that she'd heard? Whoever lived here would think she was a madwoman. Doubts moved in as darkly as the night. What would Allan be doing in a small cottage in the country? He was a man who loved luxury, fine liquor, fast horses and women with money. This place was not something she'd ever associate with the Allan Emory she knew. But it was a terrific hideaway.

Caution made her hesitate with her hand at the front door. The wood was painted dark, perhaps green, but she couldn't be certain in the night. Lace curtains hung at the windows. In the daylight, it would be a peaceful place, serene and isolated. By night, it was eerie. Instead of knocking at the door, Catherine maneuvered in the weed-filled flower beds to the window. The pattern of the lace curtains offered small glimpses into the room, but all she saw was emptiness. A dim light burned in a back room, giving just enough light for her to see several chairs, a small table. There was an air of temporary habitation about the furnishings—papers scattered on the floor, glasses on the table.

Easing around the corner of the house, she came to another window. This gave onto a small bedroom with a single cot against the far wall. The bed sheets and a dark blanket were rolled into a lump. More than anything, it was a sad room. One Robby's Lane looked abandoned, except for perhaps the neighborhood children who'd begun to use it for a getaway or clubhouse.

Feeling with one foot behind her in the flower bed, she started to back away from the window when the bundle of bedclothes began to shift. In a moment, a frail old man sat up.

He looked blindly around the room, as if he couldn't see, or maybe as if he didn't know where he was.

"Mick." She whispered his name.

"That's right. And you must be Miss Nelson."

She felt the cold barrel of the gun press into her waist and the sudden weakness of muscles jellied by fear. She fought to retain control of her legs and lower body.

"That's a good girl, no noise. Very nice. Now come away from the cottage. If you'd like to go inside, I'm just the one to arrange it for you." He laughed. "And I thought I was going to have to spend the night taking care of that filthy old man."

Catherine wanted to turn around to see her assailant, but she didn't dare. He was pressing the gun hard into her back. His voice had that cocksure quality that comes either from the young or the very stupid. It wasn't working class, but it wasn't exactly upper class, either.

"How did you know my name?" she asked calmly.

"Oh, I know enough about you to write a book." He laughed. "Mick tells a good tale about how you took over Beltene and put all of the men against you. The old fool still insists that you don't have the horse."

The barrel poked into her ribs with a jab, and she forced herself to move away from the house. None too gently, she was prodded forward, back to the front door.

"Where's Allan?" she asked.

"So, you did figure it out. I told him not to leave those ridiculous notes. Wax and seal!" The man poked her hard with the gun several times. "But Allan does have to have his little pretensions, doesn't he?"

"Where is he?" Catherine had one hope—that Allan would not allow anyone to hurt her. Allan wasn't an ethical man, but he'd been raised with a certain code of conduct. Her captor's next words stripped even that hope from her.

"I'm getting rid of the old man tonight, no matter what that prig says. He's screwed up everything he was supposed to do.

Maybe I'll make it a double deal and take care of you at the same time."

Catherine gritted her teeth and forced herself to speak normally. "Is Mick okay?"

"Righter than rain." The man laughed and prodded her up to the door. "Go on in, it's open."

She pushed open the door and entered. It had the smell of an abandoned house, a place where no one cleaned or cared. Without asking permission she went to the bedroom where she knew Mick was being held. The man with the gun made no effort to stop her as she pushed open the door.

"Mick, it's me, Catherine."

"They've got you, then." Mick sounded as if he was too tired to speak. "I never told them anything."

Fumbling for the light switch, Catherine clicked it on and hurried to the bedside. Mick was lying, eyes closed, in the narrow bed. His color was gray, his lips tinged with blue.

"Can you sit up?" Catherine put her arm around him and moved him to a sitting position. "Hey!" She called out. "Bring me something for him to eat."

"What's the point?" the young man asked. He came to stand idly in the doorway, the gun still held at his side. "Food won't mean much to him in a few hours."

"Get me something for him to eat." Catherine ground out the words through her teeth.

The man chuckled. "I forgot how you rich people like to give orders. Excuse me, ma'am. Right away, ma'am." He chuckled at his own wit and went toward the kitchen.

"You bleedin' bas—" Mick checked himself. "I was a fool to get in the car with him. A fool. My foot was hurtin' and I thought to save myself a walk. He said he knew my son."

"Are you hurt? Have they hurt you?" Catherine asked.

Mick brushed the question aside. "Where's Limerick?" He gripped her hand with surprising strength, and when he opened his eyes, there was a vitality there that had been deliberately hidden.

"I don't know. Someone took him from the hideout."

"These criminals followed us there and planned to snatch him themselves. But someone got there first, so they decided to nab me instead."

"Exactly as we thought," Catherine said. She explained the things that had happened in Clifden with Cuchulain, and how Patrick had been hurt.

"Damn! We need Patrick here." Mick looked around the room. "They've taken everything that could be considered a weapon."

There was the scuffle of feet, and Catherine shushed Mick. "Just eat this and don't worry," she said, loud enough for her captor to hear.

As Mick was finishing the last of the cold soup, Catherine heard someone at the front door. False hope sprang up, but was quickly suppressed. Patrick was the only one who could find her, and he was undoubtedly still sleeping soundly. There would be no rescue attempts on her behalf.

"Your lady friend is here," she heard the young man say. She knew then that Allan had arrived—for better or for worse.

Straightening her back in the chair beside Mick's bed, she watched the doorway. When Allan walked into the room he was dressed in a cashmere coat and wool slacks. Every hair was impeccably groomed. "Allan," she said, as if they were meeting at a friend's home for cocktails.

"Catherine." He shook his head, his worry clearly showing. "Where is that damn horse?"

"So it was you? I didn't want to believe it."

"I've got everything I own riding on the bay in the race Saturday. We both know Limerick can beat King's Quest hands down. The only way for me to win is to detain Limerick from racing. I'll win by default."

"Not very honest gains."

"Not very easy financial times. I'm afraid my luck has been running against me lately. In cards, horses and women. Ridgeway convinced me to make the bet. He said Limerick had a bad knee and that he'd make sure it was good and sore. He played me well."

Catherine recalled the day when she'd ordered Timmy to ride the big gray—at Kent's insistence that Patrick was mollycoddling the horse. So, Patrick had been correct. It wasn't surprising. At this point the only thing that surprised her was her own gullibility.

"So you and Kent have been working together," she deduced.

Allan's laughter was bitter. "Fat chance, that. I wouldn't turn my back on that wolverine."

Confusion touched Catherine. "You're not involved with Kent?"

"Not on your life. Why would I want to work with a man I can't trust?"

"Indeed," she answered, aware that Allan had missed the irony of his statement. "Do you know if Kent has Limerick?"

Comprehension spread across Allan's handsome face. "If he has him, then he'll deliberately run him." His head snapped up, his gaze riveted suddenly on Catherine. "If you honestly haven't hidden the horse away, then there's no need to hold you anymore." As he finished speaking the younger man with the gun entered the room.

Catherine smiled, and for the first time she felt the tension ease. "Thank goodness. I knew you'd see—"

"What shall we do with the two of them, Allan?" The young man spoke softly. "My, Allan, you haven't introduced me to your friend. Miss Nelson, my name is Craig. Craig Neville."

Something in his eyes made Catherine afraid, but she knew she could never show her fear. "Why, you've got to let us go, both me and Mick. Isn't that right, Allan?"

"Allan isn't making any more decisions." Craig lifted the gun.

"Look, no harm has been done to me or Mick. We can stop this now. Let us go and no one will be the wiser."

"Allan may believe you, but I'm not such a moron. Where's the horse?" Craig's eyes were deadly.

Catherine forced a laugh. "Don't be ridiculous. We don't have Limerick. The game is over. You can't simply kill us because we don't have what you want."

Allan arched his eyebrows. "He can, Catherine. And I can't stop him."

The flutter of fear nearly choked Catherine. At that moment, Craig looked perfectly capable of killing both of them. She could expect no help at all from Allan. She'd been correct—he wasn't a killer, but he wasn't a hero, either.

"Where is the horse, Catherine? You see, along with Allan's fortune, he managed to bet mine, as well. It really isn't a matter of winning or losing. It's that if we don't pay our gambling debts, the people we owe are going to kill us. This race was our last chance. You understand, don't you, that we're desperate? Totally desperate. Now I'll have the truth. Are you and Ridgeway in this together?"

"It's to Kent's advantage if Limerick doesn't run." Catherine had to keep him talking. "We're hunting him, too," she continued. "My future depends on finding that horse." She felt Mick stir beneath the covers and put a hand on his shoulder to warn him to be steady.

"I have to find that horse." Allan looked back at Catherine. It was as if he didn't know her.

"We have to get out of here and we don't have time to baby-sit your friends," Craig said. "They'll be after us, and they won't take another excuse this time. They're going to kill us both."

"Shut up, Craig." Allan's voice was emotionless.

"Allan, I can help you. Father will—"

"Thanks, but it won't work this time. I'm in too deep. Now you must tell me where the horse is."

"What would you do if you had him?" Catherine asked. "You can't run him or breed him. What good is he to you?" Catherine felt her chances slipping away.

"Make certain he won't run Saturday."

"Allan!" She started to rise.

Allan moved swiftly across the room and pushed her back down into the chair. "I don't want to hurt you, Catherine. Honestly, I don't. But I have no choice. I owe money. Lots of it. And the people I owe are going to kill me."

"In a not very pleasant way," Craig said as he walked to stand beside Allan.

"Do what you have to." Allan shook his head, suddenly weary, and walked out of the room.

SANDPAPER was scrubbing at Patrick's face. He pushed it away with his left hand, only to find himself stroking smooth fur. One eye opened to confront a golden eye glaring back at him. He opened the other eye and brought the black cat into focus.

"Familiar," he said, and the syllables sounded thick and slow.

"Meow." The sandpaper tongue swiped at Patrick's chin.

"Okay, okay." Patrick realized the cat was standing on his chest. He eased forward in the rocker, cradling the cat in his arms as he started the painful process of awakening. His head throbbed. His body felt as if he'd been beaten with a bat.

It took several minutes for him to fully remember the incident with Limerick, and he wasn't certain how he'd gotten home.

"I saw him, and I should have had him," Patrick said as he stroked the cat's back. "But now I know where to look."

"Meow!" Familiar sank sharp claws into Patrick's hands and began to tug gently.

"If you were a dog, I'd have to call you Rin Tin Tin," he said as he unhooked the cat and stood. Obediently he followed Familiar to the telephone. He saw Catherine's note and the time.

"Good Lord, it's been over two hours! She should have been back!"

"Meow!" Familiar agreed.

Fully awake now, Patrick tore the top sheet of paper from the pad, and then as a second thought took the entire pad. He wanted to remove all traces of where he was going. With Familiar on his heels, he pounded down the narrow stairs and got into his vehicle.

As the Rover sped through the night, Patrick tried to quell his growing dread. His callused hand reached out to stroke Familiar as he pressed the accelerator even closer to the floor. One Robby's Lane. He knew the area, and the isolated locale made him even more anxious.

As if sensing Patrick's distress, Familiar put both front paws on the dash and stared into the night.

Half an hour later, Patrick stopped the Rover and slowly got out. Familiar moved beside him, black on black in the tunnel of the trees. They were just on Robby's Lane, not thirty yards from the main road. He had no idea who or what lived on Robby's Lane. He didn't mind a trek, as long as it didn't take too much time. The element of surprise was crucial, and Patrick intended to have it.

With Familiar by his side, Patrick eased down the road. In less than five minutes he saw the vague outline of a house. A single light was burning in the front window, partially hidden by lace curtains. Patrick knew Catherine was inside when he discovered Mauve's car.

"Easy, Familiar," he whispered as the cat darted ahead of him.

The cat was in too big a hurry to respond. He leapt onto the windowsill and banged into the glass.

"Hey!" A cry rose from within the house.

Patrick pressed back behind a shrub and watched as the front door opened and a young man looked into the yard. "Damn black cat," he said, bending down to pick up a rock. "I'll bet I can brain him."

"No!" Catherine cried out. "He's only a cat, leave him alone."

"Craig!" Allan rebuked his friend. "Leave the stupid cat alone."

Patrick felt his fingers clutch the leaves of the shrub, but he held back.

With a yowl of rage, Familiar leapt from the windowsill toward the man in the doorway. In two bounds he was digging into the man's chest, slapping at his face with both front paws.

"Get this damn animal away from me!" The man threw up his hands and fell backward off the stoop.

There was laughter inside the house, male laughter. Patrick didn't wait. He saw his moment and darted forward. He had only the tire tool he'd brought from the Rover, and he used it with a quick, clean snap of his wrist on the man's unprotected head. Craig twitched once and then settled, motionless.

"Thanks," Patrick whispered to the cat. He heard Familiar's low growl and darted to a hiding place beside the house just before the front door opened again.

"Hey, Craig!" Allan called out. "Don't tell me a single cat bagged you?" There was tension in Allan's voice. "Quit fooling around and help me in here."

"Meow!" Tail straight in the air, Familiar marched past Allan and into the house.

"Well, I'll be damned," Allan said. He stepped into the yard. "Craig? Hey, the game isn't funny anymore." He walked down the steps and turned right. In two strides he stumbled over his partner's legs. "Son of—"

Patrick's well-placed blow caught him at the back of the head. He fell forward like a sack of oats.

"G'night, and sweet dreams," Patrick said, never loosening his grip on the tire tool.

The front door was open and he could see Familiar pacing back and forth in front of a chair. He heard a soft footstep and faded back into the shadows by the door. He had no idea how many others might be inside the house. Well, he'd get them one by one if it took all night.

"Patrick?" Catherine's voice registered hope and fear. "Is that you? Mick's here. We're alone."

"It's me." He stepped forward so that the light from the window fell on his face.

"Thank goodness." Catherine didn't bother with a step at all, she simply let herself fall into his arms.

Patrick caught her, releasing the tire tool at last. He felt the urge to crush her to him, to hold her so tightly that she might forever become a part of him. And as his hands moved over the curves of her body, the urge to protect changed to a desire to possess.

Catherine felt Patrick's lips grow more demanding, and for one moment she yielded to his need and her own. For one tantalizing spiral of time, she acknowledged the tumultuous emotions that combined to make her want and love him.

"Patrick," she whispered, knowing that with his name she'd spoken her future.

"If anything had happened to you..."

"Meow!" Familiar said from the top step.

A shadow fell across the cat, lengthening as it moved closer and closer to the door.

"It's a fine and pretty pair you make, courting in the front yard like a pair of hounds. An old man might as well be taken off by the fairies."

Catherine and Patrick broke apart, both breathing heavily. Patrick recovered his composure first. "And well I knew that no one would have an ornery old carcass like yourself. Had I been worried over you, I would have come inside."

"We'd better tie those two up before they come to. I've got a bit of magic I intend to work on them with a rope," Mick said, rubbing his wrists. "They weren't too careful with my old bones, and I intend to return the favor."

Patrick's hands moved over Catherine's body slowly, savoring each curve. He kissed her forehead before he stepped away from her.

"I was wondering how long it would take the two of you

to see what I saw from the beginning. You're mad for each other. But Patrick's family has always been cursed with a strange stubbornness. With horses they're blessed. Land and women are different matters.'' Mick moved slowly down the steps as Patrick began to drag Allan into the house.

Motioning Catherine aside, Mick touched her arm. ''I want to thank you for coming after me.''

''I only managed to get myself caught,'' Catherine said.

''Nonsense. You found me. But there's something else.'' He leaned in closer to whisper. ''Patrick isn't a man to love lightly. Don't play with him, girl. If it's a game, let him go now. He's lost his family and his home. Don't take his heart.''

Touched by the old man's concern for his friend, Catherine took Mick's hand. ''I pledge to you,'' she said, squeezing his fingers, ''that I have no intention of playing with Patrick. I'm afraid I love the man.'' She smiled, wondering at the ease of her own revelation.

''Good, then,'' Mick said, ''let's tie these rascals with forty coils of rope and go and find us a racehorse.''

''My thoughts exactly,'' Patrick said. ''Now we only have to determine where the thief has hidden him. I've given it a lot of thought. Limerick has to be within a twenty mile radius of where we saw him on the Clifden road. No matter who is holding the horse, I believe that Kent is behind the whole thing. He's the one who'll benefit the most.''

''The rider, Cuchulain, was a horseman.'' Patrick put his arm around Catherine's shoulder. ''Kent has money enough to hire anyone he needs. I don't like Kent's methods, but I can't deny that he has the skills to pull off something like this. And as I said, there are people who'd do it for the pleasure of getting even with me. The bit about Cuchulain threw me for a while, but anyone can do a little playacting.''

''Can we find Limerick?'' Catherine realized she was asking for the impossible—a reassurance.

''We can and we will.''

She felt Patrick's arm tighten, a measure of comfort and

promise, and she knew that he might disappoint her in fact, but never in spirit.

''Let's hope we find him alive,'' Mick said from the doorway.

Chapter Seventeen

"Go on now," Mick said, handing Catherine the reins to the Connemara pony. "Familiar and I will get the van and meet you across the mountains."

Catherine mounted the Irish pony and looked up the rocks to where Patrick already sat astride his horse. Dawn was just breaking. In a miracle of speed, Mick had managed to find two surefooted ponies near Clifden for them to ride up into the mountains and bogs. Patrick was determined to track Limerick—without any further delay. The ponies, native to the western coast of Ireland, were as nimble as mountain goats and extremely rugged.

"Stay away from Allan and Craig. They're fine tied up, Patrick made sure of that." Catherine could tell Mick was up to something, and she didn't like it. He was far too eager to get her and Patrick off and gone.

"I'll take care. Me and Familiar." Mick's face was stubbled with several days' growth of beard. "It's hard on an old man to admit he's wearin' thin, girl. Don't make it any harder."

Not for a minute did Catherine believe that line. Mick was definitely up to something.

"I'll join you beyond the bogs," Mick called to Patrick. "Don't worry. I'll find you." He waved them on.

Patrick locked gazes with Catherine. They were both worried, but they had little choice but to begin the search for Limerick. "Mick, go home and tend to yourself."

"I wouldn't dream of doing otherwise." Mick nodded and stooped to pick up the cat. "Come along with me, you rascal. We'll catch them down the road."

"Catherine!" Patrick called her name as he turned his pony toward the rocky path.

Catherine followed him, looking toward the mountain that disappeared into the fog. It was pure stone mixed with patches of pasture, a hard and unforgiving land. She'd often heard of the Connemara terrain, but she'd never attempted to ride across it. In places the ground was so filled with moisture that it quivered beneath the weight of the horses. On either side might be the dangerous suction of bog, where water and rich earth combined to make a type of muddy quicksand. If anyone knew the way, it would be Patrick. She held firm to that thought as they started out.

Patrick put his pony into a gallop. They had to make time while they still had road. Once they were in the mountains, it would be up to the Connemara ponies, and Patrick, to pick a path.

They rode in silence, Patrick scanning the ground for Limerick's prints. It took an hour for them to finally find one. Looking over her shoulder, Catherine could see the Clifden road far below her. They were traveling higher and higher. Mountain sheep, dotted with pink-and-blue ink to mark ownership, grazed around them. The hazy morning was broken only by the bleating of lambs and the breathing of the ponies as they climbed.

When they hit a stretch of bog, Catherine almost halted. The little mare she was riding stepped from rock to rock, but the thick mud hid sharp edges and poor footing. Several times they slipped, and Catherine could only cling to her saddle, hoping not to make the mare's work any more difficult. The sound of the hooves sliding on the rocks was terrifying to a horseman.

Up ahead, Patrick gave his own pony free rein. "Stay behind me,'' he called out to her. ''There's a path, and you have to stay on it.''

Looking around her, Catherine saw nothing except rocks, grass and the black mud. If there was a path, only Patrick knew it.

Her mare slipped suddenly, plunging chest deep into the bog. ''Patrick!'' Beneath her the horse floundered, thrashing with its front legs to find rock. The thick mud churned, sucking at horse and rider. ''Patrick!''

''Let her loose!'' Patrick called back to her. His face was drawn with worry. ''Give the mare her head, Catherine!''

Catherine loosened her hold on the reins, and the little mare lunged forward, catching rock with both front feet and hauling herself and Catherine to safety.

''Are you hurt?'' Patrick asked.

Catherine looked down at her mud-covered legs. Beneath her, the horse quivered. ''No, we're both shaken but not injured. Patrick, if they brought Limerick through this, he'll never race. He's not as tough as the ponies. His legs...the rocks...'' She faltered. It was too awful to imagine what condition he'd be in after slipping around in the muck.

''He's tougher than you know, Catherine. He comes from Irish stock, animals who've learned to survive.'' Catherine's fears were the exact same ones he'd confronted and chosen not to voice. One slip, one misstep, and it could be the end of Limerick's career as a racehorse. And if he didn't race, he wouldn't develop the reputation necessary to serve as a stud.

Instead of thinking about potential disaster, Patrick focused his rage at Kent Ridgeway. Turning his gelding back to the path, he rode on. Ridgeway would pay for this. It was total disregard for Limerick, almost a desire to cripple him. There was a perversity in Ridgeway that Patrick intended to beat out of him, pound by bloody pound.

After two hours, Patrick reined his horse around and waited for Catherine to catch up. The ponies needed a rest, and Patrick needed time to pick up the trail. They'd left the bog behind, and were glad of it. Now the ground stretching before them was all rock, and he'd lost the notched hoofprint long ago.

"My God, it looks like the moon, or some forsaken biblical land." Catherine took in the bleak landscape. Rocks jutted everywhere, some forming smooth plateaus that rippled upon themselves, broken only by an occasional scattering of gorse or heather. There was a wild beauty to the land, a defiance that brought joy and fear for Limerick.

Patrick saw the fatigue and worry on her face as he led his horse over so that he could stand beside her. "I'm going to hunt for tracks." He handed her his gelding's reins. "See that rock over there?" He pointed west.

Catherine spied the strange outcropping, a square formation of rock. She nodded.

"I played in these mountains as a child. The little people make their homes here." He put his hands on her shoulders and pulled her to lean back against him so he could whisper in her ear. "That rock is a leprechaun chair."

Even as tired as she was, Catherine smiled. "So we've given up on hunting horses and taken to hunting leprechauns?"

"Not exactly." He tightened his grip and held her securely. "But while I'm looking for tracks, you keep an eye on that chair. If we could catch one of the little men, we'd get a wish, you know."

"Ah, a wish." Catherine gave herself the luxury of one minute leaning against Patrick. One fraction of time when she didn't have to face everything alone.

"We could wish Limerick home safe and sound."

"Thank you, Patrick." She turned her head up and kissed his jaw. "Thank you."

He squeezed her to him once more before he set off over the rocks. For a while Catherine could watch him, coursing houndlike, back and forth across the rocks. Dark hair tousled by the wind, he was almost primitive against the stark stones and sky. How well he was suited to the land. In many ways he was as rugged and unyielding. And as rich and life-giving. He took a long leap and disappeared from her view.

How could anyone find a clue on the hard stone? She watched the horizon, aware of how much she anticipated his return. When she did see him, he was waving her over a good distance to the north. Leading both horses across the treacherous rocks, she started toward him. As she drew closer she saw the excitement on his face.

"What?"

He held up a finger to his lips, then pointed toward a large outcropping of rock. Catherine felt the hope shoot through her. Had he found Limerick? Certainly, if he had, the horse was alive and well. She hurried forward.

He met her and took the reins. Pointing to the rock, he whispered. "Climb up and look east. It's Limerick. Be careful, he's watching."

"Who? Kent?"

"No, Limerick. If he sees you and recognizes you, he'll call out."

"Not to me," Catherine said. "He's your horse, Patrick. Not mine. I may hold the papers on him, but he's your horse." She turned away to climb the rocks before he could say anything else. She'd spoken the truth. Right or wrong, if they got Limerick back, she was going to return him to Patrick. If he was able to race, maybe they could work out arrangements where Patrick would race him and then allow her to stand him at stud. If he couldn't race… She couldn't think about that now.

Near the top of the rock she found a ledge to hide behind. Crouched down as far as possible, she peered over the top. Far below, in a small paddock, was a big gray horse. Nostrils flaring, he was sniffing the air. He tossed his head, mane flowing in an unkempt tangle.

Catherine's practiced eye ran over him. At such a distance she couldn't be certain, but his legs looked clean, his spirit undaunted. He pranced around the small enclosure, obviously aware of something. Catherine ducked lower.

As she inched back up for another look, the door of the small hut beside the paddock opened. She caught only a glimpse of broad shoulders, lean hips and long legs. The man called out, threw something at the horse and stepped back into the shadow of the door.

"Patrick!" Catherine called his name as she hurried down. "There's someone in the hut. A man."

"Ridgeway?" Patrick looked hopeful.

"I couldn't be certain, but he's there. A big man, like you. Maybe heavier. I couldn't see his face, but it might be Kent. What are we going to do?"

"You're going to hold the ponies here." Patrick gave her the reins. "I'm going to go down there and kill whoever has Limerick."

He spoke so softly that Catherine thought at first that she'd misunderstood. "What?"

"He's a dead man. He just hasn't crawled properly into his coffin."

"Patrick!" But he was gone, striding off over the rocks without even a pebble for a weapon. As she watched his strong back disappear, she felt a moment's pity for the other man. Patrick could kill him. The question was, would he?

As soon as he was out of sight, she tethered the horses to a bit of gorse. The Connemaras were so calm, so absolutely sensible, that they stood without objection. Catherine hurried down the slope after Patrick, cursing softly to herself as she slipped among the rocks. She'd lost sight of Patrick, and she'd begun to feel that if she didn't catch up to him she might lose him completely, forever.

Working her way down as quickly as possible, Catherine concentrated on her footing. When she was close to the bottom, she looked up. Patrick was still not visible. But Limerick was watching her.

The stallion stood at the stone wall, dark eyes eagerly following each move she made. He didn't make a sound. Catherine ducked behind the largest rock she saw, hoping that whoever was in the cottage was less vigilant than the horse. The one thing she didn't want to do was alert the horsenappers that they had company.

She caught a glimpse of quick movement behind the small hut, and to her relief, Patrick ran from one rock to another. He was circling closer to Limerick, but on the off side. While she watched, Patrick disappeared behind the small lean-to that served as a barn. Sensing something, Limerick whirled and sniffed the air in Patrick's direction.

An earsplitting whinny tore the air, and Limerick charged toward Patrick.

Catherine's heart stopped. The stallion aimed directly at the fence and without a pause sailed over. Shaking his head and bucking, Limerick tore across the uneven, rocky ground toward the place where Patrick hid.

"Hey!" The door of the hut flew open. There was a scramble inside, and then the man reappeared with a rifle. As he stepped into the daylight, Catherine felt a scream trapped in her throat. The man she was looking at was Patrick Shaw!

In slow motion he lifted the rifle to his shoulder and sighted down it at the galloping stallion. "To hell with you, you sneaky devil!"

His words had a curiously flat intonation. Catherine started forward, her body moving even though her brain had yet to give the command. By three strides she was in a dead run, and on the seventh, she launched herself at the man. Everything she had, she put into the jump. Stretching and flying, she reached toward him as she watched in slow motion as his finger pulled the trigger. Her body struck his as the shot rang out. The rifle bucked in his hand and the barrel flew up. His fist came down, brutally striking her shoulder as he turned to defend himself. And somewhere in the distance there was the scream of an injured horse.

Catherine felt the man's balance give. He started to fall, and she went with him. Together they tumbled to the hard earth, the rifle beside them. Before she could scramble away from him she felt his hands at her throat. Rolling, cursing, she fought.

"What a devil," he grunted, grabbing her hair and thumping her head against the rocky ground. "A bit of spirit is a good thing in man and beast, but you're taking this too far."

Catherine saw him, then. Her first clear look at his face stopped her cold. "Patrick?" But she knew it wasn't.

As soon as she quit struggling, the man stopped pounding at her. His blue eyes assessed her and he released his hold a little, allowing her some room to breathe.

They were staring at each other when there was the cock of a gun. The barrel of the rifle swung directly against the man's head. Catherine's gaze followed the barrel up to see Patrick's finger curled around the trigger. The look on his face was cold fury.

"Welcome home, Colin." Patrick stood over his brother, gun ready to discharge. "Now let Catherine up and go stand against the wall."

When Colin didn't move, Patrick kicked his leg savagely. "You don't have your mates here now to blow up innocent people or terrorize me. You've managed to beat up a woman and shoot a horse. That's quite a record, even for Cuchulain." He spoke the last with bitterness.

Catherine gasped as Colin lifted his weight off her. Still stunned, she pulled her feet under her and stood. "Shot a horse." The phrase echoed in her ears. "Limerick!" It was half question and half cry. She started to run toward where the horse had jumped out of sight, but Patrick pulled her to him. "Don't!"

"Limerick!" Catherine surged against Patrick's grip, but he held her.

"Don't, Catherine!" The sharp tone of his voice stopped her. Very slowly, she turned back to face Colin.

With a sudden scream, she threw herself at him, her fists

pounding his face and chest. "I'll kill you myself," she screamed. "Give me the gun! You've killed Limerick!"

Patrick grasped Catherine's arm and pulled her away. The entire time he kept the gun pointed at his brother. Their gazes were steady, each unwilling to look away.

Finally Colin spoke. "So, you're still so sure I'm guilty of everything that ever went wrong in your life, aren't you? It must be nice to have someone to blame."

Patrick's gaze didn't waver. "I know, Colin. You did what you had to do. Isn't that the way you phrased it? Doing what *you* had to do, regardless of the damage to other people. Colin the patriot, the hero, the man who put country first. It sounds wonderful, unless you see the firsthand results of that behavior. I saw what happened to Ma after Lucy died. And Da'. I saw him wither and shrink, selling first one dream and then another to bail you out of trouble."

Colin shook his head. "Forget the past, Patrick, and listen to this. There's someone in the rocks behind the house." There was a low urgency to his voice. "He was aiming at the horse. That's who I was shooting at. Forget the past and believe me."

"I'm not eight years old anymore. You can't play that game with me, Colin." Patrick shook his head. "I see it all now. It always took me a while to catch on to you. Cuchulain! You were the beggar on the road. Another of your little games. What were you doing? Traveling in disguise? Well done. I honestly thought you were an old man. And I gave you the idea of resurrecting this whole Cuchulain business." Patrick's voice was self-condemning. "Didn't I always play right into your hands?"

"It was innocent, Patrick. I swear to you, that part of it was innocent. But that isn't the issue now. You have to listen to me."

"I'm not one of the suckers you can pull into your tales and rebellions. You meant to kill that horse and ruin me. Did you come home just to finish off what little I had left?"

"Don't be a dolt. I'd never shoot a horse, and especially

not that one. I was aiming at the man.'' Colin pointed vehemently at the rocks that towered above them. ''He's up there, you bleedin' idiot. He's been tailing me and the horse. He was at the place where you'd hidden the animal. That's why I took Limerick in the first place. To protect him and to protect you.''

''I'm going to kill you, Colin. For the past, and for Limerick.'' Patrick lifted the barrel of the rifle and aimed it at his brother's heart.

''Stop it!'' Catherine touched Patrick's arm. She angrily dashed the tears off her cheeks. Limerick was dead. A magnificent animal had suffered and died in a feud between brothers. But that was enough. ''Stop it now, Patrick. You can kill Colin, but you won't be able to live with yourself if you do. Besides, it won't bring Limerick back.''

''I'd like to try.'' Patrick's aim never wavered.

''If it will help your feelings, kill me. But you'd better be fast. I'm telling you, there's someone with a gun, and if you don't watch your back, he's going to catch you by surprise.''

Catherine caught either a tone of sincerity or desperation in his voice. She looked behind Patrick, scanning the horizon for any sign of a person. Behind the small barn that was connected to the paddock, Catherine saw something move. It was a shift of shadow on shadow.

''Patrick...there's something there,'' she said softly.

''Damn you!'' Patrick turned from his brother in time to see Kent Ridgeway striding out from behind some rocks and headed toward them. He carried a rifle with a scope in his hand.

''Hello, Catherine, Patrick. And this must be Cuchulain, though I see more of a resemblance to the Shaw family, so you must actually be Colin, the rebel. It would seem you've done a very nasty job for me. My thanks.'' His smile stretched even further. ''I never realized that Colin Shaw would be helping the British. But you see, if Limerick had raced, I would have lost a great deal of money. Even worse, Catherine Nelson would have owned the stallion that might well have put me out of business. It's always a shame to destroy an animal as splendid as Limerick, but then it's even worse to see yourself ruined.''

Catherine took in the gun and his expression. She knew he'd come to shoot Limerick. He'd intended to hide in the rocks and kill him. A sniper. A miserable sniper.

Patrick's face remained blank, but Colin's darkened. His intense blue gaze shifted from his brother to the man who stood so casually cradling an expensive rifle in his arms. No matter how casual the pose, Kent's finger was on the trigger and the barrel was only inches from Patrick's chest.

''You're from Wicklow, aren't you?'' Colin asked. His voice was deceptively soft. ''When I heard about the troubles at Beltene and that Patrick had been forced to sell, your name came up again and again. Does Miss Nelson know that you tried to buy Beltene out from under her?'' He smiled at the shocked expression on Catherine's face. ''I see I hit a nerve with the lady.'' He looked at Patrick. ''I came home to check on my little brother, not to make trouble.''

''Running the risk of capture, I might add.'' Ridgeway grinned. ''So you're the brother, the rebel who fled. If Patrick doesn't kill you, I suppose I'll have to turn you in to the authorities. Catherine, you can take partial credit. That would endear you to the crown, you know.'' Kent shifted slightly. The rifle he held was only inches from Patrick's chest. ''You'd better put your weapon down now, Shaw. I wouldn't want some misguided sense of family to force me to kill you or your brother.''

The true horror of what had happened was breaking over Catherine. Colin had been aiming at someone—at Ridgeway. If she hadn't ploughed into him, he wouldn't have hit Limerick. It was her action that resulted in Limerick's death.

Without thinking, Catherine bent down. She swept up a handful of rocks and dirt. ''You bloody bastard!'' She threw as hard as she could, aiming accurately for Kent's eyes.

He lowered the rifle for a second as he threw back his head

and tried to clear his vision. Patrick and Colin moved as one. Patrick hit Kent at the knees while his brother caught him from the other direction at the shoulders. The trainer went down with a knock hard enough to force the air from his lungs.

Catherine picked up Kent's rifle. Aiming it at his head she stood over him. Once he'd caught his breath, she lifted her foot. ''I'd grind your face beneath the heel of my boot,'' she said, her voice shaking with fury.

''It doesn't matter.'' Kent was still struggling for breath, but he was undaunted. ''Limerick will never race. I've won, and there's nothing you can do about it now.''

''Catherine!''

She felt Patrick's hands on her, dragging her back and away. Her finger was on the trigger and the desire to pull it was almost irresistible.

''You can't kill him.'' With a quick motion, he took the rifle and threw it to Colin. ''Watch him, will you? Catherine and I need to take care of something.''

She realized what he intended and she balked. ''Patrick, I can't. I just can't.'' She had no desire to see what her interference had done to Limerick. It was enough that he was dead.

Patrick stepped away from her, watching the play of emotions on her face. ''You can, Catherine. Trust me, you can.''

Chapter Eighteen

Catherine's breath caught on a sob as she walked beside Patrick. The place where Limerick had fallen was hidden by a dip in the ground and the barn. Patrick took her arm and gently pressed it, moving her forward.

"Catherine, it's not as bad as—"

"I'll kill Kent myself. I will." She choked on a sob.

"Catherine, please."

They turned the corner and she stopped. Limerick was on his side, his gray coat covered in blood and mud.

Catherine jerked free of Patrick and started to turn back. His fingers closed over her arm. "Catherine."

She shook her head and refused to turn around.

He gave a soft, low whistle, then another.

There was the sound of movement, and Catherine turned back. Limerick was rising. Putting both front feet out in front of him, he lumbered up. As he came toward Patrick, he stumbled, giving to his left shoulder. A fresh trickle of blood began to ooze through the mud on his coat.

"He's not dead!"

"Not by a long shot." Patrick smiled. "I doubt he's hurt much, either, but he's a damn fine actor, isn't he?"

With a cry, Catherine ran toward the horse. He greeted her with a soft whinny, but his attention was on Patrick. He blew a soft greeting, but held steady while Catherine examined him.

Her fingers moved over his shoulder, flaking away the mud. There was a clean furrow where the bullet had grazed him, cutting deep into the flesh but not striking bone or tendon.

"He looked dead." She spoke aloud, but it was as if she were talking to herself. "He really looked dead." She turned back to Patrick, still not believing what she was seeing.

"I told you Limerick and I had a few tricks. When Limerick was a foal, I amused my father by teaching the horse movie tricks. Playing dead was one of our specialties. I'm afraid my father didn't find it so amusing, though. I thought Colin was trying to kill Limerick. Just in case my brother got away from me, I wanted him to believe he'd finished the job with Limerick. I put the mud on him to clot the blood. The wound didn't look bad, but bog mud can cure many a terrible injury." As he talked, his smile grew wider. "I do believe you'll have a horse ready to race by Saturday."

"ARE YOU CERTAIN?" Catherine adjusted Timmy's silks, but her attention was on Patrick. "The agreement was a forgery. We could always dispute it, but we have to do it now, before the race." She put in the final pin and allowed the jockey to leave.

"Have you no faith in a horse that's been resurrected from the dead?" Patrick, his blue eyes dancing, looked over Limerick's withers at Catherine.

"To lose him now..." Catherine didn't finish the sentence.

"I make you a promise, Catherine. Kent Ridgeway will never own Limerick. Never." The dark promise behind those words didn't have to be spoken. Ridgeway was free and preparing King's Quest to run. They could find no evidence to prove beyond a doubt that he'd forged the racing agreement, or that he'd attempted to kill Limerick. He'd never fired a shot. His claim was that he'd been hunting in the mountains and had stumbled upon Patrick's party just in time to offer assistance.

Although Catherine had wanted to press harder to bring

charges, Patrick had convinced her to hold still. "The race will be punishment enough," Patrick assured her. "Let him lose. It will only be the beginning of what you can do to him in the future. You can drive him out of business, and that will be worse than anything else."

Only that promise had kept her from publicly declaring what a crook and coward the man was.

Now her future hung on the fact that Limerick, his shoulder sore but healing, could outrun King's Quest. Limerick had had no preparation. His pasterns and elbows were nicked and scraped where he'd run among the stones with Colin, but there seemed to be no permanent damage. Still, with his shoulder wound, it was such a risk. And Patrick hadn't even had a chance to put him on the Kildare track. Timmy would be riding him cold, not certain how he would break out of the Kildare gate. It was a big gamble. Only Patrick's calm demeanor, his steady voice and hand as he groomed the stallion, gave her any hopes of success.

"Patrick?"

She turned to the door of the stall and saw Colin Shaw. He was wearing dark glasses and a hat, a disguise made necessary by the fact that he was still a wanted man.

"Colin." Patrick's tone was softer than any he'd ever used when speaking of his brother. All through the night they'd talked, voices rising and falling as Catherine had held Familiar and sat on a bale of hay near Limerick's door. They were guarding the horse against further mischief, but the two brothers were also working through years of enmity, unwarranted beliefs and false accusations. By dawn, they had come to terms with each other. She could hear it in the way they spoke to one another. Colin had finally made Patrick believe that his return to Ireland, risking capture, had been to see if he could help his younger brother. The past could never be undone, but Colin had been able to give Patrick an understanding of events.

To give them a moment of privacy, she turned to stroke Familiar as he perched on the saddle. He'd been in the horse van with Limerick when they'd driven straight to the track, and he'd stayed at the stall the entire time.

"After the race, I'm going back to the States," Colin said.

"This is your country, Colin. If you want to stay, I'll help you fight the charges."

Colin shook his head. "As long as you know the truth, Patrick, the rest doesn't matter. Da' spent the money because he believed I was innocent. I was. Lucy—" He turned away on a muttered curse. "If I'd known what she was up to, I would have stopped her. But I had nothing to do with that bomb, or any other. It was a setup."

"I believe you." Patrick walked to the stall door. "Be careful. Once the race is over, Ridgeway will do anything he can to get even. I'm sure he'll have the authorities looking for you."

"If I ever had a desire to blow anyone up, it would be him." Colin grinned. "I'm sure I can learn the expertise if you need me to."

"We'll handle him in our own way," Patrick said, but he was smiling, too. "You can stay, you know."

"My life is in America now. I've found a home, a woman who loves me." He looked at Catherine. "She's as pretty as Catherine, in her own way. And as fiery. It seems we share a passion for scrappy women." His next remark was directed solely to Catherine. "Take care of him for me. He's always been difficult. A hard man, stubborn as a Dublin donkey. But I do think he's trainable. Just don't hold back on the bat and spurs."

Catherine laughed. Still holding the pins she'd been using to secure Timmy's blouse, she went to the stall door. "Good luck to you, Colin. If you ever decide to come back to Ireland, you have a place at Beltene. I saw you ride the night you were pretending to be Cuchulain. Beltene can always use another horse trainer with that kind of expertise."

"I didn't mean to endanger the horse," Colin said. "I knew the path, and I could see that Limerick had the heart and spirit to tackle it without any difficulty. I would never have injured him. I only took him to protect Patrick. I hope you believe that.''

''If you hadn't taken him from the hideout, Ridgeway or Emory would have hurt him,'' Catherine said. ''You did us a great favor.''

''And tweaked my brother's leathery hide a bit at the same time.'' Colin put his hand on Patrick's shoulder. ''Tell Mick goodbye for me.''

''Tell me yourself, you big oaf.'' Mick stepped up and took Colin by the shoulders, hugging him fiercely. ''Watch yourself, man.''

''And you.'' Colin grinned widely. ''I hear Allan Emory and his friend suffered some bruises on their trip to the authorities. You wouldn't have beaten men who were already tied up, would you, Mick?''

''Nah! On my mother's grave, I would never do such a thing.''

''What happened to them?''

''Can I help it if they had some difficulty rolling around in the back of Patrick's Land Rover? I'd make a curve, and they'd thump, thump, thump across the floor. I'd make another curve, and there they'd go to the other side. Was little I could do to help them, me with my hands busy driving.''

''And I'll bet you had nothing to do with ambushing Eamon McShane in the barn and beating him with a broom handle, did you?'' Colin asked.

''Not a bit of it. 'Twas the little people who got after him. Pounded him squarely, by the looks of him. But it didn't stop Kent Ridgeway from hiring him on, so all in all, there was no harm done.''

''I thought I saw McShane over by the Wicklow grooms.'' Catherine sighed. ''In a way, it doesn't seem fair. Allan and his business partner Craig will spend a long time in jail. Kidnapping is a serious charge.'' Catherine spoke softly. ''Yet Kent is completely free.''

"Free, but not undamaged, if I know my brother," Colin said. "I'll be waiting to hear what you finally do to him, Patrick."

"Well, I came by to tell you that it's time to bring Limerick out," Mick told Patrick. "Timmy's ready and the track steward is waiting."

Patrick opened the stall door and stepped out and into his brother's embrace. "Take care, Colin, and good fortune."

"The same to you."

Colin touched his hat in Catherine's direction and left.

"After all those years of hating him, it's a relief to find out I was wrong," Patrick said softly. "No matter what I've lost, I've got my brother back." He went back to tighten the girth one more time. "Ready?" He looked at Catherine. "It's time."

THE SUN DAZZLED off the mahogany coat of King's Quest as he moved toward the starting gate. Only a few steps behind, Limerick's steel gray coat seemed to absorb the light, pooling it in the dapples of his skin. King's Quest danced sideways, eager, ready for the run. Limerick looked at the gate, his ears forward and alert, his step hesitant.

Beside her, Catherine felt Patrick tense. "Limerick," he whispered, and his hands clutched the rail. Looking down the seats of laughing, gesturing spectators, Catherine saw Kent Ridgeway grin. If Limerick balked at the gate, then King's Quest stood a chance of winning.

After an initial refusal, Limerick finally walked into the chute. The back gate closed behind him, trapping him inside until the front gate opened to release the horses.

Up on top of Limerick, Timmy looked around once. Clutching his bat in his right hand, he settled as close to the saddle as possible. When the gate sprang open, Catherine felt her heart stop.

The bay leapt from the gate, striding out with tremendous

force. Catherine felt Patrick grab her hand as Limerick broke out, only a second behind the bay.

The crowd cheered, nearly drowning out the announcer who followed the horses through the first turn and the backstretch. They were neck and neck.

"He's limping." Patrick leaned forward, his grip on Catherine's fingers nearly crushing the bone. "Pull him up, Timmy! He's limping!" Patrick's yell was swallowed by the crowd.

Catherine focused on the gray. She watched him stretch and gather, stretch and gather. There seemed to be no hitch in his movement, no soreness or hesitation. But if Patrick saw a limp, she knew it was there. She kept looking.

As the horses rounded the final turn and moved into the homestretch, she saw what she'd been missing. It was a movement so slight that no one but Patrick would have noticed it. Up top, Timmy would certainly feel it. She saw the moment the jockey realized his mount was sore. Sitting back, Timmy pulled on the reins.

A roar went through the crowd as they realized the jockey was trying to halt the big gray horse.

Timmy pulled with all of his strength, and Limerick stretched his neck longer and continued to run.

The horses were neck and neck, a dark shadow and a silver streak, moving at blazing speed along the homestretch.

"Pull back!" Patrick called to the jockey, but there wasn't a prayer that Timmy would hear—or could obey. It was obvious that the gray stallion had made up his mind to run, and Timmy didn't have the strength to pull him down.

With only a hundred yards to go, Timmy gave up battling Limerick. He leaned farther down the horse's neck. His hands braced the big gray and Limerick lengthened his stride by another two inches. Hooves digging into the loam of the track, he pulled forward. Stride by stride, he moved ahead of the bay.

All around her Catherine heard the roar of the crowd. Her

hand was numb in Patrick's grip. As Limerick flew beneath the finish line, half a length ahead of King's Quest, she allowed herself one fleeting look of victory at Kent Ridgeway. To her satisfaction, he refused to even meet her glance.

"Patrick!" But she had no time to talk. Still holding her hand, he was dragging her through the crowd to the winner's circle.

Hands slapped her back as congratulations were tossed at her. She had no time to listen or respond. Patrick pulled her forward like a train. When they broke free of the crowd, she had to run to stay with him.

"Patrick!"

"His shoulder, Catherine. I thought I'd arranged the saddle so that it wouldn't rub." At those words, he moved even faster.

Instead of a grin of victory, Timmy's face reflected worry as he sat on Limerick while Mick walked the big horse around to cool him. Well-wishers and other trainers were watching, talking, laughing, offering congratulations and asking for information on the big gray.

"Timmy!" Patrick's voice was sharp with worry.

"I tried to pull him down," Timmy said. "All along the homestretch I was doing everything I could to stop him. I could feel him—" Aware of the curious onlookers, he stopped. "Limerick was determined to win, Patrick. There was nothing I could do at the last but stay with him."

Patrick reached up, as if to assist Timmy off the horse. Mick stepped forward, maneuvering between them. "Leave him be, Patrick, the horse isn't damaged!" He put his hand on Patrick's chest. "It's done and no harm, I'd say. Limerick's a bit sore on his shoulder where the saddle was rubbing, but don't call attention to it. Turn around and smile. Let Miss Catherine stand up here beside her horse for the photos." He motioned her forward. "A big smile now. Beltene is a winner today. Limerick has the good sense to recognize it."

Instead of stepping forward, Catherine withdrew something from the pocket of her jacket.

"Catherine." Mick held the reins out to her as the photographer stepped forward to snap the picture. "Come on up here. They want a picture of you and your horse." A track attendant stood by with a garland of roses.

"No." She handed the paper to Patrick. "I might own Beltene, but I'll never own Limerick. I made a vow to myself when we were on the mountain. Limerick is Patrick's horse. Perhaps we can work something out together about breeding services."

Before Patrick could protest, Catherine put the papers in his left hand and Mick gave him the reins in his right. The flash exploded and Limerick turned to blow hot air in Patrick's ear.

"Good luck, Patrick." Catherine stepped forward and stood on tiptoe to kiss his cheek. "I'll help you any way I can. You know that. If there's any way possible, I want you to consider staying at Beltene as head trainer."

Patrick signaled Mick over. He took a moment to rub Limerick's head, whispering a few words into the stallion's ear before giving him over to Mick. "I'll be back in a minute." Once again he took Catherine's hand, but this time he led her carefully through the people and back to the stables.

"I can't accept the horse," he said. "He's yours. You bought him fairly, and without him Beltene will fail."

"I'll have King's Quest, or at least the use of him. I intend to return him to David Trussell with an agreement for some breedings."

Patrick grinned. "So, you're giving it all away, everything you've fought so hard to hold."

"I think I'm doing what's fair. If you'll agree to race Limerick and allow me to buy some breedings from you, then perhaps it won't be as terrible as you think."

"There is a way you could have me as trainer and the stallion." Patrick's voice was thoughtful. "It would require more than a little sacrifice on your part, though."

"What?" Catherine waited.

"You could marry me."

Catherine stopped dead still. The noise of the crowd faded slowly away. She stared into Patrick's blue eyes and saw the future. Together they could make Beltene a great horse breeding and racing farm. She might do it alone, but that wasn't what she wanted. She couldn't imagine Beltene without Patrick. No matter where she went, she'd see him in the pastures, in the barn.

"Catherine?" Patrick held out his hand.

Ignoring it, she ran the two steps into his arms. "Yes," she agreed. "Yes."

"I always knew Limerick was a valuable animal. Little did I know he'd get me the woman I wanted from the first day I saw her."

Catherine pulled back. "You acted as if you hated me," she said.

"I wanted you, and I knew I'd never stand a chance of having you."

"Dreams can sometimes come true," she whispered.

"Ah," Patrick said, "indeed. But we have someone else to thank for all of this."

Catherine looked down. The sleek black cat stood at her feet. With a quick slap of his front paw he sent a rose scuttling against her left foot. It had fallen from the garland that was now draped around Limerick's neck.

Patrick's laugh was rich and deep. "Look, he wants to be the first to congratulate us," Patrick said.

"I do believe we may have to kidnap that cat."

Patrick shook his head. "No, Peter and Eleanor will be at Beltene to get him Monday. Mick spoke with them. They're headed to Scotland, and they want to take him along."

"There's no way they'd let us keep him? Even for a few more weeks?"

"Familiar is a very special cat. I'm afraid he means as much to them as he does to us. It was Familiar who brought Peter and Eleanor together."

"As well as us," Catherine said. Her green eyes were dancing with mischief. "It was the way you stroked him that made me think you might be human."

"Wait until tonight. I'll show you exactly how human I can be."

Catherine laughed as she bent down to pick up the rose. She stroked Familiar's fur. "Perhaps you did put a witch's spell on him—on both of us. You saved our lives, Familiar. And I thank you."

ELEANOR AND PETER should be here in the next ten minutes. I think Patrick got the idea that I'm not going back in that "kitty carrier." Jeez. Even the name is an insult.

I hear Scotland is the next stop on my travel agenda. Something about Eleanor's relatives. The dame is tall enough to have a little Scottish blood in her. Tall and striking.

I'm giving fair warning now though, no matter what they say, I'm not eating any of that haggis stuff. Sheep's belly! Whoever heard of such? I do understand that there's some perfectly lovely salmon, and if we're only visiting, I'm certain I won't go into a decline. It's a strange thing, though. I've been having a real attack for the sight of some golden arches. Just a good ol' American burger.

Here comes Catherine. You know, she even walks a little like a cat. Sort of a slinky, stalking kind of walk. Ah...I see what she's getting ready to pounce on. There's Patrick in the pasture with Limerick. Isn't that sweet? Just the three of them. One big happy family.

Here comes the car. Hello, Eleanor. Goodbye Ireland. 'Tis a fair and green land filled with fast horses and magic. But this black cat is ready to start the next leg of this journey. Scotland—and then my own Clotilde.